Bound by Murder

Also available by Laura Gail Black

The Antique Bookshop Mysteries

For Whom the Book Tolls

Murder by the Bookend

Bound by Murder

AN ANTIQUE BOOKSHOP MYSTERY

Laura Gail Black

NEW YORK

This is a work of fiction. All of the names, characters, organizations, places and events portrayed in this novel are either products of the author's imagination or are used fictitiously. Any resemblance to real or actual events, locales, or persons, living or dead, is entirely coincidental.

Published in the United States by Crooked Lane Books, an imprint of The Quick Brown Fox & Company LLC.

Crooked Lane Books and its logo are trademarks of The Quick Brown Fox & Company LLC.

Library of Congress Catalog-in-Publication data available upon request.

ISBN (hardcover): 978-1-63910-096-5
ISBN (ebook): 978-1-63910-097-2

Cover illustration by Mary Ann Lasher

Printed in the United States.

www.crookedlanebooks.com

Crooked Lane Books
34 West 27th St., 10th Floor
New York, NY 10001

First Edition: September 2022

10 9 8 7 6 5 4 3 2 1

For Patricia "Tris" Rohner,
best friend, cheerleader, brainstorming
partner, and beta reader extraordinaire.
Thank you for everything.

Chapter One

"Life is sweet." Mason stood in the open doorway to my used and antique bookstore, Twice Upon a Time, staring across the cobbled street toward The Weeping Willow. Eddy tugged at the leash in Mason's hand, and the young man stooped down to unhook it from my dog's collar before returning his gaze across the street.

I chuckled, following his gaze, spotting Lily Monahan sweeping the walk outside the pub. As the petite girl turned to go back inside, she flipped a quick glance over her shoulder and wiggled her fingers at Mason, a silly grin tugging at the corners of her mouth.

Ah, young love. But who was I to judge? My own love life had blossomed since Detective Keith Logan had finally admitted he loved me four months ago. Life was indeed sweet.

I let my gaze sweep down the street, taking in the number of couples walking hand in hand along the walkways and popping in and out of the businesses in Hokes Folly's historic district. Love was definitely in the air—likely due, at least in large part, to the new efforts of Hokes Bluff Inn, a three-hundred-room estate built in the early 1900s, to become an in-demand wedding venue. As only businesses that could have been open around the turn of the twentieth century were allowed in the historic district, couples were pouring in to the local businesses to gather items for their period-based weddings at the inn.

A familiar shock of red hair caught my eye, and I smiled as Rita Wallace—neighbor, best friend, and director of the makeup and hair department at Hokes Bluff Inn, where she primped and coifed guests into period dress and hairstyles—strolled toward my door from one of the parking lots at the end of the district. Although it was a bit of a walk, Rita had no choice, as the historic district was blocked off from anything but foot traffic in order to keep the early-1900s feel to the area.

Mason and I stepped back to allow Rita to enter, and she made a beeline to the coffeepot, pouring the dark liquid into one of the store's Twice Upon a Time mugs before giving Eddy a quick scratch on the head. He stood with his shoulder against her knee, a sloppy doggy grin on his face. He swayed his feathered tail back and forth in a slow wag before he sought out his favorite sunny spot to curl up, his silky red and white coat gleaming in the sunshine.

"What a gorgeous day." Rita inhaled the aroma rising from her mug before taking a sip of the hot liquid. "Mostly because I'm off today and don't have to help a bunch of bridezillas figure out hairstyles to match their dresses."

"Good morning to you too." I left Mason making moon eyes at the pub's windows and poured my own cup. "I take it they're turning up in droves?"

Rita plopped onto one of the stools by the counter. "You have no idea." She took another swig of coffee.

It never ceased to amaze me how hot Rita could drink her coffee. I blew on the black liquid in my mug, knowing I'd scorch the life out of my mouth if I sipped too soon. "That bad, huh?"

"Don't get me wrong." Rita set her mug on the counter. "I'm glad Elliot came up with a way to increase the inn's revenues. But the brides think they need to come in and pick everything out the minute they book. We're a bit overloaded, and it's taking time away from helping paying guests as well as the brides who are actually getting married every week."

"Can't Elliot hire someone to help them choose styles, and let you concentrate on the current clients?" I took a tentative sip of my coffee, cringed, and blew on it again.

Rita grinned. "He's interviewing today, thank goodness. Honestly, I don't think he considered how this would work out once he opened the books to weddings."

I slid behind the counter as a customer walked in, glad when Mason seemed to shake himself and turn to help them. I'd recently made him manager of the store, and so far, I'd had no regrets.

Rita propped her elbows on the counter and lowered her voice. "What's with Mason? He seems a bit out of it today."

I tilted my head in the direction of the pub. "I think he has the hots for one of the girls at The Weeping Willow. He's been staring at her all day."

"Ahhhhh." Rita nodded slowly, drawing out the word. "Does this girl have a name?"

"Lily Monahan." I chuckled. "She started working there last fall, not long after I moved here. Lately, Mason seems to be eating all of his lunches over there."

"Well, at least I won't have to worry about them coming in to plan a wedding any time soon. I have enough on my plate at the inn as it is." She tilted her head to one side and leaned in. "Speaking of weddings, how are you and Keith doing?"

I almost snorted a mouthful of coffee out my nose, barely managing to swallow it without choking. "What is wrong with you? Don't say things like that when I'm taking a sip of something."

Rita shrugged. "I just wanted an honest reaction." She grinned.

"Well, here's my honesty. We've only been dating for a few months, so it's way too soon to be asking me a question like that." I glared at her with what I hoped was a stern look before I took another sip.

"Don't I remember you saying you were engaged to that guy in Charlotte after only a month, and y'all were living together?" Rita moved to refill her coffee mug.

I sighed. "Yes. Not the best example of my decision-making skills."

Rita returned to the counter and slid onto her stool again. "Not the best example of your sanity either, from what I remember you saying."

I wrapped my fingers around my mug, letting my memory play. "Blake had his good points." I took a sip of coffee. "He had irritating points as well, which I stupidly ignored. Like the whole poetry thing. He claimed he was descended from Ralph Waldo Emerson and was always quoting poetry written by his famous ancestor. It was sweet at first, but it didn't take long to figure out he used Ralph's words because he couldn't come up with anything good on his own. Just once, it would've been nice if he could have been a bit more original, saying something from his heart, not a book."

Rita reached out and patted me on the arm. "At least he tried. They don't all do that."

"I suppose you're right." Keith popped into my head, and I couldn't stop the silly grin that slid across my face. "At least my current beau doesn't quote poetry someone else wrote. He's not famous, but he's written a few really sweet love notes to me."

Rita's mug *thunked* down on the counter. "Now that's what I'm talking about. I tell you, girl, you'd better hang on to this one. He's a keeper."

"Keeper, yes. But don't rush it." I stepped out from behind the counter. "For now, I need to worry about my store." I linked my arm through hers and tugged her from her stool before leading her toward the back room.

"Where are we going?" Rita strode beside me, still sipping her coffee.

"With all the brides-to-be flooding the town lately, I decided I needed some new books." I released her arm, stepped into the back room, and pointed at four boxes in the corner.

Rita walked to them and peered down at the labels. "And what did you buy from Chandlers Book Publishing?"

I slid a box cutter across the packing tape holding one box closed, opened the flaps, and pulled a book out to present to my friend. "You're looking at hot-off-the-press copies of *The Bride's Best Friend*, the new wedding planner for brides that came out this season."

Rita snatched the book from my hands and flipped pages. "Ooooh, this is the book all the brides are talking about when they come in. It's advertised in all the bridal magazines this spring."

"Yep, and now I have two hundred copies to sell." I tugged the book from her hands. "And since you're off today, you can help me decide where and how to display them."

"Fun, fun!" She grabbed the book back. "I'll buy your first copy. That way when I hear brides talking about it, I can jump in, ooh and ahh over it with them, and tell them about this amazing little shop that has them for sale. Of course, I have to find an amazing shop that sells them now." She narrowed her eyes and tilted her head.

"Really? That's where you're going with that?" I picked up a stack of books and headed to the counter.

Her laughter echoed through the store. "You know I'm just teasing you."

"Uh-huh." I piled the books on the counter.

Rita stepped up beside me, unloading her stack beside mine. "What about a window display?"

"That's a great idea." I hadn't changed the window display since Valentine's Day a month ago, and much of what was there could be recycled into a wedding display.

We stepped outside and walked across the street to get a full view of my store windows. "What color should I use instead of red? Maybe white?"

"Definitely white, with a touch of gold. I think I saw the perfect fabric in an order we received. I can sell you a bit at cost." Before I could protest, Rita held up a hand. "I know Elliot won't mind."

"Fine, if you're sure." I grinned, a picture of my new display forming in my mind. "How soon can we get it?"

Rita pulled her phone out of her back pocket and made a quick call. "Okay, it's settled. Carrie will meet Mason in the parking lot at the inn in fifteen minutes. Here's the total."

I rushed inside, calling for Mason as I searched for the checkbook under the counter. My hand bumped the hard binder, and I pulled it out and flipped it open to write the check.

"What's up, boss lady?" Mason stepped up to the counter.

I tore out the check and handed it to him, explaining the situation. "I'd like to get this display up as soon as possible, so don't get caught up in a conversation."

"I'm on it!" He waved the check over his head as he strode out of the store and headed for the parking lots.

Rita chuckled and shook her head. "He does love how much you've trusted him these past few months."

"I honestly don't know what I would've done without him to help me with the store." I stepped behind the counter and began removing the items from the display window, placing them on the front counter. "He's earned my trust and then some."

Rita slid the crimson velvet backdrop from the window and folded it neatly. "How's he doing in school? Wasn't he starting this semester?"

I grinned as I separated the display books into categories for reshelving: steamy romances, romantic poetry, flower meanings, and romantic cooking. "He did. I think he's taking an introductory accounting course and business math this semester. I know he's been studying in the back room when the store is slow."

"Good for him." Rita picked up the romances and the cookbooks and headed toward the stacks.

I grabbed the flower books and shelved them in their proper section, leaving the romantic poetry on the counter, and spent the next fifteen minutes pulling a few books on wedding planning from my shelves, to add to the display.

The door bells chimed, and I stepped out to see Mason entering with a bundle his arms, trying not to trip over Eddy, who had risen to greet Mason with a wagging tail and bounces of excitement.

"I'm back," he called. "Where do you want this?"

"Lay it on the counter, please." I placed the books on the counter and reached for the bundle to unwrap it. A gorgeous heavy, white satin slid through my hands, small gold threads sparkling in the light. "It's beautiful," I breathed.

"Isn't it?" Rita slid her fingers over it. "I can't wait to see a wedding dress made out of this fabric."

"Let's see how it looks in the windows." I scooped the material into my arms and took it behind the counter.

Mason worked with customers while Rita and I worked, and before too long, we had a window to be proud of. The shimmery fabric lay draped across bookstands attached to wooden blocks, leaving only the fabric in view, with elevated books nestled in its folds. Along with the new planners, I'd added the romantic poetry books and a few books on wedding planning, wedding etiquette, and honeymoon destinations. Across the bottom of the display stretched an antique veil Rita had told Carrie to include in the package with the fabric. It was only a loaner, but it was the perfect touch until I could find a replacement. I'd even gone upstairs to get Uncle Paul's and Aunt Irene's wedding bands and had placed the delicate gold bands next to the headpiece on the veil.

As we put the finishing touches on the display, Rita elbowed me. "Don't look now, but the bridezilla to beat all bridezillas is headed this way. Yesterday, she spent two hours yelling at me because I said she couldn't wear a dress slit almost to her belly button in front and call it a period wedding."

I looked up and froze. *Oh no. No, no, no, no.*

Eddy, apparently sensing my distress, strode to the door and looked out, a low growl humming in his throat.

"What's up with Eddy?" Rita turned to look at me. "Hey, are you okay? You look like you've seen a ghost."

Before I could answer, the door bells chimed, although this time the sound seemed sinister, and Rita's bridezilla walked in, her groom in tow.

"Hello, Jenna." The man's rich tones raked across my nerves.

Eddy's hackles rose, and he skittered under the counter by my feet. I reached down to rub the dog's fur, not sure if I was comforting him or me. Rita elbowed me in the ribs, startling me out of my frozen state.

My stomach roiled and I fought the urge to throw up. Instead, I smiled my professional bookseller smile and took a deep breath. "Hello, Blake."

Chapter Two

"Jenna Quinn?" The woman with Blake blinked slowly, a speculative smile sliding across her face. "How fun!" The cold look in her eyes said she thought running into me was anything but fun.

I stared at her, trying to place her face. Something about her was vaguely familiar, but I couldn't put my thumb on it.

The woman must have caught my blank stare. "Why, it's me, Missy Plott. Well, soon to be Missy Emerson." She squeezed Blake's arm against her ample bosom and placed her left hand on his chest in a possessive way that was sure to show off the sparkling diamond on her hand. "Isn't that right, love?"

Blake looked down into his fiancée's face with a tight smile and a clenched jaw and nodded once. "Of course."

Recognition sparked in my brain as I glanced again at her ring. *My* ring! The jerk hadn't even bought her a new ring. "That's a lovely ring." I forced a smile. "Wherever did you buy it?"

Missy waved her hand across in front of me. "This? Isn't it gorgeous? It's been in Blake's family for generations. I'm the next in line to wear it." She flipped her hand to stare at the diamond.

"I have to confess, I found it in his sock drawer before he could surprise me with it." She giggled.

His gaze rose to meet mine again. If I hadn't been looking, I would've missed the nanosecond of desperation mixed with disgust that marred his too-perfect features. But disgust for whom? Me? Or Missy? I honestly wasn't sure.

I was tempted to out him and tell her Blake and I had bought that ring together on the trip to the beach where he'd proposed at the water's edge at sundown.

Missy, seemingly oblivious to the exchange, rattled on. "In case you don't remember me, I worked in the admin pool at Brinks and Judson. I had been assigned to your department not too long before . . . well . . . all that nastiness that happened with you." She slapped a hand to her chest. "Honestly, after they handcuffed you and dragged you off to jail, I didn't think I'd ever see you again. How you managed to convince them you were innocent, I'll never figure out."

"Okay." My voice came out in a stutter. How was I supposed to respond to that? I cleared my throat and forced a numbness through my soul, the voice of my mother ringing inside my head, demanding I behave like a lady. I couldn't blow a gasket at this woman, with the possibility other customers might enter at any moment. "Is there something I can help you with?" Deep down, I wanted to do a number of things to her right now, and helping wasn't on the list. But I would prove I was the bigger person. Mom would be proud.

"Oh yes. I want a copy of the new bridal planner in the window." Missy pointed toward the new display. "We're getting married in five days"—she held up her hand, palm open, and wiggled her fingers—"and I want to make sure I haven't forgotten anything."

I forced a smile onto my face and reached for a stack, taking the top book and sliding it into a bag. Behind me, Mason rang up the purchase and quoted the price.

Missy swiped her card and took the bag before turning to let her gaze take in the entire store. “So this is where you ended up.” She shifted to face me again with narrowed eyes and a snotty smile on her lips. “Is this what you did with all that money you stole from the company?”

My jaw dropped, but before I could utter a word, Rita grabbed Missy by the arm and ushered her and my ex-fiancé toward the door.

“Thanks for coming.” Rita shoved her out the door. “Don’t forget to stop by the jeweler at the end of the street. He has some fantastic period wedding bands.”

Slowly sinking to a stool, I searched my brain for any sort of explanation for what had just happened. I still hadn’t said a word when Rita plopped down beside me, the offending couple halfway down the cobbled street outside.

“Are you okay?” Rita reached out to rub my shoulder.

Mason leaned on the counter. “Dude, was that *the* Blake? The guy who dumped you in Charlotte?”

Rita shot him a “shut up, Mason” glare. “I don’t think this is the best time to grill her.”

“Ohhhh.” Mason nodded slowly, drawing out the sound. “Gotcha.” He turned to go back toward the stacks. “You’re better off with Keith!” he called as he swept around a corner.

Rita turned on her stool and faced me, taking my hand in hers and massaging it. “Sweetie, talk to me so I know you didn’t have a stroke or something from the shock.”

I raised my gaze to meet hers. "I honestly have no idea what to say." I shook my head, hoping it would clear the clutter of incoherent thoughts and emotions rocketing back and forth through my brain.

"Mason!" Rita stood and moved out into the stacks, following his muffled reply. Returning shortly, she slid her arm around my shoulders and pulled me off the stool. "Come on. We're going upstairs. I've told Mason he's got the store to himself for now."

We wound up the spiral staircase, Rita urging me with gentle nudges from behind and Eddy ahead of me. At the top, we stepped into my apartment over the store. Sunshine flooded the room from the tall windows overlooking the cobbled street below, which normally gave a warm and welcoming feel to the room. Now, however, it seemed too bright, too sunny, too open. I fought the urge to go hide under the covers in bed.

After settling me on a barstool, Eddy at my feet, Rita bustled in the kitchen for a few minutes, finally setting a steaming cup of coffee in front of me. "I think you'd do better with a nice cup of chamomile tea, but you still keep resisting when I try to convert you."

I offered a watery smile at her lighthearted teasing and took a sip of the coffee, happy to find it wasn't too hot to drink.

Rita slid onto a stool next to me with a mug of her own. "I won't push you, but when you're ready to talk about it, I'm here."

Inhaling deeply, I centered my attention on the aroma and warmth, allowing my shoulders to slowly drop from the tensed ball they'd been in for the last fifteen minutes. "I still don't really know what to say. Or feel."

Rita sipped her coffee and remained silent, and I appreciated her letting me work through my emotions.

I looked down into my coffee, searching for answers. "Part of me is angry, part wants to laugh, and part wants to cry like a child." I shrugged my shoulders. "I'm not sure which one I should give in to."

"Maybe all of them." Rita shrugged. "Or none of them. Only you can know that."

"I just can't believe he gave her my ring." I pulled my gaze away from the depths of my mug.

Rita coughed, choking on her coffee. "Are you kidding me?"

"Nope." I shook my head. "We bought that ring together after he proposed. He knows I adore the ocean, and he booked a trip for us. Of course, as always, to make sure no one would know we were a couple, we had to take two cars down, and I had to sneak into the hotel room after he'd checked in."

"That man was a piece of work." Rita plunked her mug down on my counter and used her hands to make air quotes while attempting to sound male. "Don't let anyone know we're dating. Don't let anyone know we're living together. Don't let anyone know we're engaged." She dropped her hands and reverted to her own voice. "What would he have done once you were married? Made you keep using your maiden name and never let you wear that gorgeous diamond in public?"

"Who knows?" I tilted my head to one side, my gaze focused far in the past. "At the time, his reasoning of not looking like he was giving me special favors at work as one of the management team all seemed logical. I thought I loved him, so I trusted him and accepted his logic. I don't know, maybe I did love him for a while. At least in some way. Now I look back and see what an idiot I was."

Rita humphed. "No woman deserves to be treated like a nasty secret. We all deserve a man who is proud to be seen with us and who treats us like we're worth the world to him." She clinked her mug against mine. "Like Keith does."

I looked up to see the impish grin on her face and couldn't help smiling in return. "Yeah, he does." My shoulders tensed again. "I have to tell Keith about this."

"Yes, you do." Rita nodded. "You do not want him finding out any other way, or he'll think you're hiding something or maybe still have feelings for Blake." She narrowed her eyes. "You don't, do you?"

Now it was my turn to choke on coffee. "Of course not!" I caught my breath. "At least I don't think I do."

"Oh lordy. Out with it, woman." Rita stood and walked to the coffee pot. "I'm gonna need a refill for this one."

"I guess it goes back to the 'I don't know how to feel' thing." I walked to the couch, put my half-full mug on the coffee table, and sank into a corner, letting the deep cushions cradle me. Eddy jumped up next to me, cuddling tightly against me. I dug my fingers into his silky coat and kissed him on the head, needing to connect.

Rita joined me and sat on the other end of the couch, turning to face me with one leg tucked under her. "Let's go back to that. You said you didn't know whether to laugh, cry, or be angry. We'll take them one at a time."

I stared at her for a moment. What had I ever done to deserve a friend like this? "Okay, angry. I think that's easy and obvious. The man shows up here after literally tossing me out on the street about seven months ago, acting like nothing ever happened. He has a new fiancée in tow, who is wearing *my* ring—not that I want it back—but still, it was *mine*, *my* perfect dream ring that *I* picked out."

"You should've kept that ring." Rita sipped her coffee. "I'm sure you could've sold it to support yourself for a while."

I shook my head. "I didn't have it. They made me surrender everything when I went to jail. I gave it back to him for safekeeping."

Rita snorted. "Seems his idea of 'safe' was giving it to someone else, although the way she tells it, he didn't really give it to her. She found it in a drawer and jumped to conclusions."

"Whatever." I slashed a hand through the air. "That still didn't give her the right to talk to me like she did in the store. And he completely wussed out and let her, which brought up all the anger over him not standing up for me when I was accused of embezzling from the company and accused of murdering an executive who supposedly found out about my embezzlement. Blake never once visited me while I was stuck in jail for three months because they were convinced I had all that money stashed away and would go on the run. When I finally get to come home, I'm handed a key and told where the warehouse is where he's put all of my things." My voice rose to a shout. "Who the hell does that to someone they profess to love and want to marry?"

Eddy jumped from the couch and scurried into the bedroom. I barely registered that I'd run my dog off with my diatribe. The emotions were too raw, to demanding.

I leaned forward, my wildly waving hands punctuating my sentences. "He does not deserve to be happy. Not after what he did to me. He needs to be sorry and miserable and think he made a huge mistake in letting me go—not prove just how unimportant I was to him even though we were together for three years!" This last bit tore from my chest on top of a sob, and once the floodgates opened, I couldn't stop them.

Rita scooted over and put her arms around me, letting me sob into her shoulder. "It's okay." She rubbed my back softly. "Let it all out. I think you buried all of this for too long, and it's high time you washed it out and let the sun dry it all away."

When I'd finally slowed to a few huffing sniffs, Rita pulled away, stood, and went to the bathroom, returning with a box of tissues. "Here, hon, you need these."

I grabbed a tissue and wiped my eyes and blew my nose. "I'm sorry. I guess I didn't know how badly I needed to cry over all of that."

"Honey, don't you dare apologize." Rita held out the bathroom trash can she'd also brought with her. "That horrible man hurt you deeply. Until you stop burying it and deal with it, he's going to keep hurting you. He doesn't deserve that much of your attention and energy."

I took the trash can and set it on the floor next to me, tossing my tissue into it. "No, he doesn't. But with him here in town, I'll be constantly paranoid he'll show up and start more drama. I don't want to fall apart in front of him like I did just now."

"That's why we're talking through it all. It's not healthy to keep it buried, waiting for it to jump up and bite you on the backside." Rita settled back into her corner of the couch. "Now, what's the laugh part?"

"Huh?" I stopped midway through reaching for another tissue, staring at her.

"You said laugh, cry, or be angry. We got the angry and crying out of the way. We're moving on to why part of you wanted to laugh."

A chuckle burbled up, and I pulled a tissue from the box and blew my nose one last time before walking to the kitchen to wash my hands. "I guess just out of the sheer ridiculousness of the situation." I grabbed a bag of treats and whistled for Eddy.

Rita slid onto one of the stools, handing me my mug over the bar top as I turned. "I can feel you there." She mimicked a male voice again, this time with a bit of a slur. "Of all the gin joints in all the towns in all the world, he walks into mine."

I grinned at my friend's old-movie reference to *Casablanca* as I handed Eddy a few treats, trying to make up for spooking him. In the last few months, he'd really blossomed, but he was still skittish about so much. "Okay, Humphrey Bogart, but I don't run a gin joint." I dumped my cold half mug of coffee and reached for the pot to refill it.

"Fine, bookstore. But you knew what I meant."

I turned and leaned against the bar across from her. "I do. And you're right. Why here? Did he know I lived here? Or was it just some cosmic joke of a coincidence that they're getting married here, of all places?"

Rita shook her head. "I don't know. He didn't seem that surprised to see you. If he was, he hid it awfully well."

The scene when they'd walked into the store replayed in my mind. Rita was right. He hadn't seemed surprised. "You don't think he actually looked me up, do you?"

"Why would he?" Rita sipped her coffee. "You've been gone for months, and he hasn't even tried to contact you, has he?"

"No, he hasn't." My brain ran in circles, trying to make sense of the situation. "If he knew I was here, why hadn't he told Missy? She *did* seem surprised to see me."

"Who knows with that man." Rita stood and walked to the sink to rinse her mug. "I have to ask, though. Why didn't you tell her it was a ring you picked out?"

I snorted and shook my head. "I honestly have no idea. I wanted to tell her, just to see the smug look disappear from her face, but something held me back. Maybe it was my mother's training that I always be a lady and that I always be polite, no matter what."

Rita stuck her mug in the dishwasher. "I think your mom would understand if you gave that woman a what-for." An impish smile crossed her lips. "I may just have to do it for you. Oh, that ring is gorgeous. It looks exactly like the one Jenna and Blake bought when they got engaged. Imagine that same ring being in the family for all that time."

I bellowed laughter. "You wouldn't!" Deep laughter continued to push from my chest, washing the rest of the anger and hurt aside.

"I would. I really wasn't kidding when I called her a bridezilla. She's pushy, demanding, bitchy, and hateful to everyone on my staff. None of us can stand her." Rita headed toward the door. "For now, though, I need to get a few things done before I lose the entire day. Groceries wait for no woman."

As I watched Rita walk next door to her own apartment, I replayed again Blake's lack of surprise at seeing me. Had he looked me up? And if he had, why?

Chapter Three

She just had to bring up Casablanca. I rang up another customer, smiling politely while internally railing at Rita's choice of reference. Over the last few months, she'd hooked me on old movies and TV shows. She'd brought this particular movie over several days ago for us to watch while we ate a pizza, and now the entire theme song, "As Time Goes By," was playing in a nonstop loop in my head. *Play it again, Sam.* The famous line of dialogue flitted into my brain as the song started once again.

To be honest, though, Rita had been right. Of all the places in the world, why did Blake Emerson have to walk into my bookstore? Why here? Why now? Why with a fiancée in tow?

This last one brought me up short. Why should I care if he had a fiancée?

"Earth to Jenna." Mason reached across the counter and tapped me on the shoulder. "Where's Eddy?"

I jumped, realizing I'd been so lost in my own world for a moment, I hadn't heard him approach. "Oh, I left him upstairs napping, the lazy bones." I smiled at the thought. Five months ago, Eddy couldn't be left alone for even five minutes. The trauma of seeing his previous owner murdered had been too much for the poor pup. But now, he'd settled in and was okay alone for moderate periods of time.

"I wish I could go nap in the middle of the day. Lucky dog." Mason grinned.

"Me too. I tried to nap with him for a while after Rita left, but my brain would not shut down. Just too much to think about right now." I shook my head.

Mason let out a low whistle. "I can only imagine, what with that Blake dude showing up. Is he really here to get married?"

My eyebrows rose. "As far as I know. At least that's what Missy said. Why do you ask?"

"I don't know." He shrugged. "I was just watching him while you and Missy were talking, and he was staring daggers at her. But when he looked at you, it was like a kid looking through a toy store window. He sees what he wants but can't go in to buy it."

I couldn't help but chuckle at his analogy. "I'm sure you've misread things. Blake has no interest in me. He dumped me in Charlotte, and I haven't heard from him since." I hesitated before continuing. "Can I ask you something odd?"

Mason grinned. "Always. Shoot."

"Since you were watching him, did he seem surprised at all to see me here?" I held my breath, hoping he disagreed with Rita's assessment, because the alternative brought up too many uncomfortable questions.

Placing his palms on the counter, Mason braced himself and let one hip go slack, his head tilted. "You know, now that you bring it up, he didn't really seem surprised. It was like he knew you'd be in here. Not like you. You got all pale, and for a minute, I thought you were going to fall over."

"I almost did. But my mother taught me to always be polite and not to fall apart in front of others. I guess that training came through for me today." I quirked my mouth up in a half smile.

"If he wasn't surprised, that means he knew you were here. But how?"

The door bells chimed, and Mason skittered off to assist another customer. After he'd sold a book on writing your own vows and one of our new wedding planners, he joined me behind the counter, picking up the conversation as if it hadn't been interrupted.

"I mean, did he, like, google you or something? And if he did, why?"

"I have absolutely no idea." I took a deep breath and slowly released it, trying to ease the tension in my shoulders. "I haven't heard from him since before I came here. Honestly, not since before I went to jail, except for the day I got out and he answered our front door and handed me a key to a storage warehouse he'd rented for me."

"What a piece of—" His sentence was interrupted by the door chimes again, and he rose to help another client.

Customers came in a steady stream for the rest of the day, keeping us both busy and giving me something else to focus on for the next few hours. At least it stopped the song from playing over and over in my head.

As closing approached, I told Mason to go ahead and leave, and I'd close the store. After I locked the door behind him, I counted the drawer. Pleased with the day's sales, I walked to the back room and put the cash and credit card receipts in the small safe, as it was too late for a bank run. I checked the bathroom and turned off the lights in the back before returning to the front of the store to turn off the coffeepot warmer and most of the lights.

I looked at my watch. Keith was cooking dinner for me tonight at his place, and I'd better get a move on, as I was already a few minutes late. After making one last sweep of the store, I headed for the stairs to my apartment to grab my purse, a light jacket, my dog, and my car keys. I'd give Eddy a quick potty-walk on the way to the car, and we'd be on our way.

A light rapping on the front door glass caught my attention, and a knot formed in my stomach when I recognized Blake standing in the fading light of a spring sunset.

I walked to the door. "We're closed," I yelled through the door and pointed to the sign that listed our hours. "Please come back tomorrow morning if you need to make a purchase."

"Jenna, please," came the muffled response. "Please just let me talk to you for a few minutes. Please let me explain." When I didn't open the door, he placed his palm on the glass. "Please let me apologize."

This last request broke through my resolve. Hadn't I just told Rita I wanted him to be sorry? Ignoring the warning bells in my head, I opened the door and stepped back, flipping on the interior lights as I closed the door and relocked it. I turned to face him, staying in full view of the street outside. "Okay, talk."

"Jenna, I . . ." Blake reached to take my hand in his.

I stepped back and crossed my arms, hiding my hands under my arms. "Don't touch me. You wanted to talk. So either talk or leave." I nodded my head toward the door.

"Can we go sit down where we're comfortable?" Blake gestured toward the chairs in the reading nook.

I shook my head. "No. You won't be here long enough to get comfortable." I reached for the door lock, intending to usher him out, mentally kicking myself for leaving Eddy upstairs napping for the afternoon.

"Wait. Just give me a moment, okay?"

I dropped my hand from the door lock and recrossed my arms. "Then talk."

He sighed and ran a hand through his hair, hair I'd once loved running my fingers through. Hot pickles on a donut, where had that come from? I shook my head to clear away any sentiment.

"I'm sorry." Blake heaved a sigh. "For everything."

I looked at the glisten in his eyes and wondered if those were actual tears or another manipulation. "Go on."

"I should've been there for you during your trial. I should've visited you while you were in jail. I should've supported you when you came home." He heaved another sigh and reached out for me again, dropping his hand before he made contact.

"You should've done a lot of things. You should've told people we were a couple. You should've told everyone we lived together and were getting married. You should've trusted me that I wasn't a criminal. You should've had my back. Instead, you tossed me out like yesterday's trash, like you didn't give a jolly damn about me. And now you turn up with a new fiancée only a few months later? Are you hiding her like a nasty secret too? She doesn't seem the type to put up with that." I realized I'd been counting off the "should haves" on my fingers and quickly recrossed my arms. No sense in giving him the impression I wanted to hold hands.

Blake's shoulders slumped, and a dark look crossed his face. "No, she's not. She's not anything like you."

"Well isn't that wonderful for you?" I reached for the door again. "You've apologized. Now it's time for you to go."

A hand snaked around my upper arm, and Blake spun me into his arms, pressing his mouth to mine. The wet pressure of his tongue probing my pressed lips gagged me, and I turned my head to the side, pushing at his chest. "Blake, stop!"

Blake pulled me tighter, one hand at my mid-back and the other snaking up into my hair, forcing my head to be still. "Jenna, sweet Jenna." His lips moved across the side of my neck, and he tried to pull my earlobe into his mouth.

After I was attacked a few months ago, Keith had begun to teach me self-defense, and I reacted instinctively. My knee came up and connected solidly with his groin. As he fell to his knees, I brought my knee up into his chin, knocking him on his back.

He rolled to his side, cradling his crotch. "What the hell, Jenna?"

"I told you not to touch me!" I yanked open the store's front door. "Now get the hell out of my store, and don't ever come near me again!"

"Jenna, wait," Blake gasped past real tears this time, although these were likely from pain rather than emotional drama. "I love you. I never stopped."

"Well, it's a little late for that now, isn't it? Now, go!" I gestured at the still-open door.

Blake groaned and rolled to his knees. "Jenna, I don't love her. Please tell me you still love me, and we can be together."

A harsh laugh burst from my throat. "There will *never* be a time when those words come out of my mouth."

"But I'll leave her for you." He pulled himself to his feet, using the counter as support, an angry red bruise beginning to show across his chin. "She means nothing to me. Not like you. I love everything about you. I need you."

His fevered look spooked me. "If you don't leave now, I will scream at the top of my lungs. This door is open, and everyone on the street"—I swept my arm in the direction of the Weeping Willow, where two couples stood on the sidewalk talking—"will hear me and will call the police."

Blake stumbled through the doorway, turning as he exited. "Jenna, please just give me a chance."

Motion caught my eye, and I saw Keith approaching.

Keith waved and grinned, although he was close enough I could see the worry etched in his face. "Hey, Jenna, you were late, so I thought I'd pop over to see if I could help you close up."

Relief washed through me. "Hi, thanks." I smiled as he joined me in the doorway and slid an arm around my waist, planting a kiss on my cheek.

Blake's jaw dropped. "But . . ."

I slid my own arm around Keith's back, bunching his jacket up in my fist where Blake couldn't see it. I felt Keith's back tense, understanding my signal. "Blake, this is Keith Logan, a detective with the Hokes Folly PD." I gestured with a nod toward Blake. "Keith, this is Blake Emerson."

Keith's grip tightened around my waist, and he ignored Blake's outstretched hand, refusing to shake it in greeting. "Hello."

"I was just encouraging Blake to leave." I stepped back into the store, pulling Keith with me. "Please don't return." I closed the door and turned the lock.

"We're not done," Blake yelled through the door. "We have to talk. We have to straighten this out!"

Keith reached into his pocket and pulled out his badge, smacking it up against the front door glass. "I believe she asked you to move along."

Blake stumbled back before turning and staggering toward the parking lot.

Keith stared after him for a moment before turning and gathering me into his arms. "Are you okay?"

I nodded, unable to respond with my face pressed into his jacket.

After a moment, he released his tight grip on me and stepped back, tilting my face up toward his. "Are you sure?"

I took a deep breath. "Yes, I really am." I burst into laughter. It roiled up out of my chest, uncontrollable, powerful, cleansing, bringing tears to my eyes. When I could draw breath, I stumbled behind the counter to grab a tissue, and I sank onto one of the stools. "I really, really am just fine."

Keith's knit brows signaled he wasn't convinced. "Tell me what happened?"

"Let's get out of here. I'll tell you on the way."

We tromped upstairs to leash Eddy and get my things and headed to the parking lot. On the drive over, I told him about Blake and Missy's appearance at the store earlier in the day and Blake's return that evening.

When I got to the part where I put Blake on the ground, Keith burst out laughing. "I'm proud of you! Guess you really did learn a few things." He slid into the driveway at his house. He'd lived in a tiny apartment since he'd moved to Hokes Folly—one that made my loft above the store seem huge. He'd finally purchased a home, gaining more space and getting off the rent roller coaster. This was the first time he'd cooked for me since he'd moved in three weeks ago.

"It was actually quite cathartic." I giggled at the memory as we walked toward the front door. "I wish I could have caught it on video. That way I could watch it again and again." I shoved aside my inner Mom-voice telling me I shouldn't dwell on such unpleasant things.

We'd reached his front door, and he unlocked it, swinging it open for Eddy and me to precede him into his house. Silently I entered, wondering how he'd set it up. He hadn't let me help him move, unpack, or decorate, so I had no idea what to expect. His tiny apartment—less than six hundred square feet—had always felt cramped and cluttered, with no sense of design or style.

As I stepped past the small foyer, I looked into a spacious living room with a fireplace set with wood, as if ready to be lit. Noticing the white wine chilling in a silver bucket on the dark cherry coffee table, I guessed a fire was indeed on the menu for tonight's event. Across from the living room, I spied a large kitchen with light oak cabinets, as well as a double wall oven and a refrigerator with French doors and the freezer below. A light-colored granite covered the long span of counter space, adding a touch of elegance to the room. In both the dining area adjacent to the kitchen and the living room, long windows stretched from almost floor to ceiling, covered by soft golden curtains, still open to the night sky beyond the glass.

I turned to see Keith hovering, a hopeful expression on his face. "I love it. It's perfect."

Keith visibly relaxed, a grin splitting his face as he passed me on his way into the kitchen. "I'll save the bedroom tour for later." He winked over his shoulder.

I snorted. "I'll just bet you will." I unhooked Eddy's leash, and we followed Keith into the kitchen, where I sat on a stool by the island. "What's for dinner, Chef Keith?"

He slid a Dutch oven from the upper oven door, set it on the glass cooktop, and carefully opened the lid. Setting the lid to the side, Keith reached for a cooking spoon and poked around in the opaque dish. "Looks done."

Eddy hovered around Keith's feet, nose in the air working furiously. Keith took the doggy hint and dropped a tidbit on the floor for the dog to gobble.

"Whatever it is, it smells heavenly." I inhaled deeply, letting the smells of cooking herbs brush across my senses. "And Eddy seems to approve."

Keith chuckled and gestured at the dining table, already set for two, including a vase full of flowers and two previously lit candles. "Want to relight those? I had to blow them out to come check on you."

I cringed. "Yeah, sorry about that. I didn't mean to be late. We had late customers, and I let Mason go home, since he has to be there early tomorrow to start spring inventory."

"And then Blake showed up." Keith kept his voice light, but his hands tightly gripped the platter he pulled from a cabinet.

My stomach knotted. "Yes, Blake showed up."

"Do you still love him?" Keith stood still, his back to me.

I crossed the room and wrapped my arms around his chest from behind. "Absolutely not. Not even a tiny bit."

He turned in my arms and tipped my chin up. "Are you sure? No regrets? No wishful thinking? No what-ifs?"

I stared into the brown depths of his eyes, reading his hope and his fear. "Keith, I love only one man, want only one man, need only one man, and have lots of wishful thinking and what-ifs about only one man, and that man is not Blake Emerson."

Keith's pupils dilated and his nostrils flared as he inhaled deeply before lowering his lips to mine. I wrapped my arms around his neck as he deepened the kiss, and my heart lurched when he stooped down and tucked an arm under my knees, sweeping me up into his arms, moving through the house.

Softness enveloped me, and I opened my eyes to see the four-poster bed in his bedroom, my back on the luxurious mattress. "I guess we're taking that bedroom tour now, huh?" I grinned up at him.

Keith's answering kiss pushed all other thoughts from my head. Abruptly, he swung away. "Not now, Eddy."

I giggled, propping up on my elbows to see the dog's paws on the edge of the bed, a hopeful face looking at us. "He just wants to see the room too."

Keith groaned. "Yeah, well, he'll have to wait his turn." He jumped up and ushered Eddy out of the room, and I heard him talking softly to Eddy in the living room.

A couple of minutes passed, and Keith reentered the room. "We had a man-to-man talk about not trying to interrupt certain activities. I also showed him the new cushy dog bed I bought just for him, just for such situations, and gave him a few more treats from dinner. We're good now."

"Oh, I see how it is. The dog gets to eat it when it's warm and fresh, but I have to wait?" I sat up and crossed my arms.

Keith eased the bedroom door closed and crossed the room, a sexy and wicked grin on his face. "Trust me, you won't mind."

I opened my arms, and he sank onto the bed and into my embrace, and I didn't mind at all.

Chapter Four

"What's on your agenda for the day?" Keith forked his last bite of scrambled eggs into his mouth.

I scrolled through my mental planner. "I have to work on inventory with Mason. He's already there, getting a head start. I need to set up a vet appointment for Eddy. He's due for a booster with his shots. And I need to do a bit of spring cleaning at the apartment and the store."

Keith stood and took his plate to the sink, rinsed it, and put it in the dishwasher. "Sounds like a busy day and a lot more entertaining than mine. I'm riding the front desk today. Sutter called in sick."

"Isn't he due to retire at the end of the month?" I took my plate to the sink and followed Keith's example, determined not to leave a mess in his dreamy new kitchen.

Keith nodded and dried his hands on a towel before handing it to me. "He is. His full retirement hits on his birthday, which is in a few days. They're giving him until the end of March, both for bookkeeping purposes and for ease of transition. Or that's what they call it."

"How does it make it easier to force someone to retire at the end of the month instead of in the middle?" I rehung the towel on the oven bar.

"Who knows?" Keith shrugged. "Either way they do it, Sutter is furious about it."

"I'm sure he'll find some way to blame it all on me." I chuckled. The older detective had spent the last few months trying to pin a crime—any crime—on me, determined to prove he hadn't been wrong that I was guilty of the charges of embezzlement and murder in Charlotte.

Keith planted a kiss on my forehead. "I'm sure you're worrying too much about it." He strode across the room and grabbed a jacket from the hook, keys in hand. "You ready? I need to get going, or I'll be late."

I picked up Eddy's leash and hooked it to his collar, took one last sweeping look around Keith's beautiful new home, and snagged my purse and keys to follow Keith out. "I really do love it. In spite of eating a cold dinner." I flashed him a saucy grin.

Keith pulled me into an embrace on the front porch. "Let's give the new neighbors something to gossip about." He lowered his lips to mine.

A few minutes later, head spinning and lips tingling, I got into my car with Eddy and headed to my apartment for a shower and change of clothes. As I unlocked my door, Rita stepped from hers.

"My, my, my." She sashayed over to me and leaned in to sniff my shirt. "Is that a man's cologne I smell? And weren't you wearing that exact outfit yesterday?"

A grin slid over my face as I opened my door and stepped through, leaving the door open for Rita to follow. "Yes, and yes."

"Dish it, woman." Rita closed the door behind her and planted herself on one of my barstools. "I have a few minutes to spare before I need to head to work."

I laughed, filling the coffeepot. "Give me a few minutes to shower and change while the coffee brews. Can you wait that long?"

Rita stood and came around the bar into the kitchen. "I can. Let me finish making the coffee. You go get cleaned up."

I smiled all the way through my shower. Good friends. A good man. Life was sweet, in spite of the drama Blake was trying to cause. When I walked into the kitchen, clean and dressed for the day, Rita already had a mug of coffee waiting for me.

"I poured it a few minutes ago. It should be cool enough for you now." She topped off her mug and leaned on the bar.

"Thanks." I took a sip. "It's perfect."

"Okay, you're clean, you're dressed, you no longer smell like a hot date. Now dish it, sister." Rita grinned and took a sip of coffee.

"Not much to dish." I sat on a stool and propped my bare feet on the bottom rung. "He gave me a tour of his new house, and he cooked dinner for me."

Rita gave me a "yeah, and . . .?" look. "A tour, huh? Must be a house the size of Hokes Bluff Inn for it to have taken that long to see it all."

I grinned, and heat rushed into my cheeks. "Some rooms took longer than others."

Rita belly laughed. "I'll just bet they did. And who cooked breakfast?"

"I did. It was only fair." I rubbed my chilly feet on top of each other, wishing I'd taken the time to put on socks.

"Uh-huh." Rita snorted and took another sip of coffee. "What's the new house like?"

I spent the next few minutes describing the luxurious kitchen, the huge soaker tub and spacious tile shower in the master bath, the spare bedroom he'd set up as his home office, the doggy door he'd installed for Eddy so my dog could go into the fenced backyard whenever he wanted, and the gorgeous wood beamed ceiling in the living room over the stone fireplace hearth.

Rita turned to put her mug in the sink. "Sounds like you and Eddy will be very happy there when he asks you to move in."

I barely managed to keep the coffee from going down the wrong pipe, coughing a bit before I could sputter an answer. "What is wrong with you? I almost choked!"

"Just checking to see if you were listening." Rita shrugged and grabbed her purse and jacket off one of the stools. "I notice you didn't argue about the possibility."

"I . . ." Damn, she was right. I hadn't argued. "I guess not."

"Well, I just want an invitation when the time comes." Rita pulled open my front door. "And I don't mean to the house-warming party." She strode down the walkway toward the stairs, humming the wedding march.

Really? I rolled my eyes. *She just had to stick another song in my head.* I shut my door and rushed to finish getting ready to go, grabbed Eddy's leash, and headed out to give him a mid-morning potty break before work, the wedding march playing on a loop in my head.

As I approached my store from the front, I saw Missy and a group of women ahead of me on the opposite side of the street. I ducked through the propped-open doorway of a storefront, hoping to avoid Missy and her friends, turning to look out the front window to watch for when the coast was clear to make it to my own store. I was not up for another verbal sparring match with Blake's bridezilla today.

"Hi, welcome to Candle Cottage." A happy voice sounded behind me. "May I help you with something?"

I turned, realizing I'd popped into the new candle store that had opened in part of the Hokes sisters' old store. Their space had been split into two stores again, and the one closest to mine remained empty, but this one had rented out a month ago. A woman in a business suit and heels approached, her hand held out toward me.

I extended my hand to shake hers. "I'm Jenna Quinn. I own Twice Upon a Time a couple doors down from here. I just thought I'd come in and introduce myself."

Her eyebrows rose. "You do know it's okay to admit you're trying to avoid that woman out there." She grinned at me. "I'm Shelby Foster. And I may run to your store and hide next time she wants to come in here."

A laugh burst from my chest. "Shelby, it's a deal. Is it okay that I have my dog, Eddy, with me?"

"Absolutely." She reached down and stroked Eddy's head. "I love dogs."

"Thanks. We just need to hide out long enough for them to pass my store." I waved a hand in the direction of the bookstore. "Then we'll be out of your hair."

Shelby and I stood at the windows, watching the women traipse down the street. Missy abruptly turned to enter my store and almost immediately left with a frown and a huffy step.

"Do you know her?" Shelby craned her head to get a better view.

"Not really." I shifted over to give her a better view of the street. "She used to work at the same company as I did in Charlotte." I wasn't going to offer that she was also engaged to my ex-fiancé and was wearing my engagement ring. Some things were better avoided on a first meeting.

"She doesn't seem happy that you're not in your store." Shelby walked behind her counter and answered the phone, which had begun to ring.

I stared at the group hovering on the sidewalk outside my doorway. Missy obviously wanted to talk to me about something. Likely she wanted to be snotty and spiteful, as she had been the other day. An older woman stood to one side, and her face pulled at my memory. I was pretty sure that was Blake's mother. He'd kept a picture of her on the mantle when we lived together.

The woman stood with her lips pursed in a disapproving manner. Did she not like her soon-to-be daughter-in-law?

Motion caught my eye from the opposite direction as Shelby reappeared by my side. A young man, his brown hair flying in the breeze, strode up the walkway toward the women, a large bouquet of roses in his hand. My jaw dropped when he lowered himself to one knee in front of Missy, handed her the roses, and opened a ring box. I edged closer to the open door, hoping not to be seen, but unable to resist getting close enough to the doorway to hear what was said.

"I love you. I've always loved you. We belong together. Missy Plott, will you marry me and make me the happiest man on the planet?" The man's hopeful expression gleamed behind the ring box he extended.

Missy coquettishly smelled the roses before thrusting them back to the man. Laughter burbled up, and three of her friends burst out laughing, nasty grins on their faces as they mocked the man in unison.

"Why on earth would I ever want to marry you?" She waved her left hand in front of him, flashing her engagement ring. "See this?" She then snatched the ring box out of his hand and turned to wave it in front of his face. "And do you see the chip of diamond you bought? Oh, wait, of course not, because it's microscopic!"

"But . . . but . . ." He sputtered and rose from his knees. "I spent two months' salary on that ring, like you're supposed to."

Missy sneered and snorted. "That's exactly the point. Why would I trade marrying a man who can buy me this"—she waved her hand in his face again—"for one who can't even afford a diamond that's big enough to actually see? Don't you see that I'm planning a big, expensive wedding? Anything I want? We're getting married up at that big inn, and I'm on my way to buy a gown at an exclusive boutique. I'm spending more on this wedding than you'll earn in two years from your job. I got out of that furniture plant in Hickory when I got my job in Charlotte. I am *not* letting you drag me back there."

The man staggered back, dropping the roses to the ground. "But we were so in love before you got that job. I don't understand." His voice came out in a ragged gasp.

Missy's friends gathered around her like a clique of high school mean girls. All except one, who glared daggers at the bride-to-be, her jaw clenched and her cheeks flushed. Blake's mother caught my eye, and my eyebrows rose. She stood to the side, a mix of disgust and disappointment warring on her face.

"In love?" Missy snorted again. "Hardly. You were my ticket out of my daddy's house. When I got my new job, I found a better ticket. One that will get me away from the likes of you for good, Tom Jackson!"

Tom turned and fled, clutching the ring box, the roses forgotten on the sidewalk and a half sob, half growl ripping from his chest as he raced past the candle store's open door. Blake's mother stared after him, lips pursed and arms crossed.

"As if!" Missy rolled her eyes and turned to her friends. "Let's go, girls. I have a wedding dress to buy, and I plan to spend scads of money."

"What is wrong with you?" The girl who had stared daggers at Missy earlier screeched at Missy's back. "Do you not have one ounce of kindness in your shriveled up, gold-digging heart?"

Missy whirled, her other friends parting around her. "Why, yes, I do." Her mouth turned up on one corner in a snarky smile. "I invited you to be one of the bridesmaids because I had to, not because I wanted you." She swept her hand across the rest of the girls. "Can you see which one is not like the others?"

"If you mean not a cold-hearted bitch, yes, I do!" Tears began to flow down the girl's face. "And I'm well aware the only reason you asked me is because I'm your little sister."

"Then why don't you start acting like it, you ungrateful brat?" Missy snarled and stepped forward.

Holy cow on a cracker! Were they going to throw down right here in the street? I ducked a little farther back into the doorway, bumping into Shelby.

"Hey," she whispered. "Don't block my view. This is better than soap operas."

I shifted to the side a bit, and we both glued our attention to the continually unfolding drama in front of my store.

Blake's mother looked like she was about to faint from embarrassment. "Girls, girls! Let's not create a scene in public, shall we?"

Missy rounded on her. "You keep out of this, you old hag! I'll do what I damned well please, and you can't do a thing about it. My mama died years ago, and I'm not looking for a replacement." She turned to her sister. "And Connie, you're out of the wedding."

"I'm glad!" Connie pointed to the roses. "You wouldn't know true love if it bit you on the backside, you ignorant witch! You've had everything handed to you. Your fancy-schmancy job, a fiancé who lets you spend money hand over fist, and even the heart of a decent, kind, sweet man who would do anything for you. And you stomped his heart in the dirt! I hate you!"

Missy stepped forward, raised her hand and swung, landing a solid slap across Connie's cheek. "Mama only had you because she couldn't afford her birth control pills! I was seven, and I had to share everything with you. My room. My clothes. My friends. My *everything*. Then she up and died, and at nineteen, I was stuck raising a kid."

"That's not my fault!" Connie held a hand to her face. "Besides, you hated Mama."

Missy stepped forward, her fists balled at her sides. "I hated you more because you sucked what was left of my life away. I've been working the last few years trying to raise a kid when I was barely a kid myself."

"Stop treating me like a child!" Tears streamed down Connie's face, and her shoulders shook with sobs. "I'll be eighteen in two months, and when I graduate from high school, I hope I never see you again."

"You think you're such a grown-up?" Missy laughed and poked a finger into Connie's chest. "Fine, go be a grown-up. I've found what I want. I've found a way to never be dirt poor again, and you're not going to mess this up for me. If you think Tom is so amazing, *you* go get him." Missy waved her hand in the direction Tom had gone.

Connie staggered back, ducking as if she thought Missy was going to strike her again. "I hate you! I wish you were dead!" She stooped and grabbed most of the roses in one sweep and rushed off, following Tom.

Blake's mother, eyes wide and face pale, again tried to regain control. "Ladies, let's just move on to the dress shop and see if we can find period-appropriate gowns for all of you." Her hands shook as she waved them around, as if herding the girls to her.

"Whatever." Missy turned and trounced off down the street, her mean-girl bridesmaid trio and a flustered mother-of-the-groom behind her.

Shelby whistled low and stepped back. "I wouldn't have believed it if I hadn't just seen it with my own eyes."

"I just saw it, and I'm still not sure I believe it." I shook my head. What did Blake see in her?

"At least that didn't occur inside one of our stores." Shelby crossed her arms. "That woman caused enough drama as it was. I've never had this much trouble just trying to sell a set of unity candles."

"Well, they have them now. At least she shouldn't be back, right?" I grinned and headed to the door.

"Thank goodness for that." Shelby chuckled as she headed toward the once-again ringing phone. "Feel free to hide out again if you ever need to. I'll try to stick a few dog treats behind the counter for Eddy."

I laughed as I left, glad to have found a new friend in town.

Chapter Five

"Oh, man, you missed it. Wait 'til I tell you." A huge grin split his face as Mason rushed toward me.

"I saw. I was hiding out in the new candle store down the street." I set my purse behind the counter and turned to look out in time to see Missy and her troupe enter a bridal shop that had opened down the street. Maybe she'd find something that didn't show her navel. Rita would be thrilled.

"Yeah, but you didn't hear what she said when she came in here." Mason's smug look matched his crossed arms.

I laughed. "Okay, spill it. What did she say?" I unhooked Eddy's leash, and he followed me behind the counter, where I sat on one of the stools.

"She breezed in the door, asking if you were here, all fake smiles." Mason sashayed, his hips swaying and his hand on his chest, mimicking a female voice. "Is Jenna here today?" Mason dropped his hand from his chest. "When I told her you weren't in yet, her nice-nice act stopped. She said to tell you she'd be back to talk to you and that you'd better not be avoiding her."

"Oh my." My eyebrows shot up and my eyes widened. If I kept being surprised this often, I was going to get permanent wrinkles on my forehead. "To be fair, I *was* avoiding her. But no need to tell her that."

Mason looked out the window again, craning his neck as if to see if there were more drama unfolding. "Did you see the old lady?"

I looked out the window and back at Mason, taking a moment to realize whom he meant. "Yes, I saw Blake's mother."

"Wow." Mason propped his elbows on the counter. "I'd hate to be her. Going by the look on her face, she is *not* happy about Missy. But then, after all Missy shouted about marrying Blake because he made more money, I can't say I blame her."

I recalled the older woman's look as she stared after the retreating ex-boyfriend. "Did you see how she watched Tom when he left?"

Mason nodded. "It was weird, like she wanted to go after him or something."

"You don't think . . ." I rolled the replay through my head. "What if she told Tom where to find Missy and set this all up?"

"Like to break up Missy and Blake?" He shoved back from the counter. "Man, that would put a twist in things, wouldn't it?"

The door chimes sounded, cutting off my answer. But Mason had been wrong. This whole thing had more twists than the Blue Ridge Parkway.

The rest of the afternoon passed with a steady flow of customers. I'd spent over an hour with four ladies who lugged in almost a dozen boxes of old romances they wanted to trade in for credit. I had to go through each book and check to ensure we didn't have a huge overstock of that title, as well as check the book's condition. I didn't accept books that smelled of smoke or animal pee, and unless it was a really popular title in high demand, I didn't take books with anything more than gentle wear on them.

After leaving several books with missing covers and more with severely broken spines and pages falling out in one box and a dozen older romances for which I had no need, I tallied up their totals and off they went into the stacks to shop with their credit.

As I'd tallied, I'd organized the books as much as I could in order to make shelving them easier. Mason had already lugged one box down the romance aisle, and I reached for a second box and had made it partway across to the aisle when the door chimes sounded again.

I turned and froze, gripping my box tighter. "Can I help you?"

Missy's three bridesmaids stood just inside the door, looking as if they'd rather be anywhere than here. The one in front turned back to whisper something, and all three came alive with smiles and Southern charm. Each wore a painfully bright white tennis outfit and light tennis shoes. Where in the world were they going to play tennis in this town? I didn't think Elliot had installed a court at the inn.

The bridesmaid who had apparently assumed the leadership role in Missy's absence stepped forward, extending a hand in greeting, making sure to flash the expensive diamond bracelet that sparkled on her wrist. "Hi, I'm Mandy, and they're Molly and Mickey." She gestured to the women on either side.

I managed not to guffaw. Missy, Mandy, Molly, Mickey. Could it get any more bizarre?

Mandy must have caught my blink of a grin before I'd buried it. Her face drew down in a frown. "We call ourselves the M Squad."

My mother's training took hold, and I stepped to the counter and put down the box to reach out and shake her hand. "That's great." I smiled in a friendly bookstore owner way. "What can I do for you today?"

Mandy pasted a fake smile on her face. "We're hoping to find a great gift for Missy for the wedding. She bought us these amazing bracelets as bridesmaid's gifts." She flashed her wrist again, mimicked by Molly and Mickey. "We want to find something unique to get for her in return."

I resisted the urge to ask why they'd think Missy would want a book, even if it was expensive, as a gift. She didn't impress me as much of a reader. But who knew? Maybe I was judging Missy based on my dislike for Blake. "I'm sure we can find just the right book."

"Books?" Mickey, or was it Molly, frowned and crossed her arms. "I thought we could buy her, like, some expensive crystal thing to sit on a shelf and look nice."

Well, there went the theory that Missy liked books. "I'm sorry, we only sell used and antique books." I smiled again. "But some of the antiques are very valuable and would look good as a display piece." I noticed the third woman had disappeared, and I caught a flash of white as it rounded a corner on the other side of the store. "Is your friend looking for something in particular?"

"Used?" Mandy sniffed and wrinkled her nose as if she smelled something rotten, completely ignoring my question. "You don't have anything new?"

I tried to take in a deep breath through my nose without making it obvious, hoping Eddy hadn't let go with one of his room-clearing farts. Nope, all I smelled was the coffeepot a few feet away. "The only new book we carry right now is the wedding planner in the window. Missy already has a copy of that book."

"Then I guess your store is completely useless," she huffed and pursed her lips as the third girl reappeared. "Let's go, girls. I'm sure some store in this backwater little town has something decent for a gift."

They flounced out of the store, and as they passed my windows, they quickened their paces.

I'd picked up the box of traded-in books and headed toward the romance section when a screech ripped through the room.

"Fire!" One of the ladies who had traded in the books ran out of the antique section of the store.

Eddy leapt from his nap in a sunny spot, barking at the woman as she ran past him and out the door, followed by her friend.

The box of paperbacks dropped from my hands, and I raced toward a small column of smoke spiraling up over the shelves. "Mason! Get the extinguisher!" Rounding the corner, I saw a small pile of books on the floor, a flame burning in their center, growing rapidly higher and spreading to the carpet.

Mason's footfalls sounded behind me, and he pushed me aside, aiming the nozzle of the extinguisher and pressing the lever. White goo shot out and covered the flames, smothering them into the pile of damaged books.

A siren wailed in the distance. Great, that's all I needed.

The door chimes sounded, and a moment later, the woman who had found the fire peeked around the corner. "I called nine-one-one! I think I hear them coming!"

The sirens drew closer, and I realized they were coming up the alleyway behind the store. Hot pickles on a cupcake. All I needed was for some well-meaning firemen to break down my back door.

I ran through the store, Eddy barking at my heels, and ripped the door open just as the firemen began to pound. "It's fine. The fire's out." My words rushed out in a tumble.

The front fireman signaled to the others that the coast was clear and turned to me, pulling off his helmet. "Aren't you the lady we pulled out of the burning library a few months ago?"

I cringed, remembering one of my less intelligent actions of late. But I'd been trying to solve the murder of a colleague. "Yes, I am. But I don't need to be rescued this time. Everything's fine."

He stepped through the doorway. "We have to check it out and write up a report any time we're called, ma'am."

I stood back and let three men in burly fire gear walk through the back room and into the front room, snaking my fingers through Eddy's collar to keep him from getting in their way. "It's over there." I pointed in the direction of the burned pile of books.

The man nodded. "I know. We can smell it, although I don't think it's strong enough to have caused any smoke damage to the walls."

Smoke damage? Crap, I hadn't considered the stench might have soaked into any undamaged books nearby.

Mason stepped back as we approached, striding toward a beckoning fireman. The man reached out to check the extinguisher and shared a few words with Mason before handing the equipment back to my employee. Mason nodded, his face drawn into a serious frown.

When he looked up, I motioned at Mason and pointed down at Eddy.

Mason crossed to where I stood. "Want me to take him upstairs?"

"Please." I surrendered my hold on the dog. "The door's unlocked. Sit with him a minute or two to make sure he calms down."

Mason headed toward the spiral stairs, leaning a bit to the side to keep his fingers looped through Eddy's collar. Over the tops of the shelves, I watched their feet disappear onto the second floor.

My chimes jangled angrily as the door was flung open, and I jumped.

"Jenna!" Running footsteps were followed by Keith rounding into the aisle and dragging me into his arms. "Are you okay?"

"Not if I can't breathe." I pulled back and looked up.

He loosened his arms. "Sorry. All I knew was that your store was on fire." His brow wrinkled as he looked over my shoulder. "Is that all that burned?"

I slid out of his arms and turned. "Yeah, thanks to a customer, we found it right as it started."

The fireman stood. "This was deliberately set." He held up the burned remains of a matchbook smeared with white goo.

Way to go, Captain Obvious. "Yeah, we kind of figured that, since the books aren't normally in a little pile in the floor."

The man chuckled. "Yeah, I get that."

Keith flashed his badge before reaching out to take the matchbook cover. "It's too damaged to see where it came from. Can you tell anything else?"

The man shook his head. "Not really. The chemicals in the spray diluted any small amount of accelerant that may have been used. It would take a lab to sort it all out."

I tugged on Keith's arm. "There's no need. I'm pretty sure I know who did it, but there will be no way to prove it." I explained about Missy's bridesmaid trio and how one of them had sneaked off into this corner for a few minutes right before they left.

I turned to the fireman. "Do I need to sign anything? Will my store be shut for any length of time?" All I needed was to lose sales over something this ridiculous.

He shook his head. "No, ma'am. I think we can handle it from here. It seems pretty simple and straight forward, and with the police here, I think we're done." He turned and motioned to the other firemen, and they tromped toward the back door.

Mason called from across the room. "I'm back. I'll go lock up behind them."

I turned to the pair of shoppers, who had apparently deemed it safe to stand at the end of the aisle and watch once the firemen were present. They whispered between themselves excitedly. This was probably the highlight of their shopping day.

"Ladies, if you don't mind, I need to close the store for the remainder of the day." I gestured for them to follow me to the counter, where I rang up the books they'd already picked out and gave them credit slips for the remaining credit on their traded books, thanking them for shopping—and for their quick thinking, which had saved my store—and waving to them as they left.

I turned after locking the door and realized Keith hadn't followed me. I crossed the store and walked down the aisle toward the burned pile. "The fire's out. No need to keep watching it."

He stood, arms crossed while he stared at the pile of books. "So, what really happened?"

I frowned. "What really happened is exactly what I told you happened. I had a group of ladies trade in a ton of books. Right after that, Missy's bridesmaids came in wanting to buy her a gift, but apparently not a book. One of them disappeared over here for a minute or so, and then they left. Right after that, one of my traders screamed there was a fire."

"Nothing else?" He looked up and cocked his head, his eyes boring into me.

I shook my head and shrugged. "Nothing else. I'm just glad the shoppers were still here, or it would have gotten a lot worse before Mason or I saw it."

Keith sighed and reached out, grabbing my hand to pull me into his arms again, this time without the death grip he'd used when he'd almost crushed the breath out of me earlier. "I'm just glad you're okay."

"I know." I pulled out of his arms and turned, kneeling beside the burned books. "It just doesn't make sense. Why would those women want to set fire to my store?"

"You did physically attack Missy's fiancé." He knelt beside me and pulled a book from the stack.

"Hey, that was in self-defense, and you know it." Did he honestly think I shouldn't have done whatever it took to get away from Blake?

Keith shrugged. "I know that, but you have no idea how Blake could have spun things. They might have been trying to impress Missy by striking out at you over it."

"Maybe." I pulled the book from his hands, recognizing the tome. "Oh. Oh no."

"What is it?" Keith leaned in.

I wiped the chemicals away from what was once a rich green cover. This had been the top book on the stack, and burns covered what I knew had been a picture of five children frolicking with a yellow farmhouse in the background printed directly onto the cloth covering the book.

The title page had curled in the flame, but I knew the book by heart. "The Five Little Peppers and How They Grew. It was written in the late 1800s, but this copy was from 1909."

"You know the dates on all your books?" Keith took the book back and flipped it closed, running his hands over the burned cover.

"Only a few special ones." I touched the cover again before pulling my fingers away. "My mother used to read that book to me when I was little. Her mother had read it to her, too. When I ran across a copy at in a box of books from an estate sale, I almost took it upstairs. Now I wish I had."

"I'm sorry, Jenna." Keith reached out to squeeze my hand. "For everything."

"Me too," I whispered.

Mason rounded the corner, shattering the moment. "I'm gonna keep shelving books, if that's okay. That way it'll be done before we open tomorrow."

After he trotted off, I reached for the other two books in the pile. "I hate to see any of these books damaged for such a petty reason. They made it this far, through readings, handling, sometimes moving several times, and in such good shape, only to be set on fire." I shook my head.

Keith pulled one from my hands. "What were they?"

I peered at the brown cover he held and barely made out the remains of the title *Marian Grey* stamped in gold on the spine. "That was a gothic romance novel originally published during the Civil War, although I think this copy was from the 1880s. I read a copy of it back during my *Jane Eyre* days."

This book hadn't been as badly damaged, and Keith flipped to the first page and read. "'The night was dark and the clouds black and heavy which hung over Redstone Hall, whose massive walls loomed up through the darkness like some huge sentinel keeping guard over the spacious grounds by which it was surrounded.' Man, that sounds like something Snoopy would write."

I laughed. "It was a dark and stormy night, huh?"

Keith grinned at me and pointed at the third book, which I held. "What's that one?"

As it had been on the bottom of the pile, it's green cloth front cover was relatively unscathed, as was the ornate title stamped in gold. "*Songs of Three Centuries.* It's a compilation of lyrical poetry, published in the late 1800s. The many authors included Blake, Tennyson, Longfellow, Milton, both Robert and Elizabeth Barrett Browning, Emerson, and even Shakespeare. None of any author's longer works were included. Only their short stuff."

Keith stood. "Emerson, huh?" He sighed through his nose.

I picked up the three books and stood. "I doubt the fact that Blake's ancestor was in this book, along with well over a hundred other authors, had anything to do with it. I think she just grabbed the closest books she could reach."

Keith looked down and shuffled a foot through the scarred spot on the floor. "I hope your insurance will cover this."

The carpet on that section of floor had blackened where the heat had hit it, making a distinctive pattern on the otherwise gray-colored flooring. "It is what it is. We'll figure it out."

"They're getting married this weekend?" Keith snaked his arm around my waist as we walked toward the door. "They're gone after Saturday?"

I nodded and grinned, trying to ease the tension. "Only three more shopping days to go." At his reproving look, I added, "Look, they have to realize I know it was them. I don't think they'll try it again."

Keith brushed his lips across mine. "Let's hope you're right." He turned and left, the door chimes tinkling a soft goodbye.

I walked back to stare at the black scar on my burned carpet, fingers of brown in a starburst around it.

The door chimes sounded again, and Mason appeared around the corner. "There's someone asking for you."

Heaving a deep, emotionally exhausted sigh, I turned and headed toward the counter, delighted when I saw who stood there. "Shelby. What brings you by?"

She planted her hands on her hips. "Are you kidding me? Firemen? A big firetruck in the alleyway behind the stores parked right behind your door? And you ask why I came down here? I'd have been here sooner, but I had a customer." She stopped, taking a long sweeping look around the store. "I don't see any issues. And this store is amazing. I love books."

"Let me give you the nickel tour." I led her away from the burned area, hoping she'd forget why she ran down. "This is our fiction section, organized by genre and author."

Over the next ten minutes, I walked the aisles with her, moving at a snail's pace by the time I got to the damaged area. I shifted my body, blocking her view down the aisle. "And this is our section with our antiques, including poetry books, history, foreign language, reference books, and novels."

Before I could turn her away, she brushed past me and pulled a book from the shelf. "Imagine the stories this book has seen, not just the story behind its cover." She ran her fingers gently across the cover and slid the book back onto the shelf. "If only they could talk."

I grinned. "I know, right?"

Her nose wrinkled. "Is something burning?"

The smile fell from my face. So much for that hope. I stepped aside and gestured down the aisle toward the burned carpet. "No. We had a small . . . accident."

"Oh no!" She strode toward the damage, turning a full circle when she reached the blackened flooring. "How would a fire start here? I don't see anything electrical or dangerous here."

"Um . . ." There was no way to answer this without opening a can of worms. "Someone sort of helped it along."

"What?" She stooped and ran her fingers across the charred carpet. "You mean someone set this? Why?"

"It was Missy's bridesmaids." I sighed and shoved my hands in my pockets. "But please keep that to yourself. I don't want the negative publicity." Especially since I'd already had three murders linked to the store in the past few months.

"Missy. You mean the bridezilla who all but got into a brawl in the street a while ago?" She stood and brushed her fingertips off against each other.

"Yep." I nodded. "That's her."

"Did you call the police?" she asked.

"Keith came. He said he thinks it's because of my ex." I cringed, realizing I hadn't told her about my personal drama wrapped up in Missy's earlier outburst.

"Ooooh." Shelby grinned and rubbed her palms together. "This sounds interesting. Dish it, sister. Who is Keith, and who is the ex?"

I sighed and shook my head, wishing I'd been more vague. "I need coffee for this."

"Hey, wait a sec." Shelby ran the toe of her pump across the burned spot. "Do you see that?"

I knelt and probed the spot, finding a tiny hole burned all the way through. I pulled at the ruined threads revealing a sliver of wood.

Shelby tucked her skirt and squatted, knees together, beside me. "Girl, I think that's hardwood. My daddy used to work for a flooring company." She stuck a finger into the slightly larger hole and tugged, pulling apart more of the damaged carpet. "It is!" She squealed excitedly. "Do you think the owner will let you pull up the old carpet and get to this yummy wood? Might be cheaper for them than paying to replace the carpet."

I stood. "I'm the owner."

She jumped to her feet, amazingly not tottering on the spiked heels. "Then you *have* to redo this floor."

Caught up in her excitement, I could almost envision hardwood floors in place of the utilitarian-gray, commercial-grade carpet. “Maybe. But I’d have to wait a couple of weeks. Mason, my employee, has exams next week, and I don’t want to start a huge project like this that would take away from his study time.”

Shelby waved her hand in a dismissive gesture then looped her arm through mine to walk toward the front of the store. “Pish posh. We don’t need Mason. I’ll help. And if we get stuck with something, I can call Daddy.”

I laughed, walking with her to the door. “I may just take you up on it.”

When we arrived at the door, Shelby abruptly stopped. “Hey, wait a minute. I never got to hear about who Keith and your ex are.”

So, so close. “That’s sort of a long story.”

She looked down at her watch and grinned. “I’m supposed to close in twenty minutes, and since I’m the boss, I’m closing a few minutes early. Let’s go grab something to eat across the street.” She tugged at my arm.

I hated to leave Mason alone, but he waved me on with an assurance that he’d clean up the rest of the mess caused by the fire and the extinguisher goo and would lock up when he was done. It was good to have a store manager.

When Shelby and I were seated at a high-top table near one of the stained-glass windows and had ordered drinks and a couple of burgers, she turned toward me, hooked one heel on the bottom rung of her stool, and crossed her legs. “Okay, dish it, girl. I have a feeling this is going to be good.”

Chapter Six

I rolled my eyes. "You have no idea."

I launched into an overview of Blake's and my history, glossing over my arrest with the phrase "accused of indiscretions, but I was cleared."

Shelby raised her eyebrows. "Indiscretions? I heard you were arrested for stealing from your company and murdering one of the bosses."

"Um . . . yeah." I squirmed in my seat.

She reached across the table and touched my arm. "Don't worry, I don't make snap judgments based on hearsay." She grinned. "A customer who came in recently to buy some decorative candles mentioned it. I can't remember her name, but she was with some crime prevention group."

"Let me guess. The Women's League on Public Safety?" The group had focused on me as the sole cause of crime in Hokes Folly after a death in one of the historic district parking lots.

Shelby nodded. "That's the one. While we chatted, I mentioned I was new in town and that I was looking forward to getting to know all my store's neighbors. She warned me to avoid you like the plague."

I rolled my eyes. "Yeah, they don't care for me much."

"Who cares?" Shelby waved a dismissive hand. "The point is, you don't have to tiptoe around your story. I've already heard the rumor mill version. Now let's hear the real story."

I sighed and fidgeted with my napkin on the table, half relieved she had treated my past like it was no big deal and still wanted to get to know me and half worried she really would want to avoid me like the plague once she heard all the drama that had surrounded me since I'd moved here. "Someone embezzled from my company using my credentials. Then one of the junior partners was murdered, supposedly because he found out about the embezzlement. I was arrested for both crimes and was held in jail for three months while I awaited trial."

Shelby's eyes widened. "But you were acquitted, right? I mean, you wouldn't be out on parole this soon."

"Yes, I was acquitted." I filled in the missing gaps in my history with Blake leading up to my move to Hokes Folly. It seemed, as with Rita, I wouldn't have to convince this woman I was innocent.

"Oh, that rat bastard." Shelby pounded her palm on the table when I got to the part about Blake handing me a key to a storage slot.

"It gets better." I took a fortifying sip of wine. "Remember that woman I was avoiding who created the scene in the street the day we met?" At Shelby's nod, I continued. "Her fiancé is my ex."

Shelby squealed and clapped her hands. "I knew this was going to be fun."

Tension broken, I chuckled at her enthusiasm. "Yeah, fun isn't what I'd go with, but you do you."

She sobered. "Wait, this was just in late July? That was only eight months ago. What's he doing here with a wedding date at the end of the week? Was he cheating on you?"

That brought me up short. I honestly hadn't considered that possibility. "I don't think so." Even I heard the doubt in my voice. "No." I shook my head. "I know he wasn't. There were no late nights, no skipped dinners unless he was working late, and I was usually working late on the same projects. There were no surprise trips, no going out after he was home, and no hiding in the bathroom with his phone unless he was reading on the throne of power."

"Throne of power. I have to remember that one." Shelby guffawed. "But if he wasn't cheating on you, isn't it a bit soon to already be walking down the aisle? Especially after he delayed your wedding for years."

"I guess so." I shrugged. "I mean, they could've hooked up while I was in jail, since he never once came to see me or tried to contact me. But that would only add two or three months at most."

Lily approached the table with our drinks. "Hi." She smiled shyly at me. "You're Mason's boss."

"I am." I returned her smile. "And you're Lily. He talks about you."

A blush crept up her cheeks, and her smile widened. "Cool. I brought your drinks, since your server was busy." She set our drinks in front of us, a martini for Shelby and a glass of Chardonnay for me.

Shelby leaned close after Lily walked away with the tray. "That girl has it bad. How does Mason feel about it?"

I nodded my head in the direction of Lily's retreating back. "See how gooey she got when I mentioned Mason?" At Shelby's nod, I continued. "Mason's worse."

"Perfect." She sat back and raised her martini glass. "Here's to young love. May it always stay true and innocent."

I raised my glass to the toast and took a sip, wishing I could have met Keith before I lost my trust in innocent love at the hands of Blake Emerson.

"So your ex shows up with his new chick, getting married in your town, walking into your bookstore." She shook her head. "I can only imagine how that felt."

"It wasn't easy, I tell you." I slowly swirled the wine in my glass, watching the alcohol make patterns on the sides. "I'm over him, but it was still a shock, and it's dragged up a bunch of emotional drama I thought I'd already dealt with. But I'm getting there."

Shelby stirred her martini with a toothpick stuck through two large green olives. "You know, I'm a martini drinker. I'm only thirty-two, and I know as a millennial I'm supposed to like fruity drinks, Cosmopolitans, daiquiris, sweet mixed drinks. But I like a simple vodka martini."

I tried to follow her abrupt change in subject. "I like Chardonnay," I offered tentatively.

Shelby laughed. "I do have a point." She pulled the olives from the drink, grabbing one with her teeth and chewing it while she gazed at me intently. When she swallowed, she said, "I also like green olives in my martinis. But I prefer garlic olives. The garlic olive juice and olives stuffed with toes of garlic give a great flavor to the drink."

I nodded as if I had any clue what she was getting at.

"Is Blake your garlic olive? Are you looking for a nice plain olive when you're really wishing you had garlic-stuffed olives?" She pointed the toothpick at me, a green, pimento-stuffed olive skewered on its tip.

I burst out laughing. "Definitely not. Keith is my garlic olive by far."

Shelby sat back. "And who's this Keith guy?" She popped the olive into her mouth and dropped the toothpick on a bar napkin beside her drink.

"He's a detective with the police department. We started dating not long after I moved here." I sipped my Chardonnay. "And I'm going to have to tell him he's my garlic olive. Think that would fit well in a romantic card?"

Shelby snorted. "Honey, if he doesn't already know he's your garlic olive, you're doing it wrong." She paused to sip her drink, eyeing me thoughtfully. "Are you sure he's not just a rebound? You did start dating him right on the heels of several back-to-back traumatic events. You lost your job, lost your man, lost your home, got arrested and went to jail, and your uncle was murdered, all in a span of a few weeks."

"I worried about that a bit at first, but no, I don't think he's a rebound." I considered the strength, the solidity of my relationship with Keith, even though it was new and had started under freak circumstances. "Okay, it could technically fit the term 'rebound,' but that doesn't mean it isn't real and won't last."

"True that." Shelby nodded and raised her glass to me again before setting it on the table. "Here's to real rebounds."

I shook my head. "You're too much."

Our burgers arrived, and I took the opportunity to push the spotlight in the other direction. "What about you? Any garlic olives or even green olives in your life?"

Shelby swallowed and dabbed at her lips with her napkin. "Not right now. I've had my share of olives, but my last relationship ended two years ago when she moved across the country. Her parents were less than thrilled that she wasn't too keen on men, and her mother just could not understand how she would ever get grandbabies if their daughter married a woman."

"What about insemination or adoption?" I bit down on a fry, savoring the salty burst.

"That wasn't good enough for my dad, any more than it would have been for her mom. He wanted someone to carry on his bloodline." She took another sip of her martini. "What he doesn't know is that I can't have children. I lost my virginity to a boy who had an STD when I was sixteen. I was drunk at a party and did it on a dare. Afterward, when the pain started, I was too scared to tell my parents I'd even been at the party, much less caught a disease from losing my virginity to the guy who would screw anything. It got really bad before I cut school one day and drove two towns over to go to a health clinic, where I lied about my name. By this time, it had permanently damaged my uterus."

"I'm so sorry." I wanted to hug her. What she'd been through could have happened to anyone. But she was the one who had paid the price. "Do you want children?"

"I do." She nodded. "One day. But don't be sorry. I've known for fourteen years that I'd likely adopt. I have no problem with giving a loving home to a baby that I didn't carry. Genetics don't determine love. How about you? Planning on any children?"

"Maybe one day." A mental image of Keith with a baby in his arms flashed through my mind. Whoa, where had that come from? Rita was putting some freaky ideas in my head lately. "Just not any time soon."

"Maybe one day for both of us." Shelby dipped a fry in ketchup. "Just not today."

"Definitely not today." I raised my burger in a salute and took a bite.

Companionable chitchat flavored the remainder of our meal. After we finished and paid, I walked across to my store, letting myself in through the front door. Everything was still, and I found the silence comforting. I walked through the room, touching a book here or a shelf there, grateful the fire hadn't consumed it all.

Eddy barked, reminding me he needed a walk. Up the stairs I went, and we headed out for his nightly constitutional. Keith had already said he wouldn't be able to stop by this evening, as he had to be in to work before six the next morning. In his absence, my evening consisted of binge watching a few episodes of *Murdoch Mysteries* until I fell asleep on the couch and dreamed of a dozen baby cribs surrounding Keith while he rocked each infant to sleep.

Chapter Seven

"Jenna, wait. Please let me talk to you!"

Blake's shouted words followed me up the stairs to my apartment. I'd spent the morning peacefully enough, considering all the tossing and turning I'd done in the night. When he'd shown up, I'd told him Mason would assist him, and I'd headed upstairs.

Suspecting this wouldn't hold him off for long, I kissed Eddy on the nose. "Sorry, sweet boy. I need to grocery shop, and I can't take you in with me. I'll be back soon."

Trying not to feel guilty over his sad puppy eyes when I shut the front door, I strode across the walkway and down the back stairs toward the parking lot. I spied Blake entering the lot as I pulled out, and I pressed the gas, scooting out of sight, I hoped.

At the small grocery near my store, I smiled at the owner, Benny Dixon, who waved from behind the checkout counter. I grabbed a cart and started my rounds. Cereal, check. Waffles, check. Eggs, check. I'd also picked up meats and veggies to cook for Keith, as well as paper towels, toilet paper, and aluminum foil.

With a half-full cart, I rounded the end of an aisle, headed toward the frozen pizzas, and almost bumped into Blake, who stood stock-still in the center of the aisle, blocking my way.

"Jenna, please let me talk to you."

I kept the cart between us, ready to run over his feet or ram it into him if he got aggressive again. I looked up, searching for the cameras, just in case I needed proof of anything. "There's nothing for us to talk about." I kept my voice as even as possible, eyeing the dark bruise that spread across his chin. He'd definitely have to use some of Missy's makeup to cover that for the wedding photos. "I said all I had to say to you two days ago. Now please get out of my way." I scooted around him and continued down the aisle.

"Jenna, please."

Whether it was my sense of sentimentality or my curiosity, I wasn't sure, but I swung the cart around to face him. "Just what is so important that you have to hunt me down me in a grocery store to tell me?"

He took two long strides forward and rested his hands on the rim of my cart. "Jenna, I need you to understand I never meant to hurt you."

I propped my foot on the cart's bottom rack but kept my grip on the handle. "Then why did you?"

"I . . ." He shoved his hands in his pockets. "I didn't have a choice."

"Uh-huh." I dropped my foot and tugged my cart back from where he stood. "That explains everything. Thanks for the chat."

"Jenna, I mean it. I really didn't have a choice. Missy . . ." He stopped and pursed his lips.

"Missy what? Just what is it that she has on you, Blake?" I shook my head. "I've seen you together, and I don't see a couple in love. I see her be rude and cutting to you. I see you, who always had to be in control to the nth degree, suddenly kowtowing to a shrew. I'm seeing you, but I don't recognize you at all. None of this matches the man I was going to marry."

"I'm still me, Jenna. We can be us again if you'll let it happen," Blake said.

"You just don't get it, do you?" I shook my head. "There is no us anymore. And there won't ever be an us again, whether or not you choose to let Missy destroy the rest of your life."

He shuffled his feet. "Missy's had a hard life, but she has her good side too."

My eyebrows shot up. "Good side? I've seen a reincarnation of every mean girl in high school all rolled into one person."

"She's just spent the last six years taking care of her sister, trying to give her a life. She's worked hard, scrimped, saved, and even moved, dragging along a passive-aggressive teenager who didn't want to go." He reached to grab the cart again, threading his fingers through the bars.

"Let me see if I have it straight. You dumped me at the lowest moment of my life, when everything was falling out from under me, even though I did nothing wrong. I lost my job, my home. I went to freaking jail, Blake. And you dumped *me*, the woman you professed to love so deeply that you wanted to marry me, with whom you had lived for the last three years, so you could rescue *her* from *her* difficult life?" I yanked back on the cart.

Color flooded his face, but his grip remained tight on the cart. "I'm sorry, Jenna. I really can't even begin to tell you how sorry I am for all of it."

"And what are you most sorry about, Blake? That Missy won't let you run the show, and I let you walk all over me, making every decision for me? Or how about that Missy is spending your money hand over fist, and you made all the money decisions for us when we were together, even when it came to *my* money that *I* earned. Or how about that you see that I'm successful and happy without you and that I've found someone who loves me for me, encourages me to be me, and doesn't want to control my life, and it burns you up because someone else has the toy you want?" I planted my feet and yanked the cart hard enough that I ripped it from Blake's fingers.

He staggered forward a couple of steps. "Jenna, no. Please. I do love you. I always did."

"I don't even think you know what love is. Love is not control. Love is messy and hard and worth every tear and laugh." I stepped back, turning the cart. "I'm sorry you don't seem to have ever truly felt what it is to love." I chose to skip the frozen pizzas but grabbed bread and chips on the next aisle, dropping them into my cart. I strode down the aisle, skipped back to the center of the store, and moved toward the checkout.

Blake stepped in front of me at the end of the aisle, grunting when I couldn't stop my cart in time to keep from running into him. He straightened. "I'm sorry, I didn't mean to startle you. But there's more I need to tell you. It's important."

"Nothing you have to say is important at this point." I eased my cart around him. "Please quit stalking me."

"You know I'd never hurt you, Jenna." He fell into step beside me.

"Wouldn't hurt me?" I rounded on him. "What do you call sending your girlfriend's buddies to try and burn down my store? Now, leave me alone, Blake. I mean it."

Benny approached. "Miss Quinn, is there a problem with this gentleman?" He narrowed his eyes at Blake.

"I'm sorry, Benny. I hate to do this"—I gestured at my mostly full cart—"but I need to get out of here."

"Don't you worry about a thing." Benny winked at me. "I've got this handled."

I strode out of the store, casting a glance back over my shoulder when I heard Blake shouting at Benny to let him pass. Benny, bless him, had blocked the exit door. I jogged the rest of the way to my car, and as I sped from the lot, I saw Blake push past Benny and race to his car.

I made several unnecessary turns on my way to the grocery chain store across town, hoping to have lost Blake. However it turned out, I still needed groceries. As I pulled up to the stop light beside the store, I remembered it was across from Phillie Hokes's plant nursery. Turning right instead of left, I pulled into her lot and found a choice spot up near the front door.

Phillie looked up from behind the counter when I walked in. "Jenna. What a lovely surprise." She came toward me with outstretched hands.

I gave her a quick hug. "Just thought I'd pop in and see how my favorite plant lady is doing."

"Business is booming, I tell you." The older lady ushered me to the back office where we sat, her behind the desk, and me on a chair across from her.

"See, I told you you'd be great at this." I grinned, reminding her I was the one who had suggested she open a nursery after she decided to close the antique clothing store she'd owned with her sister Olivia.

"You did at that." Phillie nodded and reached to her back pocket, pulling a phone out and laying it on the desk. "There, that's better. Now tell me why you're really here."

I chuckled. "I'm that easy to read?"

"As easy as any book in that store of yours." Phillie crossed her arms and leaned back. "Now out with it."

I sighed, my shoulders sagging. "I think I'm being stalked."

"What?" Phillie sat up, her hands plopping on the desk. "Have you told Keith?"

I nodded. "He knows." I filled her in on my run-ins with my ex-fiancé. "And that's how I ended up here today."

Her eyes narrowed. "Little blonde woman? About my height? Slightly wavy, long hair, green eyes?"

"That sounds like Missy." I turned and looked out the doorway, half expecting to see the bride-to-be hanging out in the lobby.

"Sit back and stop being paranoid. She's not here." She rose to close the door and returned to her seat. "Now you don't have to keep looking."

I let go the breath I'd been holding when I thought the bridezilla had found me, although what she'd be doing in a nursery, I had no idea. "Then how did you know what she looks like?" With those expensively manicured nails she'd flashed at Tom, I doubted she'd ever stick her hands in the dirt to garden.

"She was here yesterday." Phillie shuffled reached into a folder on her desk and withdrew a notepad, flipping through to find the right page. "Here it is. She wanted a rare orchid that I carry. She wants them in her bouquet. However, florists won't carry them because they don't do well as a cut flower."

"What was she going to do? Carry a potted plant down the aisle?" I snorted, picturing the scene.

Phillie laughed. “Now wouldn’t that be something to see when it came time to toss the bouquet?”

The rest of the tension left my shoulders as I shared a laugh with my friend. “Definitely one for YouTube. But seriously, how did she think you would be able to help her?”

“She wanted me to wait until an hour before her wedding, cut all the flowers from my orchids, rush them to the church, and let her stick them in the bouquet just before she walked down the aisle.” Phillie flipped the pad closed and slid it back into the folder.

My jaw dropped. “Are you kidding me?”

“Dead serious.” Phillie shook her head. “I told her I wasn’t destroying the value of my plants for her wedding. Besides, those flowers wouldn’t last long enough to make it through the wedding, and her bouquet would look horrible. She would have to make do with the cut flowers the florist could provide.”

“How did she take your refusal?” I was pretty sure Phillie wasn’t going to say her response was gracious.

“She grabbed up a pot and threw it to the ground, destroying the pot and scattering dirt across the floor. Then she stomped on the orchid and screamed, ‘How’s the value of the plant now, bitch?’” Color flooded Phillie’s cheeks and she put her fingers up to them. “I can’t tell you when I’ve ever been angrier, not even when Olivia did her best to break up your uncle and me.”

My jaw dropped and there went my eyebrows shooting up again. Yep, wrinkles for sure at this rate. “What did you do?”

“I ordered her from the store and told her never to come back. A nice young man I recently hired herded her out.” Phillie snorted. “Who knew I’d need a bouncer at a nursery?”

I belly laughed at both the image of Missy being manhandled out of the store and Phillie's reference to a bouncer. "Well, at least you're okay, and she only destroyed one plant."

Phillie nodded and turned to a shelf behind her. "I've been meaning to bring these by to you." She held out two books to me.

I slid them onto my lap. "These are your Godey's Ladies' Books from your clothing store. Do you want me to sell them for you? I'm sure I could get a fair price for you."

"Oh no, dear. These are a loan." She looked across at the books in my lap. "I thought it might be fun to highlight one or two of them in your store. You could put them in a case and turn pages every day or so, showing the dresses, giving folks something to come look at when planning their weddings. If you look, I picked two that are from the late 1890s. Some of the last issues they ever produced, since they stopped in 1898."

"Why, Phillie Hokes, there's a bit of the book collector in you after all." I gently closed the book in my lap.

"I never disliked Livie's book collecting. I just didn't like the *same* books as she did." She pointed at the two in my lap. "If those go over well, I can change out and lend you another couple later if you like. I have twelve of them."

"Perfect!" I pulled the books to my chest. "I'll take good care of them. I promise."

"Pish posh." Phillie stood. "If I doubted that, I wouldn't have handed them to you."

I stood and followed her out into the showroom. "I'd better get going. I still need to grocery shop while I'm on this end of town, and I need to get back to the store to help Mason."

We hugged once more, and I walked to my car and gently laid the books in the front passenger seat, almost screaming when someone rapped on the window on the other side of the car.

"Blake, leave me alone!" I warred with whether to run back into the store or try to shove past him to get into my car.

Blake propped his arms on my car's roof. "Jenna, I need to make you understand. I didn't have anything to do with Missy's crazy friends. I want to find a way to fix things."

"How, Blake? You just told me you don't have a choice but to marry Missy, although you didn't bother to tell me why." I slammed my passenger door, instantly sorry for taking out my anger at Blake on my poor car.

"I know." He heaved a sigh and rested his forehead on his arms. "I don't know what to do. I don't love her. I never did. I still love you." He raised his eyes to meet mine. "More than you know."

I snorted. "That and five bucks will get me a coffee at Starbucks."

"If you told me there was a chance, even just a tiny one, I would leave her and do everything in my power to prove to you that I love you, to make up to you everything that happened, consequences be damned." He pushed away from the car and strode around the back. "We can fix this if you'll let me try, if you'll try with me."

As he approached, I scurried around the front of the car and yanked open my door, jamming my key in the ignition as I pulled it closed and pressed the door-lock button. "Leave me alone, Blake! I mean it!" I shouted through the closed window and pulled away.

In my rearview mirror, I saw him pull out of a spot, speeding across the lot as I turned out onto the street. Groceries be damned. I cut the fastest route I knew, and within a few minutes, I pulled into the parking lot of the Hokes Folly Police Station and slid my car into a spot near the front door.

As Blake pulled in a few spots away, I stormed inside, rushing to the front desk. "I need to see Keith, please." I looked back over my shoulder.

Detective Frank Sutter turned around behind the glass, giving me a nonplussed look. "For?"

I gritted my teeth. It had been a couple of months since I'd last been the recipient of his rudeness. He'd gone out of his way at the police department Christmas party to make sure I knew he was still convinced I'd done the things I was accused of in Charlotte.

"Detective." The word slid out with the utmost of self-control. "Today is not the day to mess with me. Get. Keith. Now." I threw another glance over my shoulder.

Sutter must have somehow understood my desperation, because he didn't argue. "Logan. Your girlfriend is up here with some drama. No, I don't know what it is, nor do I care. You can come deal with it." Sutter plopped the phone back into the base and turned his back to me, rifling through a stack of papers.

Within moments, Keith strode through the locked door between the lobby and the back offices. "What's wrong? Are you okay?"

I looked back over my shoulder, spotting Blake pacing back and forth beside my car. "Blake has been following me all day, and I can't get him to leave me alone." I turned back to Keith, briefly telling him the sequence of events. "I didn't know what else to do."

Keith's jaw tightened. "You did the right thing." He strode out the front door.

I peeked through the windows and watched him approach Blake. As the two men spoke, Blake stepped toward Keith, gesturing wildly at the windows where I stood. A uniformed officer spotted the fracas and approached, hand on his utility belt. Keith motioned for the officer to stay back and spoke to my ex-fiancé once more. Blake put up his hands and stepped back, got into his car, and left the lot.

I sagged with relief when Keith came back inside. "What happened?"

Keith hugged me tightly. "I think he won't be bothering you anymore. He kept insisting he needed to tell you something, but I told him if he continued to harass you and stalk you, I would encourage you to file a restraining order, which would not look good on his record."

I leaned back, searching his face. "Really? I could do that?"

"Absolutely." He nodded. "And with me as witness to his behavior, you'd get one."

Laying my cheek on his shoulder, I mumbled, "Thank you."

"If you two are done playing Dick and Jane"—Sutter emphasized the name Dick as if he were using it more as a slur on Keith than a name—"we can all get back to work."

Keith's arms tensed around me, and he took a deep breath, exhaling slowly as he relaxed. He walked to the counter. "Sutter, I suggest you remain civil and professional when you're behind that glass."

Sutter sneered. "Or what? They'll fire me?"

"Yes," came Keith's quiet response. "You know you're on thin ice already, and they're trying to be nice and let your pension reach maximum level at twenty years, which is right after your fifty-fifth birthday next week. Keep on intentionally antagonizing those entering the station, and they will revise that stance."

Sutter paled. "They wouldn't." The sneer returned to his face. "I'm too close."

"Care to wager your retirement funds on that guess?" Keith casually leaned on the counter with one elbow and looked at his watch. He turned to me. "I have to go. I have a staff meeting in a few minutes." He bussed a quick kiss across my cheek and strode to the door.

Sutter had crossed to the back of the desk area, ignoring Keith's attempts to go through the door. Finally, he turned and reached under the counter and a faint buzz sounded.

Keith yanked open the door and strode through, stopping to duck his head into the front office area and speak quietly.

Sutter's face paled again, and after Keith disappeared, Sutter appeared at the front window. "Will there be anything else I can do for you, Miss Quinn?" His nostrils flared, and he gritted his teeth, belying the polite tone.

"No, thank you, Detective. I'll see myself out."

I drove to the store, wondering what Keith had said to Sutter to make him behave. On the way, I called Mason, who swore he hadn't seen hide nor hair of Blake Emerson since the morning. Relieved, I headed up to the apartment to grab Eddy, who was more than ready for his afternoon walk. When he was done, he dozed under the coffee station table in the store, and the afternoon progressed pleasantly with a steady stream of customers. Until it didn't.

Chapter Eight

"There you are!" Missy Plott entered the store, her three bridesmaids with her, each wearing a matching smirk, with Connie bringing up the rear. The bridesmaids all flashed a manicure to exactly match Missy's bright coral-pink, but Connie had opted for a pale purple with sparkles. Good for her.

I pasted on my helpful-store-owner smile. "How can I help you today, Miss Plott?" I kept my words civil, as I had another customer in the store. However, I purposely ignored the three bridesmaids. I caught sight of Mason hovering near the end of an aisle, staring at the three intently. At least he could follow them if one decided to try for a second arson attempt.

"Why, just a friendly little ol' chat." Missy smiled a predatory smile and sashayed up to the counter, her entourage surrounding her, feeding her their strength. "I just wanted you to know I'm watching you."

"Excuse me?" What the hell? Did I have another stalker?

"I know you want my Blakey back." She gestured to the girls around her. "We've all noticed it."

The trio of look-alikes nodded in unison. Connie rolled her eyes. I liked this girl.

"I have no desire—"

"Don't you dare try to deny it. He told me all about how you asked him to come over here a couple of nights ago and threw yourself at him, kissing him and begging him to come back and how he had to force you away from him. He was only here because he felt sorry for you." Missy's sweet girl demeanor disappeared, and she leaned toward me over the counter, her ample bosom splayed across the surface. "I've gone through too much, done too much, given up too much, to get where I am now, and you are *not* going to ruin it for me."

I took a step back then shook my head, warring with a compassion I didn't want to feel for this woman, thanks to Blake's words. Wait a minute. This was *my* store. What was with these people thinking they could come into my store and try to intimidate me. I stepped forward, placed my hands on the counter, and leaned toward Missy, forcing her to take a step back, removing her boobs from my counter. I made a mental note to wipe the counter down after she left.

"One. I have no desire whatsoever to ever be in a relationship of any kind with Blake Emerson. Not a romantic relationship, not a friendship, not even an acquaintance." I strode around the counter toward the women, edging them toward the front door. "Two. I have not at any time tried to"—I used my fingers as air quotes—"'get your Blakey back.' Nor do I want to in any way. For your information, *he* showed up here uninvited and unexpected as I was closing the store. *He* begged me to come back, *he* tried to kiss me, and *he* got a knee to the groin and to the chin for it."

I continued moving toward them as they backed toward the doorway. "Three." I held the door open and ushered them out. "If you ever come here again and try to threaten or intimidate me or my employee, or if you ever send your BFFs to try to burn down my store again, I will call the police and have you arrested for harassment, vandalism, and attempted murder. Am. I. Clear?" By this time, my voice had risen to a shout, and Missy's sister and friends had skittered through the doorway ahead of her, leaving her to face my ire alone.

Missy's face flooded with red, and her back stiffened. Her mouth opened and closed a few times before sound emerged. "You just stay away from him, and we'll be fine. He's mine." She turned on her heel and stalked away, her trio of bridesmaids in tow.

Connie, a few paces behind them, turned and mouthed, "I'm sorry," before continuing down the walkway behind her sister's crew.

I shook my head as I walked back into the store. That girl did not belong in the same family as Missy. Or maybe her family was all sweet, more like Connie, and Missy was the odd one out. Who knew? Honestly, who cared, as long as Missy and her crew left me alone.

Mason whistled from behind the counter. "What a load of crap. But at least we know why she was looking for you yesterday. Did I hear her say Blake told her you were throwing yourself at him?"

"You did." I held up a hand. "And before you ask, no, I didn't."

Mason laughed. "I didn't think you would. You're too smart for that. You've got a great guy in Keith. I don't see you being dumb enough to go back to a guy who treated you like dirt." He took a clipboard out from under the counter. "It's slowed down some, so I'm going to work on inventory until closing, unless it picks back up."

"Sounds like a great idea." I followed him down an aisle, discussing how far he'd gotten and how he was tracking the books. After getting a feel for his system, which impressed me, to be honest, I grabbed a clipboard and started on another section of the store.

We worked in tandem—inventory, I helped a client, inventory, he helped a client—rotating turns until it was time to close. When we'd closed the store down and I'd locked the door behind Mason's retreating back, I heaved a sigh of relief and headed up the stairs to my apartment, Eddy in tow, opening the door to a wonderful smell.

Eddy rushed past me into the kitchen, where Keith stood, an apron across his middle, stirring something on the stove.

"Hey, buddy." Keith reached down and scratched Eddy's head, handing him what looked to be a piece of cheese.

Eddy happily gobbled the treat and wagged his tail.

"No more cookies before supper, young man." I walked past the dog and picked up his food bowl. After filling it, I put it in his usual place in the kitchen's corner by the pantry.

Eddy bounced to his bowl and enthusiastically dug in to his meal.

I grinned and turned to Keith, glad I had given him a key for a Valentine's Day present the previous month. "Whatever you're cooking smells delicious."

He put down the spoon on a spoon holder and turned, pulling me into a light embrace. I figured if you'd been run off from two grocery stores, you might not have much to cook around here. I made a quick trip to pick up staples for you. Even if I missed something, I figure you're good for a few days." He gestured toward the pantry and fridge.

I opened the pantry and scanned the shelves. He'd bought my favorite cereal, paper towels, toilet paper, and four boxes of macaroni and cheese.

I pulled a mac and cheese box out and held it up. "Am I going on a binge here? Four boxes?"

He shrugged. "I know you like it. I wasn't sure what else you needed, and it's not like it'll go bad."

I laughed. "True." I slid the box back onto the shelf and turned to the fridge. Milk, butter, cheese, eggs, and two thick steaks. "Are we grilling?"

"Those are for me," he said, not turning. "I picked them up to take home and cook for my other girlfriend."

"Hey!" I laughed. "Give her the mac and cheese, and leave me the steaks."

Keith sighed, still stirring the pots on the stove. "I suppose I could. After all, she's not as nice as you, and she doesn't have a dog."

At this, Eddy raised his head and whuffed before returning to his meal.

"Thanks, boy." I reached down to ruffle his fur before crossing to wrap my arms around Keith from behind. "I think I'll keep the steaks *and* the mac and cheese. If you want either, you'll just have to let the other girl go."

"As you wish." Keith nodded, quoting the line from *The Princess Bride*, one of my all-time favorite movies.

I giggled. "I do."

"Well, if food is what makes you happy, then get plates out. This is ready." Keith lifted a pot and poured pasta into a colander in the sink.

I busied myself setting the table with flatware and napkins and putting two plates on the counter beside the stove.

Keith served the pasta with a pink cream sauce with crab and lobster bits crumbled up in it. "I hope you like it." He put a plate down in front of me.

I slid my fork into the pasta and took a bite. "Delicious," I mumbled around the rich flavors bursting through my mouth.

Keith grinned and took a bite of his own.

When I'd swallowed, I asked, "What did you whisper to Sutter to get him to be nice to me this afternoon?"

He shrugged and reached for his napkin, carefully blotting his lips before rising. "I forgot the wine." He walked into the kitchen and returned with a bottle of chilled Chardonnay and two glasses.

I took the glass he poured and asked again. "Sutter? What did you say?"

Keith set the bottle down and retook his seat. "I told him if he didn't toe the line for the next couple of weeks until his retirement, I would personally see to it that he spent the remainder of his days pulling janitorial duty cleaning vomit out of the cruisers after we pick up drunks."

I guffawed, glad I hadn't just put a bite of food in my mouth. "You did not!"

He nodded. "I did. We often have very unpleasant messes to clean out of the cars, and we usually hire out to a janitorial service to do the cleanup. But I assured Sutter we could make an exception in his case."

Shaking my head, I snickered. “If you end up doing that, please let me come by one day and see it.” I sipped a bit of the Chardonnay.

Keith crossed the fingers of his right hand over his heart in an *X*. “I promise, cross my heart.”

Chapter Nine

Friday morning matched my mood. Clouds blanketed the sky, and a wind cut around the corners of the building, moaning as it rushed past.

Keith hadn't spent the night, and I'd tossed and turned, plagued by dreams of Missy and Blake chasing me through grocery stores and parking lots. Now I was grumpy, but I knew I wouldn't get any more rest, even if I stayed in bed.

I rose and moved through my morning routine. Dress and walk Eddy. Return and feed us both. Shower and put on work clothes. Walk Eddy once more before we headed into the store. By the time we arrived, however, my mood had improved, probably from a combination of eating Keith's leftover pasta for breakfast and the bracing wind perking me up as we walked the green space near the parking lot.

We entered the store, and I spent the day bustling between inventory and customer care. Mason helped me set up a display area for the Godey's books Phillie had loaned me, and we rearranged the seating area to highlight them. Before the day was done, at least three brides had looked through the books and taken pictures of several of the styles.

On Fridays, I kept the store open an hour later, closing at eight, but I usually let Mason go at our regular closing time of seven. However, tonight, due to the recent happenings, Mason had gallantly insisted he stay, refusing to leave me to close the store alone. While I didn't technically need him to be there, I was grateful for the company after the last few days.

As we compared notes on inventory, marking down the last few shelves Mason would need to tackle in the morning before opening, a loud screech sounded outside the door.

"Don't touch me!"

Mason and I raced to the windows to see Missy stagger off the sidewalk, almost falling, and stumble into the cobbled street. Blake strode after her, trying to keep her from falling.

"Get your lying hands off of me!" Missy screamed, yanking her am from his grasp and staggering again.

"Is she drunk?" Mason whispered.

"Looks like it," I answered, still glued to the scene unfolding in the street. What was with this woman and airing her drama at the top of her lungs in public? My mother would have had my hide if I'd behaved like this.

Blake approached her again, talking too quietly for us to overhear, but his gestures seemed like they were intended to calm her and get her back inside the restaurant.

Their words raised a notch in volume, and I realized Mason had slunk to the door and had eased it open a few inches, propping it with a book, allowing us to hear better. I stifled a chuckle.

"Honey, please." Blake rubbed her back. "Let's just go back inside. I'll get you some water, okay?"

"Water?" Missy swatted his arm away. "You think I want water?" Her slurred words rang through the damp evening air.

Connie appeared in the restaurant doorway, holding up a phone to snap a picture. Movement from a darkened doorway caught my eye as Tom stepped off the curb a few doors down, as if to interrupt the bridal drama.

Connie ran out and intercepted him, tugging at his arm and pulling him back onto the sidewalk toward the bench outside The Weeping Willow. Even at this distance, I could see the goo-goo eyes she was making at the young man, but Tom couldn't tear his gaze from Missy in her distressed state.

Missy burst into tears, throwing herself into Blake's arms. "I love you sooooooooo much," she slurred. "How can you do this to me?"

Blake wrapped his arm around her back, holding her up, yes, but not with affection. It looked more like resigned duty. "I've done nothing to you that you haven't brought on yourself. Shall we go back inside now?"

Missy pushed away, raising her voice again. "You tricked me into coming here! You knew she was here!" She swept her arm in my store's direction. "You let me believe this stupid hotel here was the best and fanciest place to get married and told me how amazing it would be. But you knew! You *knew* she lived here!"

Mason and I ducked down a bit, and I hoped the dim lights hid the cracked door.

"I've seen you making moon eyes at her." Missy waved her arm again, as if my store was the offending party.

"Missy, darling, I love only you." Blake's voice rang through the night with all the conviction of a professional liar.

Even I could hear the sarcasm in his tone. Missy would have to be a lot drunker to have missed it.

"Love me?" Missy barked out a harsh laugh, or maybe it was a hiccup. "That's funny! If you really love me, why do you keep trying to be near her?"

Blake ran a hand through his hair. "Do we really need to do this now?"

Missy staggered back and pointed at The Weeping Willow. "You even demanded we have the rehearsal dinner here in this shitty little restaurant across from her store. Why, if you didn't want to see if you could meet up with her later?"

"Oh damn, she went there." Mason tensed next to me and shot me a glance.

"Wipe that look off your face." I rolled my eyes. "You know I'm not meeting him anywhere, any time."

Blake apparently met the end of his patience. His voice roared as loudly as hers, his hands punctuating his sentences. "If you weren't bleeding me dry with this wedding fiasco, trying to prove to everyone how you're marrying someone a lot richer than I really am, we wouldn't have to hold our rehearsal dinner at a cheap pub instead of somewhere more elegant!"

"Me?" Missy screeched. "You're blaming *me* for all of this?" Missy waved her arm in my store's direction once more. "If I see you anywhere near her or her store again"—she swung her arm around to point at Blake's chest—"I'll destroy you! I'll destroy both of you!" She turned and staggered down the sidewalk toward the parking lot. "How dare you blame me?" Her parting words echoed through the damp night air.

Blake stood in the street, head ducked. He glanced up at my store, and our eyes met. His mouth opened as if he wanted to say something, and he took one step in my direction before turning and striding down the walkway after Missy's retreating form.

Tom jumped forward as if to follow, but again Connie pulled at him, speaking too softly to be overheard. Whatever her words were, Tom finally listened, nodded, and strode off in the opposite direction, leaving Connie to sit on the bench for a few moments, staring into the darkness before rising, straightening her back, and following Tom into the night.

"Well, that was sure fun." Mason moved beside me, walking over to close and lock the door.

"Yeah, okay. We'll go with fun." I rolled my eyes. "At least it wasn't in my store this time." I flipped off the lights, while Mason went to the back room to check the back door lock.

"All locked up tight." Mason strode through the room. "I'm ready to head out. Will you be okay?

"I'm fine. Just be careful going to the lot." I turned the lock and opened the front door. "Stay away from Missy and Blake. No need for you to get into the middle of this mess."

Mason grinned. "I'm parked in the opposite lot, so I won't even see them."

Relieved, I watched Mason walk toward the lot at the other end of the street, finally closing and locking the door. As I started to turn away, I noticed a figure approaching out of the darkness. Blake. His head hung low, and he looked like he'd lost his last friend.

As he drew near my store, he turned to lock his gaze on me. Raw pain burned in his eyes, and he paused, shoving his hands in his pockets. I pushed away any sentiment of compassion or empathy. He'd had all of those from me that he'd ever get. I'd never fall for his lost little boy act again.

His chest rose and fell with a deep breath before he turned to walk back into the Weeping Willow, letting the night fall full and dark. I hoped its eerie feeling was simply in my head, and not a portent of more to come.

Chapter Ten

Saturday morning, I took my time with my morning routine. Mason didn't need me for the last few shelves of inventory. I'd be there in time to help him open the store. It would likely be a busy day, as Saturdays usually were, but at least I wouldn't have to worry about Missy or Blake showing up to harass us, since their wedding was in a few hours. They'd soon be on their way out of town, and my life could get back to normal.

I enjoyed the crisp morning air as I walked Eddy, returning to put kibble in his bowl and scramble a couple of eggs for myself, rather than racing through my usual bowl of cereal. When they were piled on a plate next to two lightly browned pieces of buttered toast, I took them to the coffee table in front of the couch to watch the morning news while I ate.

I turned on the TV and headed to the kitchen to grab a mug of coffee, returning in time to see Connie Dunne and Jonathan Greer give their opening spiel for the Channel Five Morning News, which always came on an hour later on weekend mornings than during the week.

"Today's top story," Connie cheerfully announced, "is the disappearance of Missy Plott, a bride from Charlotte, who was scheduled to get married this afternoon at the Hokes Bluff Inn."

I almost choked on my coffee. Hot pickles on a Pop-Tart, what now?

Jonathan took over, turning to face the camera with his I'm-serious-and-trustworthy tone. "During a rehearsal dinner, attended by the bridal party as well as the bride and groom, Ms. Plott left the restaurant after an argument with her fiancé, Blake Emerson, also of Charlotte."

The camera swung back to Connie, and a picture of Missy and Blake, smiling and posing, likely for their engagement picture, hung on the screen over Connie's shoulder. "According to sources, the couple continued the argument in the street outside the restaurant, finally going to the parking lot. A short while later, Mr. Emerson returned without his intended, stating she needed to rest in the car for a bit. Ms. Plott hasn't been seen since."

Once again, the cameras swung, and a phone number was displayed at the bottom of the screen, under Jonathan's sincere pose. "If anyone has any information, please contact the Hokes Folly Police Department. The investigation will remain open until Ms. Plott has been found."

The news story swapped to one about the fire department chief retiring, and I muted the volume. Before I could make it back to the kitchen with my now-cold eggs, a pounding sounded against my front door.

Rita barged through when I opened it. "Have you heard?"

I nodded. "I just saw it on the news."

"I'm heading in. I wasn't supposed to be there today, but Elliot has asked me to come in to help with damage control. The police have been there for an hour, questioning Blake, his mother, the bridesmaids, and even the groomsmen, who didn't even arrive until late last night after it was all over." Rita made a beeline to the coffeepot. "But I just had to get your take on things before I left."

"And that makes a hair and makeup emergency?" I asked, unsure how Rita would be able to help.

"Honey, everything can be a hair and makeup emergency." She snickered. "But no, he just needs a babysitter for the bridesmaids. They're crying and wailing at the tops of their lungs, and he's hoping I can quiet them down by appealing to their vanity."

I scraped my eggs off into Eddy's bowl, knowing he didn't mind cold eggs. "I honestly don't know what to think. But I'm pretty sure Blake was the last one to see her."

Rita turned and plunked her mug on the counter. "You don't think he did something to her, do you?"

I snorted. "No. He doesn't have it in him. He's too afraid of what everyone will think of him to do something nefarious."

"Well, something happened to her. No one can find her." Rita took a long draught of her coffee. "The bridal party looked for a couple of hours. The bridesmaids and her sister drove up and down, hunting for her, and Blake headed back to the hotel, in case she showed up there."

"What about his mother?" I thought back to the news report. It hadn't mentioned Mrs. Emerson.

Rita shrugged. "She's at the hotel, demanding justice, demanding a statewide search, and insisting Missy has likely been kidnapped. She's creating quite the scene, and the news media is eating it up." She dumped the rest of her coffee and set the mug in the sink.

"Missy was pretty drunk last night. I'd guess she probably passed out somewhere and hasn't woken up yet." I followed Rita on her way to the door. "I'm sure she'll stagger in soon enough, and all the drama will have been for nothing."

Rita turned. "How do you know she was drunk?"

I recounted what Mason and I had witnessed the previous evening. "When she does wake up, she'll have one humdinger of a headache." I tried not to enjoy that thought.

Rita opened the front door and stepped out. "Either way, I'd better get going before Elliot has a duck over all of this."

I laughed, picturing the elegant man. "If Elliot has a duck, he'll take it home, and he and his partner can have foie gras."

"Ew, liver." Rita wrinkled her nose. "Never could stand that. Or escargot or caviar either. Guess I'm not cultured enough."

"Then you'd better get going so Elliot can remain duck free." I pointed in the direction of the parking lot.

As she strode down the walkway toward the stairs, Eddy appeared by my side, intently staring at the alleyway, a low hum in his throat and his hackles raised.

"Rita, wait," I called after her retreating back as I knelt by Eddy's side. "What is it, boy?"

Rita's footsteps got louder. "What's wrong?"

I shook my head, draping my arm across Eddy's tense back. "I don't know. Something's got Eddy all keyed up."

Rita leaned over the railing, scanning the alleyway. "I don't see anything."

Eddy sprang into motion, and before I could stop him, he was in a dead run to the stairs.

"Eddy, stop!" I ran after him. "Come back here!"

Rita jogged along the top rail. "There's a cat!"

I jumped off the last few steps and rounded into the alleyway to see a large orange cat arch its back, hissing and growling at my dog. Eddy bounded toward the cat, barking and yipping, as if trying to figure out the new game.

I picked up my pace, hoping to avoid a trip to the vet for a sliced open nose or an injured eye if the cat went all ninja on Eddy. As I passed the dumpster, my toe snagged on something, and I fell forward, landing hard on my knees, the palms of my hands scraping on the grungy asphalt as I caught myself from face-planting. My fall startled the cat, who turned and skittered away. Eddy ran to my side to lick my face, the doggy version of first aid.

Rolling to one side, I plopped down on one hip and swung my legs out straight. My jeans were torn, and blood seeped through the jagged tears. I raised my hands to look at the scrapes lining my palms.

Rita skidded to a halt at my side and dropped to her knees. "Are you okay? You scared me to death." She grabbed one of my hands to look at it.

"I'll live." I struggled to stand. "What did I trip over?" I scanned the asphalt.

Rita reached out and picked up a heavy gold chain attached to a small black purse "Was this it?" She held it up to me.

I gingerly took the purse, trying not to get blood on it from the cuts on my hands. "Could be." I opened it to find a lipstick, a compact, and a couple of tissues. "No ID."

Rising to stand beside me, Rita clutched at my arm. "Jenna." She pointed a finger.

I followed her pointing finger, freezing when I saw something that didn't belong. "Is that a shoe?" I pointed at a small protrusion sticking out from behind the dumpster.

Rita nodded. "I think so."

My mind spun, refusing to accept what I knew we had found. "Wait here." I pulled away from her and tiptoed closer, following the line of the shoe and looking behind the dumpster. My stomach rolled, and I scurried back to Rita's side. "Hand me your phone."

Rita dug in her purse, still slung over her shoulder, and held the phone out.

I took it and dialed Keith's number, breathing a sigh of relief when he answered.

"Hey, Jenna. Sorry I didn't come by last night. We've been searching for Missy Plott." I could hear the frustration in his voice. "We're still at it, so I can't really talk now. Can I call you later?"

"You can stop looking." I turned my back on the dumpster, wishing I could blot out the image of what I'd seen. "I know where Missy Plott is."

Chapter Eleven

Detective LaTisha "Tish" Riddick sat across my dining table from me, her phone on the table. "Are you okay?" True concern shone from her eyes.

I nodded and wrapped my hands around my coffee mug. "I'll survive."

"Finding another body." Tish shook her head. "You do have the best luck."

Rita snorted and took a seat beside me, a fresh mug of coffee in her hands. "Not a lucky streak I'd want."

Tish straightened, her brows drawn together, marring her cocoa skin with temporary wrinkles. "Keith is taking point on this one. He asked me to interview you two, figuring a familiar face would make it easier."

"Thanks." I managed a watery smile and took a deep breath. "What do you need to ask?"

Tish tapped her phone's screen a few times with a long, dark finger. "I'm going to record this conversation to make sure I don't miss anything. Okay?"

"What, no little black notebook for you?" Rita sipped her coffee.

Tish snorted. "I'm a little more high-tech than these old-school guys I work with. I write slowly, and I have horrible hand-writing that even I can't read." She picked her phone up and wiggled it. "This works better for me. I don't have to ask anyone to repeat themselves, and I don't have to ask anyone to help me decipher what I wrote. I just have to make sure folks understand they're being recorded."

"Kind of a cover-your-backside thing?" Rita asked.

Tish nodded. "It is." She slid the phone across the table until it rested between Rita and me. "Are you ladies ready?"

I glanced at Rita. "We are."

"Start from the beginning. How did you discover the body was behind the dumpster?"

"I didn't intend to." I looked down at Eddy. I wrapped my arms around myself and shivered. "He didn't give me a choice."

"Explain?" Tish gestured to Rita, pantomiming a cup of coffee.

Rita nodded, rose, and went to the kitchen.

"Rita had come over for a morning chat, which we often have." I glanced up as Rita returned to the table. "When she was leaving, Eddy followed me out onto the walkway. He kept growling and raised his hackles. I called Rita back in case there was something dangerous down there that had upset Eddy."

Rita slid a fresh mug of coffee across to Tish, along with creamer and a sugar bowl. "I wasn't sure how you take it."

"Thanks." Tish reached for the creamer and poured a generous helping into the mug before reaching for the sugar bowl. "Could you see the body from your porch area?"

I reached down to Eddy's head and gave it a scratch, wishing my hands would stop shaking. "Nope. Neither could Eddy. He was more interested in chasing the stray cat than in finding a body."

"A stray cat." Tish grinned. "Dogs will be dogs. I have a rough collie who was raised by cats, so she knows better than to chase one."

"Believe me," Rita said. "Jenna wishes Eddy knew better too." She gestured at my legs. "There are some seriously skinned knees under those pants."

Tish's eyes widened. "You fell? Are you okay?"

"I'll live. I may limp for a day or two, but that's about it." I'd changed clothes before Tish arrived, tossing my ruined pants into the wash. They'd do as work pants, or maybe I'd cut them off as shorts this summer. "A collie is like Lassie, right?" I needed something lighter to focus on for a few moments.

Tish rolled her eyes and plunked her mug on the table. "Yes, and I've heard all the 'Timmy down the well' jokes. She's not a sable, though. She's a tri."

"A tri?" I asked.

"Sorry." Tish picked up her phone and tapped the screen then turned it to face me. "Tri as in tri-color. She's black, white, and tan. Sables are the ones like Lassie and like Eddy."

"She's gorgeous." I looked down at my dog. Sable. Well, now I knew what his color was called. He was my first dog, so it was all new to me.

"Back to business." Tish placed her phone on the table between us again. "Eddy chased a cat, and you fell."

"Yes, and she scared me half to death." Rita sipped from her mug. "She tripped over a little black purse with a long gold chain for a strap." She stood and crossed the room, returning with the bag. "This one."

Tish took the bag and opened it. "Not much in here. We'll find out if it's Missy's."

"I'd bet it is." Rita sat. "It was too near the body to be a coincidence. We were all but standing on top of the poor woman. One minute Jenna is looking through the purse, and the next, I see a shoe sticking out from behind the dumpster."

"I went to check, and there was Missy." My shoulders tensed, and I wrapped my arms around myself, fighting a chill that had nothing to do with the temperatures.

"Did you touch anything?" Tish sipped delicately at her mug.

"No, I didn't. There was no need." I closed my eyes, wishing I could blink away the image of Missy's crumpled body lying on its side behind the dumpster, dark, dried blood matted in the back of her once-brassy blonde hair. "I knew she was dead."

Tish nodded, tapped her phone's screen, and rose. "I guess that's it, then."

When Tish was halfway to the kitchen with her mug, Rita whispered, "Tell her the rest."

Tish turned. "The rest?"

"Wow, that's some sense of hearing you have." Rita chuckled and nodded at me. "She saw something last night that you need to know."

"Hang on." Tish returned to the table, set down her mug, and pulled out her phone again, tapping the screen several times before laying it on the table. "Okay, what happened last night?"

I recounted what Mason and I had seen, which probably hadn't been more than several others had witnessed.

"Was there blood on Emerson's shirt or pants when he returned alone?" Tish asked.

"Not that I could see." I thought back, picturing the scene again in my mind. The rumpled hair, as if he'd run his hands through it. The turned-up sleeve cuffs. The pain in his eyes when they had met mine. No, I was sure there was no blood.

"What about this other man who was there?" Tish sipped her coffee again, wrapping her fingers around the mug and crossing her legs.

"Tom apparently used to be Missy's boyfriend." I explained about the proposal in the street the day before. "Missy dumped him because Blake had more money, but Tom still seemed to be carrying a torch for her."

Tish leaned forward. "And this Tom left your view just after Missy stormed off?"

I nodded. "He ran off in the opposite direction, though, and Connie followed him a few minutes later."

"I see." Tish reached for her phone. "Anything else?"

"Not that I can think of." I rose when Tish stood, following her toward the kitchen. "Do you know who killed her?"

Tish barked a hard laugh as she dumped her remaining coffee in the sink and rinsed her mug. "If we knew that, I would be sitting here enjoying the rest of my coffee rather than grilling you about finding a body."

When Tish had closed my front door behind herself, Rita turned to me. "They must have some sort of idea."

I'd refilled my mug and had walked to the couch, tucking my feet under me. Eddy had joined me, his head in my lap.

"How can they?" I shook my head.

"It's obvious that ex of yours did it." Rita plopped down on the other end of the couch and propped her feet on my coffee table.

"I don't know." I replayed the conversation with Tish in my head. "I think he's not the only one who had an opportunity."

"You mean Tom?" Rita asked.

I shifted my legs, sliding them out and settling Eddy's head deeper into my lap. "And Connie. If you look at it, within two days of her disappearance, Missy publicly humiliated Tom, Connie screamed her hate and anger at Missy, and Missy threatened to destroy Blake and me if he came near me again."

Rita chuckled. "You realize you just put yourself on the list of folks having a reason to kill her. After all, you were the one who tossed her out on her ear the day before yesterday."

I lobbed a small, decorative couch pillow at her. "Then you'd better watch out if I'm the killer. I made the coffee."

Rita, having caught the soft missile, propped the pillow behind her low back. "She was hit in the head, not poisoned. Besides, I haven't pissed you off that I'm aware of."

"Point taken." I chuckled but quickly sobered. "I just don't like it that I'm in the middle of all of this again."

Rita stood and moved to her purse, where her phone dinged a text. "There's Elliot asking when I'll be there."

"Don't tell me. Elliot's had that duck because you weren't there to help out."

"No, and I hope he doesn't." Rita slipped the phone back into her purse and slid the purse's handles over her shoulder. "But with the tone of questioning changing, the bridesmaids are up in arms with the whole 'how dare you ask us things like that' attitude. Elliot wants me to help keep them from making a scene in the common areas."

"Oh no!" I followed her to the door. "Hug Elliot for me. I hope you don't have to learn to like foie gras."

Rita rolled her eyes and strode out the door. "Yeah, like that will ever happen."

After she left, the silence in the apartment swamped me. I didn't want to go downstairs and see the police or fend off lookie-loos. I considered watching TV to take my mind off of dead bodies and murder and weddings and drama. But that eliminated police dramas, reality dating shows, and soap operas, leaving only the home shopping channels, sports, and infomercials, which didn't appeal to me on any level. And even the novel resting on my bedside was a murder mystery.

Instead, I grabbed Eddy's leash for a walk, choosing to exit my apartment by the spiral stairs down into the store rather than get a bird's-eye view of the alleyway out my apartment door. As I'd suspected, the morbidly curious onlookers had already swarmed the area and were congregated at either end of the street, trying to see into the alleyway past the yellow police tape.

Making my way around the crowd, I scooted Eddy toward a grassy area, encouraging him to hurry up about his mid-morning business rather than take his usual leisurely stroll, sniffing every tree and bush before making his choices. As if he understood, he hiked his leg toward the first bush he came to, finished, and tugged me toward the store. Guess he didn't like the crowds and drama any more than I did.

The store was empty when Eddy and I walked in. I unclipped his leash, and he sought out a sunny spot while I searched for Mason.

"Hey, boss lady." Mason exited the back room, a smug look on his face. "We've been really slow today, and I was able to finish all of the inventory."

I hated to shatter his pleasure at completing inventory, but there was no way around it. He'd never forgive me if I didn't tell him. "I see you haven't heard."

The smile slid from his face, and he walked with me to the front of the store. "What's going on?"

I sighed and sat on one of the stools behind the counter. "I found Missy Plott's body behind the dumpster out back."

Mason's jaw dropped, and for a moment, he stared at me before finding his voice. "Dead? But how? What happened?"

"They're not sure yet who killed her, but her head was bashed in. I'm late this morning because Tish had to interview Rita and me," I said.

"Rita, too?" Mason shook his head. "Man, I miss all the excitement around here."

I patted him on the shoulder. "Don't worry, I'm sure they'll be in to talk to you too, since I said you witnessed a bunch of the stuff with me."

"Is that why I kept hearing noises out back?" He gestured toward the back door. "I knew I should've looked. But I wanted to finish the inventory and surprise you. I figured if it was important, someone would tell me."

"Getting the inventory done was the most important thing you could do," I assured him. "Besides, they wouldn't have let you watch anything anyway."

Mason shrugged. "I guess so."

Keith strode through the front door, coming to my side and gathering me into his arms for a bear hug. "I'm glad you're okay."

I sank into his embrace, reveling in its warmth. "I am. I promise." I wanted this moment to last, shutting out the dead body a few feet away, the thought of a zippered bag on a gurney, the search for murder weapons and guilty parties. I wanted to just think about how good Keith smelled and how warm his arms were where they surrounded my shoulders. I wanted to lose myself in the solidity of his shoulder beneath my cheek and let the world fall away.

Mason rose and headed across the store. "I'll give you two some privacy."

"Wait." Keith called Mason back, pulling away from the embrace after brushing a kiss across my lips. "I need to talk to you both."

So much for my dreams of hiding from reality. I shot Mason an I-told-you-so look as Keith stepped back from me.

Mason shoved his hands in his pockets, a somber look on his face. "How can I help?"

"I need you to tell me, in your own words, just what you saw last night, and for the last few days since Blake and Missy hit town." Keith pulled out the old-school little black notebook that Tish refused to use.

"Well, it all started when Missy and Blake walked into the store on Tuesday, and Missy was really rude to Jenna."

I closed my eyes and listened closely, comparing Mason's rather lengthy version of events to mine, glad to realize I hadn't dreamed up the ugly looks and the snotty attitudes. At the same time, I was disappointed to realize I'd been right about it all.

"Then on Wednesday, Missy tried to find Jenna, but she wasn't here. But some guy tried to propose to Missy just outside our door, and she was a hateful witch." Mason recounted in detail the same story he'd told me when I'd gotten back from hiding in the candle shop.

Still I sat silent, letting Mason push through without breaking his train of thought.

"Thursday, she came back and all but threatened Jenna."

I looked up to see Mason imitating me herding Missy and her friends toward the door. "And Jenna said, 'If you ever come back, I'll call the police!' Missy said something about staying away from Blake. But Jenna doesn't want to be near Blake anyway."

Keith had flipped several pages and continued to take rapid notes. "And last night?"

"Last night was freaky." Mason recounted the same story I'd told Tish earlier. "Later, I picked up Lily from work—she was serving last night at The Weeping Willow—and she told me that Missy was really pissed off even before they came outside."

Keith turned another page and held his pen poised. "Did she tell you why?"

"Something about how Blake's mom never showed up for the rehearsal dinner." Mason shrugged.

Keith nodded and made a note. "Others in the wedding party told us the same thing."

"Missy got up and went to the bathroom, and her sister followed her. Lily was in one of the stalls. She said that Missy was saying how Blake's mom kept disrespecting her, and she'd had enough of it." Mason used his fingers as air quotes. "She said 'that woman' was going to be really sorry if she didn't stop disrespecting her and went on about how she was going to be Blake's wife."

I cringed. It was never a good idea to come between a man and his family. I'd never met Blake's mother, but right now, I was in her corner. I wouldn't have wanted Missy for a daughter-in-law either.

"Lily said Missy refused to let anyone order food until Blake's mom arrived." Mason pantomimed raising a glass to his lips. "But she sure kept drinking. Lily said the more she drank, the madder she got, and the madder she got, the louder she got. Blake kept trying to calm her down until she finally turned on him and started screaming at him about Jenna. He tried to argue with her, but she jumped up and ran out into the street, and Jenna and I saw the rest."

Keith flipped his booklet closed and pocketed it and the pen. "Thanks, Mason. This fills in a couple of gaps and lets me know I need to chat with Lily. Do you know if she's working today?"

Mason nodded. "Since she has the lunch shift, she's probably there by now."

Keith brushed a kiss across my cheek, hugging me tightly. "I'll be back when I can to check on you. I love you."

"I love you too." I wanted to hang on, to pretend things were back to how they were before Missy and Blake had plowed into my life, turning it into a roller coaster of emotion and drama. Instead, I let my arms drop and watched him walk out the door.

After Keith left, Mason plopped down in the chair at the end of the counter. "I'm betting it was the sister."

I thought of the girl who had finally grown a spine and rebelled against her sister's bullying tactics. "Why do you think so?"

"Well, it couldn't have been your jerk of an ex." Mason raised his hands up, his shoulders in a shrug. "Because it's never the one you want to be guilty. It's always the one you don't expect it to be, which would be the sister, and we both heard her say she wished Missy was dead. At least that's how it would work out in TV shows and books."

A true laugh burst out of my chest, lightening my mood. "You do realize this isn't an episode of *Law and Order* or one of those thrillers." I waved my hand at the mystery and thriller section of the store.

Mason stood and walked around the counter, reaching under to pull out the duster. "I know. But still. My money's on Connie."

I watched him walk away, considering his points. I agreed Blake was almost too obvious, but wasn't that how it worked in real life? I hated to think either the guy with the roses and the puppy-dog eyes or the girl with the purple sparkly nails who'd apologized for Missy's rudeness might be a killer. But what if one of them was?

Chapter Twelve

"I can't believe you're defending him." Keith paced his living room.

Eddy jumped up from his corner bed by the fireplace and hopped onto the couch, snuggling up against me.

I slid an arm across him, soothing him with my hands. "You're upsetting Eddy."

Eddy and I had come for dinner at Keith's house Sunday evening, and this time we'd eaten while the food was warm before Keith had dropped a bombshell on me.

"Upsetting Eddy?" Keith paused his pacing and raked a hand through his hair. "What about the fact that you've decided to take your ex-fiancé's side after we've arrested him?"

I sighed and wove my fingers into Eddy's coat, not sure if I was comforting him or myself. "I'm not taking anyone's side."

Keith sat on the raised stone hearth in front of the unlit logs and propped his elbows on his knees, his gaze focused on me. "Did you not just say you thought we'd arrested the wrong person?"

I nodded. "I think you have."

Keith jumped up again, and his pacing resumed. "See? There you go defending him."

"It's not defending him." I stood and planted myself in front of Keith, forcing him to stop pacing and look at me. "I know this man. I lived with him. I ate meals with him. I worked with him."

Keith crossed his arms and cocked his head. "For how long?"

"How long what?" Did he think Blake and I were secretly back together or something?

"How long did you live together? You've never said, and I've never pressed it." Keith remained frozen in place, his gaze boring into me.

"Three years." I crossed my arms and returned his icy stare.

He threw his hands in the air. "And in all that time you never once saw anything that might lead you to believe he might hurt someone?"

I dropped my arms, my fists balled at my sides, and raised my voice to match his. "We've only been a couple for six months, and I'd like to think I already know you well enough to know you wouldn't kill anyone either!"

Keith stilled, the ire in his gaze turning to hurt, and his voice dropping to barely above a whisper. "I can't believe you just compared me to your ex."

My heart clenched. "I'm not comparing you. I've never compared you, because there is no comparison." I reached out to touch him on the arm. "Why are you making this out like I'm still in love with him or something?"

"Are you?"

His whispered words brought me up short. "That's what this is about?" I dropped my hand from his arm. "If it were any other suspect, any other crime, you'd value my input, my ideas, my insights. But because I used to live with Blake, used to share his home, share his bed, cook for him, clean for him, and wear his ring, my inside knowledge of what makes the man tick is now completely invalid because you're afraid I still want him? Is that it?"

"Three years is a long time." The pain in his gaze matched the gruffness of his voice.

"Keith, you can't be serious." I reached for his cheek, cupping it in my palm.

Keith pulled away from my touch. "When is the last time you spoke to him before he arrived?"

"The day he handed me my key and told me where my stuff was stored." I dropped my hand and stepped back. "The day he walked into my store was the first time I heard word one from him after that."

"Then why is he convinced you want to get back together with him?" He stilled and his gaze bored into me.

"How the hell am I supposed to know that?" I raised my hands in the air and dropped them. "I'm not a mind reader!"

Eddy whined, huddled on the couch.

Keith stepped to the couch and dropped down beside my dog. "It's okay, boy." He stroked the dog's head. "There has to be more to this. The man obviously thinks he's got a shot."

"Are you accusing me of lying to you?" I planted my hands on my hips. "Please tell me you're joking."

Keith took a deep breath and huffed it out. "What would you think if an ex of mine suddenly showed up and was all over me? Wouldn't that make you question things even a little?"

"Questioning is one thing." I knelt in front of him. "But not believing the answers is another."

"What am I supposed to think, Jenna?" His hand on Eddy stilled, and he swung his gaze to meet mine. "That this guy, who you've said never made a move without overplanning it and making sure every detail is perfect, would accidentally appear here and go completely off the cuff? It doesn't fit his profile."

I stood. "Great then. I guess you have it all figured out, like I'm supposed to have been secretly in contact with him all these months, trying to set this up with him behind your back so I can go running back to a relationship with a man who was smothering and demanding and critical and—"

"And rich and handsome and with whom you have a long history." Keith clenched his jaw.

"There it is. The real reason." I crossed my arms. "It's your insecurities. You think I think he's better looking than you and I want his money. Do you really think I'm that shallow? Oh, wait, apparently yes, you do."

Keith sighed again and stood. "I think you should go."

Acid flooded my stomach and bile rose in my throat. "You're asking me to leave?"

Keith nodded and reached for Eddy's leash, walking to the couch to snap it on and scratch the dog's head. "I think it would be best."

"Fine." Tears welled in my eyes, but I refused to let them fall. I grabbed my purse from the table by the door and called to Eddy.

As I loaded my dog into my car, I turned to see Keith silhouetted in his open front door, shoulders slumped, before he turned, shut the door, and flipped off the porch light.

Tears fell freely on the drive home, where I curled up on top of my bed, my dog at my back, and cried myself into an exhausted sleep.

I woke to moonlight pouring in through the window and looked at my watch. Four AM. The soft glow of the kitchen light, which I hadn't turned off before I'd collapsed onto my bed, shone through my open bedroom door. I sat up, realizing I hadn't even taken off my shoes, much less undressed or gotten under the covers.

My head pounded from all of the crying, and my eyes felt crusty. I rolled off the bed, pulled a towel from the closet, and headed for the shower, hoping the warm water would revive me a bit.

Once clean, I dressed, knowing I wouldn't be able to sleep more after last night's fight with Keith. How could he think I wanted to be with Blake Emerson? How could Missy have thought that? How could Blake believe it? Was I giving off some sort of I-want-Blake vibe that I was unaware of?

I padded into the kitchen and rummaged in my medicine cabinet for a bottle of ibuprofen. I poured a glass of water and downed three of the little orange pills before putting on a pot of coffee. When I had a full mug, I took it to the couch and turned on the TV, finding a channel showing back-to-back episodes of *I Love Lucy*, hoping it would make me laugh or at least distract me from the roller coaster of emotion plowing through my brain.

It didn't.

At seven, I dragged myself from the couch, popped two more ibuprofen, ate a bowl of cereal that might as well have been chunks of the cardboard box for all that I could taste it, and leashed Eddy for his morning walk. I took him out the front door and down the walkway, purposely avoiding looking down into the alleyway.

Eddy took his time, sniffing every spot of grass and trying to nibble a few bites of it before I shooed him away from it. After he'd had time to pee on at least ten different spots, I'm sure as a result of the crowd of people tromping around in his territory the day before, we headed back to the apartment.

As I unlocked the front door, Rita exited her apartment and waved a greeting. "Morning, neighbor. I didn't expect to see you home this early." She grinned and walked over to me, her face paling. "What happened to you?"

"Nothing. I'm fine." I shrugged.

Rita took my arm and dragged me into my home, leading me to the bathroom and planting me in front of the mirror. "That does not look fine to me."

My shoulder-length dark blonde hair stuck up at odd angles on one side of my head. It must have dried that way while I lay on the couch after my shower. My blue eyes were heavily hooded by swollen eyelids. My tan skin was pale and blotchy from the crying. "No, I guess it doesn't."

Rita turned me to face her and took my hands in hers. "Whatever it is, I'm here. Now what happened?"

Tears welled in my scratchy eyes. "Keith and I had a fight last night."

"Oh boy." Rita tucked her arm in mine and led me to the couch. "Sit. We need coffee for this."

She bustled about in the kitchen for a few minutes, returning with two steaming mugs, setting hers on the coffee table and pressing mine into my hands. "Okay, I'm fortified. Now spill it."

"They arrested Blake, and I told Keith I thought they'd arrested the wrong person." I clenched my hands around the mug like it was a lifeline. "We argued and he threw me out."

"Threw you out?" Rita scooted closer and laid a hand on my arm. "Are you sure you didn't misunderstand?"

"His words were, 'I think you should go.' Kind of hard to misunderstand that." Tears fell down my cheeks.

"And did he say not to come back again?" She reached for a Kleenex box on the end table and held it out to me.

I pulled out a tissue and blotted my cheeks and eyes. "No."

"Did he say things were over and he never wanted to see you again?"

I blew my nose and rose to throw away the tissue and wash my hands. "No."

Rita sighed and followed me to the kitchen. "Honey, fights happen. This is just your first one with Keith. Didn't you and Blake ever fight?"

I shook my head. "No."

"Ohhhh." Rita smiled and hugged me. "That explains it."

"Explains what?" I asked.

"Why you're acting like you've just lost everything." She led me back to the couch, tucking me back into my comfy corner.

"But he threw me out!" I waved my hands. "We didn't just fight. He accused me of still being in love with Blake!"

"And are you?" she asked softly.

"Not you too." I shook my head. "Why does everyone keep asking me that question? No, I'm not. I haven't been for a long time. I have no desire to be in love with Blake. I don't miss being in love with Blake. To be honest, I'm not sure I ever *was* in love with Blake when I think about how I feel about Keith. I didn't have those same feelings for Blake. I just didn't know any better."

"Have you looked at it through Keith's eyes?" Rita raised a hand and ticked off items on her fingers. "First, you lived with a guy for years, and you were engaged. It's not a stretch to figure out you loved him. Second, it's only been a few months since things ended, which isn't that long of a time. Third, you rebounded into the relationship with Keith almost immediately upon landing in Hokes Folly."

I sat up, sloshing a few drops of hot coffee into my lap, my conversation with Shelby rushing back. "Now everyone is saying Keith's a rebound! Is that really what you think?" I grabbed a tissue and blotted the hot liquid from my pants.

Rita's face softened, and she dropped her hand. "No. But that's how Keith could be seeing things."

"Oh." I sagged back, realization washing over me.

"Yeah, oh." Rita continued her list. "Four, now Blake has shown up again, professing his love for you, albeit in a creepy and pushy way. But from Keith's perspective, those three years far outweigh the few months you two have been together. That's three years of history, of laughter, passion, and challenges you overcame together that you and Keith don't have."

"He accused me of comparing him to Blake." I looked down into the depths of my coffee. "But he's the one who's comparing himself to Blake, isn't he?"

"Now you're getting it." Rita sipped at her mug. "He's trying to figure out why you want to be with him and not this man who has more money, who is willing to do anything to get to you, with whom you have a ton of history, and now, in Keith's eyes, a man you're standing up for."

We sat quietly for a bit, sipping our coffee. My mind spun, going over the argument again and again, and each time, I understood more and more about where Keith was coming from.

"Should I call him?" I asked, sitting forward and putting my mug on the coffee table.

Rita shook her head. "No, not today. I'd give it a day to calm down. Give him time to let his emotions settle and think things through. You need that same time."

I sighed. "You're probably right. But what if he thinks I really do want to be with Blake?"

"Honey, if one day to let things settle breaks the relationship, then it wouldn't have survived in the long run anyway." Rita stood and crossed to the kitchen to put her mug in the sink and grab her purse. "It's Monday. What are you doing today?"

Many of the stores remained closed on Mondays, mine included, and I knew she was concerned I would sit here and wallow all day. "Mason and I are meeting at the store to go over the inventory results. We want to discuss possible improvements. We were supposed to do it Saturday, but after finding Missy . . ."

Rita ignored my trailed-off sentence. "I'm sure you'll think of lots of fun things to do with the store today." She walked to the couch and sat down to give me a quick hug before heading to the door. "Now get a move on and show this town what you're made of."

After I'd fixed my tousled hair and held a couple of teabags over my eyes for fifteen minutes, trying to get the swelling down, I headed to the store to meet Mason. We started the day with a bit of spring cleaning, dusting shelves and books, vacuuming under the shelves as best we could, reorganizing the back room and under the front counter, and fully sanitizing the bathroom. The steady physical work did wonders for my mood, and Mason refrained from asking why my eyes were still a bit puffy, although I did catch a few concerned glances when he thought I wasn't paying attention.

After lunch, we tackled the inventory sheets, assessing where our thin spots were and whether or not these sections had enough sales to warrant trying to beef them up. Lost in conversation, we almost missed the tapping at the front door.

I looked up and saw a tall, elegantly dressed woman with her hand cupped around her eyes peering through the door.

My stomach tightened, and I wanted to do anything but open the door to the woman, but we'd already been seen. The woman clasped her hands together in a pleading gesture then motioned to the door. Whatever Blake's mother wanted, I was not in the mood to hear it.

I walked over and turned the lock, cracking the door open a few inches. "We're closed today," I said through the crack. "But we're open tomorrow morning at nine."

"Jenna, please," the woman begged. "I know you don't know me, since Blake never let us meet. But I know who you are, and I need your help."

Chapter Thirteen

I swung the door open, letting the woman enter, and turned the lock behind her. I didn't want a random customer to walk in if there was going to be drama. And at least today, Mason was here to have my back or to be a witness, depending on how things went.

"How can we help you?" I turned to face the woman, my face carefully kept as blank as I could manage.

"I'm Gwendolyn Emerson, Blake's mother." The woman extended her hand in greeting, smiling expectantly.

"I recognize you from the picture Blake kept on the mantle." I crossed my arms, ignoring my inner Mom-voice fussing at me for being rude. I simply didn't have it in me to be fake today.

Her smile slipped a bit, and her hand dropped. "Yes, well. I suppose that's to be expected." She cleared her throat. "I know my son kept us from meeting during the time you were seeing one another. He and I are not what you would call close."

I nodded. "Yes, he told me." I thought back to the times he'd gone to see her alone, and I assumed he'd wanted to keep me a secret from her as well. I'd never understood why, and despite the discussions we'd had about it, he'd never explained. "Mrs. Emerson—"

"Please, call me Gwendolyn." She tried to perk up her smile and failed. "After all, we were almost family."

"Yes, well, your son took care of that, didn't he?" I still hadn't moved from beside the door, but I caught Mason out of the corner of my eye, settling in behind the counter to listen.

Gwendolyn looked at Mason and gestured toward the seating area across the room. "May we please sit and have a quiet conversation?"

"Sure, why not?" I swung my arm in the direction she'd indicated. "Mason and I would be happy to chat with you."

"Oh, I thought we could chat privately." She took a tentative step toward the comfy seats.

"I would prefer we didn't." I motioned for Mason to join us and take the middle seat, making a mental note to apologize to him later for sticking him between me and my former mother-in-law-to-be.

Once we were all settled, Gwendolyn cleared her throat. "I know you don't really know me and don't owe me anything. But you loved my son for a long time, and I think that means something."

I remained silent, not confirming her statement.

After a moment, she shifted in her seat and crossed her ankles. "Yes, well. I just feel you're the only person in this town I can turn to."

Against my better judgement, I asked, "For?"

Gwendolyn smiled, seemingly relieved that I'd actually responded. "You know my son. You know he's not a killer. I need your help proving he's innocent."

"We have a very competent police department, Mrs. Emerson." I deliberately used the formal title for her, watching her smile slip away again. "I'm sure they're very capable of ensuring the correct person is put in jail for this crime."

She waved her hand in the air, as if dismissing my statement. "You know from personal experience that the police often arrest the wrong person. After all, you went to jail for all that mess in Charlotte, didn't you?"

I gritted my teeth. "And I was later released when they found I was innocent."

"Innocent or not, you spent time in jail for a crime you supposedly didn't commit." She uncrossed her ankles and leaned forward a bit. "You know how that feels."

I imitated her and leaned in, lowering my voice. "I also know how it feels to have someone who professes to love you completely cut you off and toss you out like yesterday's trash."

Mason coughed, and I glanced over to catch wide eyes and what I thought might have been a stifled grin.

"Do you hate my son that much?" Gwendolyn's voice was barely audible.

My stomach tightened. Maybe I did. Was I so hardened that I would allow someone else to go through what I had?

"I'm not defending what he did to you in the end. I know my son's failings." Gwendolyn reached out a hand toward me as if to touch me, letting it fall back when she couldn't reach that far. "But would you really let him go to jail for a crime you know in your heart he did not, could not, commit? Do you really need revenge that badly?"

My sense of justice warred with my desperate need to have nothing more to do with the Emerson family. Maybe it was revenge. I wasn't sure. Maybe it was just karma coming full circle. "My belief is irrelevant to the police. They're interested in proof. Evidence. Facts. I have none of those things." I stood and gestured toward the door. "I don't see how I can help you."

Gwendolyn followed me to the door, turning before she exited. "Blake says you're friends with one of the police officers here. Please, Jenna. Talk to him. Make him understand who my son is. If you ever loved Blake, make your friend see Blake is not a killer." She laid a hand on my arm and locked her gaze with mine. "Please consider it."

I stepped back, and her hand dropped away, a sadness in her eyes that pulled at my heart. Gwendolyn sighed deeply before stepping outside and walking toward the parking lot, her shoulders drooping under the weight of her distress.

I locked the door behind her and sagged against it.

"You okay?" Mason's hand landed on my shoulder. "I can call Keith if you need me to."

I straightened. "No. I'll talk to him about it later." But I knew I wouldn't.

"That woman had a lot of nerve asking you to help out after all that Blake did to you." He hooked his arm through mine and led me behind the counter to sit on the stools. "I mean, I know you used to date him, but do you really owe him anything after all that?"

I shook my head. "No, I don't owe him anything." But did I owe it to myself? Did I need to show myself I could be the bigger person, the person on the side of justice, not because it was Blake, but because it was the right thing to do?

"I don't think Keith would like it." Mason looked through the window in the direction of The Weeping Willow. "I know if an ex-boyfriend of Lily's turned up asking for her help, I'd have a really hard time with it."

"Wouldn't you trust her to do the right thing, even if you didn't agree with how she did it?" I followed his gaze, but my mind's eye only saw Keith framed in his door, slowly closing it and turning off the porch light.

"I don't know. Maybe." Mason shrugged. "But I'd like to think she wouldn't stick up for a guy who treated her like garbage. If she did, it would make me wonder why she stayed loyal to him." He looked down at his watch. "Speaking of Lily, I'm due to pick her up for dinner. We're grabbing a pizza and going to a movie."

I shooed Mason out the door and locked it, though his words still rang in my head. Did Keith feel I'd been disloyal to him? Was that the key? If so, how did I convince him I had to be loyal to myself and loyal to the truth, and that it didn't mean I wasn't loyal to him?

I continued to wrestle with Mason's and Rita's words as I made a simple salad for dinner and ate it in front of the TV. When Tuesday morning rolled around, and I still hadn't heard from Keith, I knew I had to do something, whether Rita agreed or not.

Leaving Eddy in the store with Mason, I headed to the end of the street and entered The Cookie Cutter. Inhaling deeply of the myriad of baked goods aromas, I let my senses take control of my brain for a brief moment, giving it a respite from the latest drama.

"Hey, Jenna," called a plump woman with a sunny smile from behind the counter. "What can I get you today?"

"Hey, Dana." I walked along the row of glass cases, looking at all the delectable treats. Dana Nichols had known Uncle Paul, but I'd only recently begun to frequent her bakery, much to the downfall of my previously somewhat-healthy diet. "I'd like four dozen cake pops." I pointed at the two-inch-round balls of cake dipped in hardened icing, sitting on lollypop sticks.

"A variety box?" She reached under the counter for a box.

I nodded and continued to stroll, picking out a few baked goods to take home for tomorrow's breakfast.

"Did you hear about that murdered bride?" Dana handed the box of cake pops across the counter to me and grabbed another box for my other items.

"I found the body." I cringed, having answered before thinking it through. Dana was sweet, but she couldn't keep a secret to save herself. Soon every store owner would know. Too late to take it back now, though.

"No!" Her eyes widened. "What happened?"

"Eddy chased a big, orange cat down the alleyway, and I found her behind the dumpster."

"Oh. My. God." Dana put a hand to her chest. "I would have died on the spot." She fanned herself with her other hand. "But you know what? I think I know who did it."

"Really?" I shifted the cake pop box, stacking the other box on top while I swiped my card. "Who?"

"Well, the day before she disappeared, that sister of hers—Karen, Kelly, something like that—"

"Connie." I dropped my card into my purse, making a mental note to put it back in my wallet later.

"Yeah, Connie. That's it." Dana washed her hands after touching the cash drawer, talking to me over her shoulder. "Well, she was in here with that man who tried to propose to Missy."

My ears perked up. "Tom Jackson." Maybe I was going to get information Keith could use. If I could get him to talk to me. I tightened my grip on the cake pops.

"Was that his name?" Dana waved a hand as if dismissing it. "Well, let me tell you. Connie was all over him, begging him to stop loving the dead girl, although she wasn't dead yet, God rest her soul." Dana crossed herself, showing her Catholic roots. "Anyway, Connie was all 'you deserve better, you need to be with someone who loves you the way you need to be loved, you need someone who respects you, you need someone who doesn't care if you're rich or not' and on and on and on."

A couple walked in, and Dana excused herself to assist them with their purchase of bear claws and coffees. They took their snacks to one of the pink tables with chairs with heart-shaped backs and sat.

Dana waved me over to the far end of the counter. "Anyway, she was going on and on, and he kept telling her the dead girl was the only girl for him. He loved her so much and had always loved her. He couldn't live without her, and until that guy she was going to marry came along, she'd said she couldn't live without him either." She leaned closer and waved me to do the same, whispering, "Then Connie says, 'What if she's not around anymore? Will you stop living? Will you waste away waiting for a woman who disappears from your life?' And he says, 'While we're both breathing, there's still hope for us,' and he turns and walks out, leaving her standing here. As she's walking away, she says, 'And what if she's not breathing anymore?' Then she turns around, as if she realizes I heard her say it, and she runs out of the store after him."

Connie? Little, sweet Connie? There was no way. I'd sooner believe Blake actually did it than believe Connie had. But if

Dana had overheard her correctly, maybe Connie was really a killer at heart. "Are you sure that's what she said?"

Dana pulled back and put her hand on her chest. "Hand to God, I swear it was as clear as what you're saying to me now, not that I try to listen to other people's business."

"Have you talked to the police yet?" I knew Keith would want to know this. Or at least Tish would.

Dana shook her head. "Nope, uh-uh. No way am I getting involved. I don't butt into other people's business."

I caught myself before laughing at that statement. Instead, I thanked her, picked up my boxes of baked goods, and headed home. There were other people who had wanted Missy dead, apparently including her own sister. How terrible did you have to be for your sister to want you dead? I shook my head. I'd never had a sister, but I couldn't imagine hating one that much, no matter what happened.

Chapter Fourteen

I took the time to enjoy one of the chocolate-cream-filled donuts I'd bought for myself, hoping to fortify myself for what was coming. On a sugar and chocolate high, I straightened my spine, grabbed the box of cake pops, and headed out the door to the police station.

When I arrived, I cringed to see Sutter behind the front counter again. "Hello, Detective. I'd like to see Keith, please." I held up the box and smiled what I hoped was a friendly looking smile, even though I did not count Sutter among my friends. "I brought baked goods."

Sutter humphed and narrowed his eyes, looking at the box. "Logan's been in a bad mood for two days." *Grunt.* "Y'all have a fight or something?"

Guess this wasn't going to be easy. "I believe he asked you to be polite. Shall I tell him you weren't?"

Sutter's face reddened even more than his normal ruddy complexion, and I hoped he wasn't going to have a stroke or something.

He clenched his jaw before snaking a meaty hand under the counter to press the door-release button. "You know the way." *Grunt.*

I'd never figured out why Sutter grunted that much, but it really didn't matter. Soon enough, I'd never have to see him again. I pushed open the door and paused. Before I could second-guess myself, I turned and opened the box, stepping into the doorway to the front office. "Would you like a couple before I take them to the back?"

Sutter narrowed his eyes at me before looking at the box. "What's in them?"

Oh my god, did he think I was trying to poison him? "Cake. That's what's in them. Do you want any or not?"

Grunt. Sutter sniffed and reached into the box as if expecting a snake to bite him if he moved too quickly. He grabbed two stems and pulled them out, holding them like a little boy at a candy counter as he turned back to his post.

Ungrateful much? I started down the hallway toward Keith, hoping he'd be happier with my offering than Sutter had been.

"Hey, Quinn!" Sutter's voice rang behind me.

I turned, expecting to see his typical sneer and was surprised by an actual smile on his face. "Thanks." He waved an empty stick at me. "These aren't bad."

Wow, had Sutter just called a truce? "You can get more at The Cookie Cutter if you like them." I returned his smile, and this time it was genuine.

With a lighter step, I wound my way through the bullpen of desks to Keith's and Tish's desks, which faced each other.

"Hello, Jenna." Keith's formal tone and cold expression almost made me turn and run.

I stiffened my spine and plowed through. "I brought cake pops for everyone." I put the box on his desk and opened the lid.

Several nearby officers crowded around, snagging stems from the box before heading back to their own areas.

Keith hadn't touched them. "Why are you here?"

His tone was like a slap, and I fought the tears that threatened to swamp me again. *Not here, Jenna. Suck it up.* "I wanted to make peace. I miss you."

Keith raked a hand through his hair. "Damn it, Jenna, I—"

"Hey!" Tish approached. "I heard there was food. Specifically, those." She reached into the box and pulled out a pop, taking a bite. "Mmm. These are incredible. I've never had one before."

"I get them from The Cookie Cutter. It's a bakery near my store." I avoided looking at Keith, using Tish's interruption to regain control over my emotions.

"Remind me to never go there." Tish laughed, biting into her second pop. "If I do, I'll end up as round as these things." She gestured toward the cake pops still in the box.

I laughed and turned to Keith. "Peace?"

He sighed deeply and nodded. "Peace. But Jenna, I want you to stay out of this case."

"Uh-uh," Tish mumbled around a bite of her third cake pop, hurrying to swallow. "She can't do that."

"The hell she can't." Keith crossed his arms and glared at Tish. "There's no reason for her to be sticking her nose into this case."

"Get off it, Logan." Tish wiped her mouth on a napkin. "You're just itching to pin it on the guy we arrested because he hurt Jenna in the past. It's why they decided to swap and put me in charge."

My jaw dropped. Was Keith really pulling a Sutter, not looking at everything because he wanted it to be a specific person?

"I do not want him to be guilty. I just don't want her trying to prove he's innocent!" Keith slammed himself down into his chair, which groaned under the onslaught.

Tish sat on the corner of the desk. "Uh-huh. Sure. And I'm the chief."

Propping his forearms on the desk, Keith leaned forward. "We have enough evidence to put him away for a long time."

"But we also have evidence that someone else could have done it." Tish closed the cake pop box, sliding it across the desk and out of her immediate reach, as if removing the temptation to take a fourth pop. "Evidence we've not been able to link to Emerson yet."

"But Jenna doesn't have to be involved in that." Keith reached for the box and took out a pop, twirling the stem in his fingers.

Tish shook her head. "I disagree. She could have insights into Emerson's state of mind, she was a witness to several critical altercations, and she found the body."

Tired of being talked around like I didn't exist, I cleared my throat. "Excuse me."

Both heads whipped around to stare at me, as if they'd forgotten I was standing there.

Talk about being in the spotlight. "I've also had other people come to me with information since we talked last." I tried to put a good spin on it by sealing it with a smile.

Keith threw his hands up, the cake pop sailing off the stick and skittering across the room to roll under another desk. "Great, here we go. Next thing you know, someone will try to kill her again."

Tish laughed as she walked over to grab the loose cake pop and drop it in a trashcan. "Is that what you're worried about? I think we're okay on this one. I doubt Jenna is eager to jump that deeply into things. But we do need her insights."

"Nope, not eager at all," I assured them both, wishing I didn't feel like such an outsider, just standing there watching them argue.

"Who talked to you this time, Jenna?" Keith reached for another pop and stuck the whole thing in his mouth.

I hoped he didn't choke on it when he heard who it was. "Blake's mother. She asked me to help her prove his innocence and begged me to talk to you about it."

Keith jumped to his feet. "After all that man did to you, you're going to pal up with his mom and get him out of jail?" Anger flashed from his eyes.

Tish stepped in front of him. "Whoa there, Ghost Rider. Let's take a few calming breaths, shall we? Jenna didn't say that was why she was here, just that it's what Mrs. Emerson asked her to do." She looked over her shoulder at me for confirmation.

I nodded. "Exactly. I told her no. I told her the police department would handle it."

A deep, ragged breath pushed from Keith's chest, and he rubbed a hand over his face. "I swear, woman, you're going to give me a heart attack one day."

Tish laughed and gently pushed his shoulder until he sat in his chair again. "I think you're giving yourself that heart attack by jumping to conclusions and worrying about what hasn't even happened yet."

Man, too bad this woman hadn't been at Keith's house two days ago. Maybe she could've calmed him down before it got to this point. "Look, I don't want to get into the investigation. I just wanted to pass along what she said."

"I'm sorry," Keith mumbled. "Go on."

Tish nodded encouragingly at me and reached for another cake pop. At my grin, she said, "What? They're too good to resist. Please don't bring more of these here. Bring donuts. Donuts I can resist."

Both Keith and I chuckled, the tension broken, at least for the moment.

"She tried to play on the angle that I know Blake too well to think he would kill anyone, and that after being in jail for a crime I didn't commit, I should be the first person to want to help him not go through the same thing."

"After he left you to rot with no support and then dumped you for Missy when you got out?" Keith slammed his palms on the desk. "Oh hell no. Does she not know what that man did to you? Is she that stupid?"

"I wouldn't know!" I cringed when my voice came out in a shout, drawing stares from others in the room. Lowering my volume, I said, "I've never met her before." So much for the broken tension.

"Wait." Keith cocked his head and crossed his arms. "Are you saying that in three years together, you never once met his mother? Even after you got engaged?"

I shook my head. "Blake said she wasn't someone he wanted in our lives. I never could get a straight answer as to why. It was weird, too, because he kept a photo of her on the mantle."

"Then she wasn't trying to play on your relationship with her to get you to help." Tish crossed her arms and chewed on her bottom lip, her brows drawn together. "Why would she think you'd want to help him then, if she didn't even know you?"

I shrugged. "I have no idea. I told her I couldn't help her. But she's determined to prove he's innocent."

"As any mother would be, I'm sure." Tish slid into the conversation, stopping Keith's tirade before it started. "Who else has talked to you?"

"The baker and the candlestick maker." I grinned.

Tish laughed. "Okay, start with the baker, since I'm eating their food now."

I reached behind Tish and rolled her chair out from behind the desk, sliding it around to face both of them. "According to her, Connie was all over Tom Jackson, Missy's ex-boyfriend." I lowered myself onto the chair. "Dana overheard Connie whisper something about wondering what would happen if Missy wasn't breathing anymore. Dana's convinced Connie killed her."

Tish tsked as I finished. "That little snip of a girl? I don't know. I think Missy would have broken her in half."

"Missy was too drunk. Anyone could have pushed her over." Keith crossed his legs, one foot on top of his other knee, sliding his chair closer to mine in the process.

Did I dare hope it was on purpose? "Pushed her over?"

"Yeah." Tish closed the box lid and reached over to place it on the other side of the desk. "She apparently fell and hit her head against an old concrete block in the alley, although bruising on her chest indicates someone slammed their palms into her, causing her to fall."

"How hard would someone have to push her to bruise her?" I tried to picture Connie mustering up the force required.

"Not that hard, really," Tish said. "With the amount of alcohol in her blood, she would have bruised pretty easily. Now what about the candlestick maker?"

"I don't know if she actually makes the candles, but she owns the candle shop." I told them about hiding in Shelby's store while Tom proposed to Missy. "According to her, Missy has pissed off about every store owner on the block. Maybe one of them killed her if she pressed their buttons too many times."

"A bit weaker, but we'll look into it." Keith reached for a pad and grabbed a pencil. "Any idea who all she pissed off?"

I listed the wedding dress place, the candle store—even though I hated to toss Shelby onto the list—and the florist. "I'm sure you could find more if you canvassed."

"You just stay out of it." Keith pinned me with a hard stare. "Am I clear?"

Guess my hope that he was softening was unfounded. "Crystal."

As I left the station, I peeked in on Sutter. "If you liked the cake pops, there are still some left in the box on Tish's desk."

Sutter eyed me warily. "Thanks." *Grunt.*

So much for that truce too. Guess it just wasn't my day.

Chapter Fifteen

The afternoon spread out in a steady stream of customers keeping Mason and me busy. Most were legitimate, although there were the expected curiosity seekers who wanted to see if we knew anything about the murder. I played dumb, and thankfully, Mason followed my lead.

When we finally caught a break in the traffic, I noticed Eddy pacing by the front door.

I grabbed his leash and snapped it on. "I'm taking Eddy for a quick walk. Back in a few!"

Mason stepped from the back room, one of the donuts I'd brought him in his hand. "Okay," he mumbled over a mouthful.

I hurried down the walk, Eddy all but dragging me like a sled dog in his race to relieve himself. As he hiked on the first bush he came to, I tilted my head back to the warm sun and closed my eyes, soaking in the spring warmth. We took our time, Eddy sniffing and labeling his territory and me basking in the blue skies and gentle breeze, letting it whisk away the day's stresses, if only in part.

We eased our way back toward my store, in no hurry now. As we passed Candle Cottage, I saw Shelby waving at me, as if she wanted me to enter.

I swung the door open to the soft *bing-bong* of an electronic door chime. "Hey, Shelby."

Eddy tugged me forward, aiming straight for the treat Shelby was wiggling at him.

As he crunched happily on the bone-shaped dog cookie, Shelby gave me a quick hug. "Glad I caught you. I've been too busy to try to run down to your store today. This is the first break I've had in traffic all day."

I grinned. "Same for us. Isn't it great when it's busy?"

Shelby pointed at her high heels. "When I have to be on my feet all day in these, I daydream of the slow days. At least you have help in your store."

"You know you don't have to wear dresses and suits to work every day here." I gestured toward my own work outfit, which consisted of jeans, a light-teal spring sweater, and a nice pair of flat-soled leather shoes. "If you have to be on your feet all day, go for comfort. The sales will still happen. I promise."

"I guess I'm still in the bigger-city-job mindset. There's no way I could have gotten away with wearing what you've got on at my old job." She waved a hand at Jenna's jeans. "I worked as an executive secretary for the president of a small, high-tech company in Raleigh."

"Raleigh? What brought you here?" I shushed Eddy, who was actively begging for another cookie from his new friend.

Shelby smiled and reached behind the counter, obliging Eddy's demands. "I don't mind. He can have another. As for how I ended up here? I'd visited Biltmore several times. It's one of my favorite places. Then a few months ago, I actually won two hundred thousand dollars with a scratch-off. I hated my job. I couldn't stand my boss. I decided to open my own business, but Raleigh was too expensive, too crowded. I'm not into the night life or the concerts or the drama that comes with big-city living. I grew up in a small town and only ended up in Raleigh for a job. When I started looking around for a new place, a girlfriend who's getting married told me about the Hokes Bluff Inn and the cute little town with the historic district. I checked it out, fell in love, found these spaces were available, and the rest is history."

I looked around the store, taking in the wide variety of candle styles and colors. "Do you make them or order them in?"

Shelby crossed the room toward a display of carved candles with multicolored curls and grooves. "I make these, but I order the plainer ones. Eventually I'd like to make them all, but I don't have enough space in my tiny back room. As soon as I can find a better place to live, one with room for a studio, I'll be all set."

"Aren't you living upstairs?" I pointed at her ceiling, imagining what fun it would be for her to be on the other side of Rita. The three of us could have some serious fun together.

"I am for now," she said. "I bought it along with this store slot, or rather, I'm buying it. The bank technically owns it." She grinned. "But there really isn't a way to cordon off an area in that open space for a full candle-making studio. Not without giving up half my house."

"I guess you're right." I looked through the candles, picking up one with an outer shell of dark blue with curled windows showing soft lavender and pale peach. "How much for this one?"

Shelby quoted a price and added, "It's scented with orange and lavender. Don't just keep it for display. I always make more, and I sell them at a price so folks can keep buying them to burn and enjoy."

I held the candle to my nose and inhaled, letting the mix of smells relax me. "Yummy. I'll definitely be back for more."

She rang up my purchase and slid it into a bag. "Just remember not to put it in a sunny window, or it can droop from the hot sunshine."

"Thanks." I took the bag and my dog and headed toward the door.

"Oh, wait," Shelby called. "I almost forgot what I called you in here for."

I turned and saw the papers she waved at me. "What are they?"

"A petition and a pamphlet." She laid them on the sales counter side by side. "I figured you'd want to see these."

The pamphlet was a rah-rah piece for the Women's League on Public Safety, and the sheet of paper contained a series of lines and three signatures: Helen Grigby, Elizabeth North, and Lavinia Scoddin. I cringed, picturing the three women who had all but accosted me in my store a few months ago.

"They came in here, wanting to leave the signature sheet. I recognized one of them as the lady who told me to avoid you." She picked it up and scanned it. "I planned to toss it in the trash after I showed it to you. They're petitioning to permanently block off our alleyway, station twenty-four hour police officers in the parking lots, and have you banned from living here."

My head whipped around to stare at her. "Me? Why me?"

"Same thing she said before. Your store is a hotbed of crime and murder, and I should never darken your door if I want to stay alive." She grinned and winked. "I didn't tell them I'd already been there and we'd had dinner together.

Heat flooded my cheeks, and my fists clenched around the pamphlet. "I can't believe this. None of this is true."

Shelby laughed. "Too bad. It made your store sound more interesting."

Relaxing my death-grip on the offending paper, I took a deep breath and exhaled slowly. "Okay, yeah, I've been involved in several murders since I got here a few months ago. But only one took place in my store." I stopped, realizing I wasn't making this any better.

"Ooh, this sounds juicy." Shelby stepped out of her heels and plopped on a stool behind her counter. "You only told me about finding your uncle after you moved here. I want details."

Inwardly kicking myself for getting sucked into discussing it, I skipped over finding my uncle's body at the base of the spiral stairs in the store the day I arrived in Hokes Folly but gave her a brief overview of the murder of my supposed cousin, finding a murdered visiting librarian in the parking lot after an event at my store, and finding Missy Plott behind the dumpster. "I'm just the unlucky person who finds some of the bodies. And as I said, only one was actually in my store. The latest one didn't even have anything to do with my store. That's the only dumpster back there for the stores on this row, and it's behind my store because I'm in the middle."

Shelby's eyes sparkled as she hopped off her stool, stepped back into her heels, and pointed to a woman peering in the windows at her display. "Girl, I have got to spend more time at your store, but for now I have to sell some candles." She chuckled. "And yes, I still plan on tossing those." She snatched the papers from the counter as a young couple entered and dropped them into a can behind the counter. "There, nothing to see here."

As she greeted the couple, Eddy and I quietly slipped out the door and made our way to the bookstore, catching Mason making goo-goo eyes at Lily as she once again swept the walkway outside The Weeping Willow.

"See anything interesting?" I unhooked Eddy's leash and stuck it under the counter.

Mason blushed and cleared his throat. "Um, no . . . I mean, yeah . . . what?" He blinked a few times, his blush sliding down his neck and out to his ears.

"You'll never guess what I just heard." I plopped my purse on a shelf and turned. "The Women's League on Public Safety is at it again. This time they want me banned from the district."

"No way!" Mason leaned on the counter, one hip slack. "Isn't that the group with those women who came in here after Linus Talbot died?"

I nodded. "The very same three." I gave him the nuts and bolts of what Shelby had said. "I just hope none of the other store owners buy into it."

Mason shook his head. "No way," he repeated. "They're crazy if they do."

"Either way, until I'm kicked out, we have a bookstore to run." I swept my arm around the room. "How were sales today?"

Before he could answer, the door swung open, and Tish Riddick walked in. "Hey, Jenna. Glad I caught you. Can we talk for a few minutes?" She looked at Mason over my shoulder. "Privately?"

"Of course." I turned to Mason. "I'll be back as soon as I can. Call me if you need anything." I started up the stairs to my apartment, motioning for Tish to follow. "We'll be more comfortable up here than in the cramped back room."

Once we were settled on the couch, I asked, "Is Keith okay?" I couldn't see any other reason she'd want to talk to me alone and without him in tow.

She waved a dismissive hand. "Oh no, he's fine. But he's part of the reason I'm here alone. He's really having a hard time with this case because of your past history with our prime suspect. I figured it would be easier to ask you a few questions without him constantly interrupting."

Tension released from my shoulders as relief poured through me, and the breath I'd been holding slipped past my lips. "How can I help?"

Tish reached in her back pocket and pulled out her phone. "Recording again." She tapped the screen. "I'd like to ask you about your past relationship with Blake Emerson."

The tension I'd let go flooded back with a vengeance. "I'm not sure what I can tell you that would be helpful."

"In the time you were together, did you ever see signs of violence?" Tish laid the phone on the coffee table? "Were you ever afraid of him?"

"No," I answered without hesitation. "He was actually kind of a wuss. Oh, he'd bluster and try to get his way, and he could be controlling, but he was never physically violent with me or anyone else that I ever saw. He was more of a verbal manipulator than a physical bully."

"Did he ever say things like 'I'd like to punch him' or 'just wait until I get my hands on her' or 'I'm going to kill him?'"

I dropped my gaze, staring past the pattern in my throw rug, searching my memories. "No, I honestly can't remember a time when I ever heard him say anything like that." I shook my head slowly, still mentally scanning. "No, I'm positive. He never said those types of things." I looked up and met her gaze. "Why do you ask?"

Tish reached for her phone. "I'm trying to get a feel for him." She tapped the screen again and slid it back into her pocket. "Something about all of this just doesn't feel right."

"How so?" I tucked my feet under me and pulled a pillow to my chest, wishing I'd brought Eddy up with me, not sure which one of us depended on the other more these days.

Tish pulled out her phone again and looked at the screen. "Sorry, just making sure it's not still recording. I shouldn't be discussing this part with you, but I'm hoping you might have some helpful insights on his motivations and attitudes." She tucked the phone away. "I know he's hiding something. I can smell it. But I can't quite put the pieces together." She shook her head.

"But you're not convinced he killed Missy?" Maybe Gwendolyn would get her wish after all. It seemed at least one police detective wasn't buying Blake as a cold-blooded killer any more than I was.

"No, not really." Tish sighed and her shoulders slumped. "But I'll be damned if I can see a way to prove that. The evidence against him is pretty hefty. He's a much stronger suspect than anyone else connected to this case, including you." She held up a hand. "No, don't worry, I'm not going all Sutter on you."

I grinned back at her. "Although, if I know Sutter, he's probably filled your ear with how I'm the killer."

A laugh barked from her chest. "He has indeed. Man, I will be glad when he's gone in a couple of weeks. Things will get a lot easier at work without him trying to hammer everyone with his harebrained ideas."

"From what Keith has said, Sutter used to be a really great detective." I stood and headed to the kitchen. "I'm getting some lemonade. Want some?"

"Sure." Tish stood to follow me. "And I've heard the same about him. Too bad I never got to see it. All I see is an angry conspiracy nut with persecution issues, mostly centering around you."

I pulled two glasses from the cabinet and turned. "Well, we both know I didn't kill Missy. Tell me what you have on Blake that convinces everyone he did it, and why you don't agree."

Tish settled onto a barstool, holding up a hand to tick points off on her fingertips. "One. He was seen publicly arguing with Missy right before her disappearance. Two. He followed Missy to the parking lot and came back without her, making him the last person to see her alive."

"That you know of." I opened the fridge door and pulled out the lemonade, giving it a swirl in the pitcher to make sure it was still well mixed.

"True." Tish nodded. "But we can't prove anyone else was anywhere near her after Emerson came back to the restaurant alone."

"Yet." I dropped ice cubes into the glasses and poured the lemonade, sliding one across to Tish before putting the pitcher back in the fridge.

Tish sighed and wrapped her fingers around the cool glass, staring into its depths as if it might reveal an answer. "That's just it, though. Almost everything points to Emerson. The timing, his proximity, his motivation of her bleeding him dry. Even you heard that. The fact that he's been begging you to come back to him and saying he'll leave her. But there are a few things that just don't fit."

I propped myself against the sink and crossed my ankles. "What doesn't fit."

"If I tell you this, you can't let Keith know. He'd blow a gasket if he thought I was dragging you into this any deeper." Tish leveled a stare at me that would have done any Southern mama proud.

I set my glass on the counter and raised one hand in the air, placing the other across my heart. "Yes, ma'am. I swear."

"It's three things, really. First, we know she was killed about forty feet from the dumpster. We found the bloody spot on the asphalt. If Emerson had dragged her that far and then manhandled her behind the dumpster, he'd have ended up with blood on his clothes, even if just a few drops. The likelihood of him coming away from that with no blood on him is so close to impossible it's not even worth mentioning." Tish finally took a sip of her lemonade. "Hey, this is really good. Is this homemade?"

I nodded and grinned. "Yep, my mother's recipe. We didn't drink the powdered stuff when I was a kid. She bought lemons and made it from scratch. See the bits of lemon floating in the liquid?" I picked up my glass, holding it up to let the light shine through it, watching the liquid swirl before lowering it and taking a sip. "As for Blake being bloody, I can't see him doing that either. If he'd killed her, I'm pretty sure he'd have let her lie there rather than touch her and risk getting dirty. He's kind of a neat freak."

"See, that's what I mean about your insights." Tish set her glass on the counter, her hands twirling it on the surface.

"What's the other thing?" I asked.

"We found a button"—Tish held up her thumb and first finger in a circle about an inch across—"about this big. Shiny gold thing with a pattern on it. Too big to be a man's suit cuff button, although we did check Emerson's jacket."

"He wasn't wearing his jacket when they came out into the street or when he came back from the parking lot later." I replayed the scene in my head, picturing the brouhaha that had occurred outside my store. "Just slacks and a dress shirt with the sleeves rolled up a couple of turns."

"That matches what others have said." Tish nodded, continuing to swirl her glass in the sweat that had pooled under it. "We also checked his clothing for blood and didn't find any, just in case you were wondering. They were in a stack of clothing he was prepping to send out to be cleaned."

"Did anyone else have anything on that would've matched that button?" I pictured the perky little dress Connie had worn and the jeans and untucked shirt Tom had on when he leapt out of the darkened corner. I couldn't see a large, ornate button fitting on either of them.

"Not that we've been able to find. Logan think's it's a random piece of trash and that it could've been there for weeks before we found it. But something tells me it's connected." She looked at her watch and stood. "Speaking of Logan, I'd better get back before he misses me. I didn't tell him I was headed here."

"Wait." I set down my glass and followed her to the door. "What was the third thing?"

"Her engagement ring had been pulled from her finger, and an expensive diamond bracelet was also missing." Tish hovered in the doorway. "Logan is saying that Emerson took the ring because it was yours and the bracelet to make it look like a mugging gone wrong. But I don't see a mugger dragging a body forty feet to hide it behind a dumpster."

"For what it's worth, I think you're right. I honestly don't think Blake could be a killer." I stepped out onto the walkway with her. "If you think of any other way I can help, let me know."

"I will. Thanks."

I watched Tish as she walked down the walkway toward the stairs. I'd come to like and respect Keith's new partner. I just hoped we'd find the killer before the investigation destroyed my relationship with the man I loved.

Chapter Sixteen

I watched the dappled sunshine dance across my lap as it filtered through the trees above, and I tried to concentrate on the steady *clop clop* of the horses' hooves and the sway of the carriage rather than the lunch I'd agreed to have with Gwendolyn Emerson at the Hokes Bluff Inn. When I'd reached the inn's gated parking lot, I'd sat in my car for a full fifteen minutes, debating whether or not to actually go through with it.

Keith would be pissed if he knew. But it was another instance where someone would tell me things they wouldn't tell the police, and I owed it to Tish. At least that's the excuse I used to force myself out of my car and into the horse-drawn carriage for the two-mile ride to the inn.

When I alighted from the carriage in front of wide curved stairs leading to a shaded porch that stretched for at least sixty feet and was dotted with benches, chairs, and tables, I pulled two carrots from my pocket and thanked the horses for a lovely ride, a habit I'd formed after my first carriage trip up the tree-lined lane.

I climbed the stairs and entered what served as a lobby, marveling yet again over the beautiful paintings; ornate, hand-knotted rugs; soaring ceilings; and delicate-looking but sturdy furniture. Entering Hokes Bluff Inn was truly as close as I'd ever come to taking a step back in time.

As I crossed the room toward the dining area, I passed Elliot, the inn's manager, his soothing tones aimed at a distraught older woman.

"Mrs. Blankenship, as you know, we're already booked out for a year for weddings in the main hall, and that time line keeps extending."

"I don't care. My baby has decided she wants a June wedding, and we're not waiting until next June. Don't you realize who my husband is?" The woman's loud voice carried through the massive room and bounced off the walls, echoing into every corner.

"My good woman, I understand your plight, and I would be happy to accommodate you and your husband, our district's senator." Elliot maintained his turn-of-the-twentieth-century mannerisms, which matched the early 1900s clothing he wore. "I may have a solution for you and your daughter. You say you want June? Let me look in our calendar. We have an exclusive room we hold in reserve for only our best clients. I'm sure at least one weekend in June will still be open."

The woman preened and her nose rose another notch, if possible. "That would be wonderful of you." She looped her arm through his offered elbow and allowed herself to be escorted toward the front desk.

I managed to hold in my snort. I knew all about the overflow room, usually used as a children's entertainment area while adults enjoyed the main hall during booked events. I'd heard him use that trick before, and it seemed it worked every time.

I stepped through the doorway to the dining hall, impressed again by the two huge fireplaces, stacked with unlit wood, which stood at either end of the hall. Rather than the original long table, the room was filled with small and medium tables, allowing for more privacy for guests, one of the hotel's few concessions to modern desires.

An arm waved in the air, and I saw Gwendolyn half rise from her chair. I returned her wave and made my way across the room.

Gwendolyn air-kissed at me before sitting. "I'm glad you could make it. I wasn't sure you would come."

"To be honest, I almost didn't."

A footman appeared from a corner and pulled out my chair. I sat and thanked him, tucking my purse strap over the back of my chair as he walked away.

"Yes, well, I'm still glad you're here." She fussed with her flatware, arranging each piece to space them evenly across her napkin.

"Why am I here, if you don't mind my asking? Especially since I already told you I can't help you." I settled back and crossed my legs, letting my hands rest in my lap with my fingers laced.

"Did you talk to your police friend? Did you tell him Blake isn't a killer?" Her eyes held an almost frantic look, compounded by the white-knuckled grip she had on her fork, as she'd paused while shifting it to the other side of her knife.

And there it was. I sighed and rose. "I've already told you, Mrs. Emerson. The police are more than capable of solving this without my assistance."

Gwendolyn gripped my wrist in a lightning-fast strike. "Please don't go."

I hesitated a moment but realized I was drawing stares. Elliot had enough drama going on right now without me adding to it. I sat and stared pointedly at her grip on my wrist until she let go.

She tucked her hands in her lap. "His bond hearing is later today. Will you come?"

I barely stopped the ugly retort that wanted to pop out of my mouth. I counted to ten, letting the manners my mother had instilled in me take over. "Why would I go?"

Gwendolyn shifted in her seat, squirming a bit under my gaze. "I was hoping you'd be a character reference. After all, you lived with him for over three years. Who else would know him better?"

I gritted my teeth and counted to ten again. This woman did not like to take no for an answer. However, if I was stuck talking to her for a few minutes, the least I could do was try to gain some juicy information for Tish. "That's just it. I don't think I really did know him."

Her eyebrows shot up. "Why would you say that?"

"I did live with him, for three years in fact, after he proposed. Even then, he didn't want to rush the wedding. Every time I tried to bring up setting a date, he stated he needed more time before he'd even discuss wedding plans." I tilted my head and crossed my arms. "So explain to me why he would be getting married this quickly?" I recalled my discussion with Shelby. "He only broke up with me in July, and I moved here in August. The Inn began taking wedding bookings in December. For Missy to have gotten them a date this fast, she would have needed to book before the end of last year, as they were filling up pretty fast. Even if they started dating while I was in jail, that means they were together less than six or seven months before the wedding was booked. Was she pregnant?"

A gasp escaped Gwendolyn's lips and her hand fluttered to her throat. "I . . . I hope not." Tears sparkled in her eyes, and she blinked rapidly. "A grandchild," she whispered. "I never thought . . ."

I took pity on the woman. "I'm sorry. It was rude of me to suggest she was forcing Blake to marry her over a baby." I reached in my purse and pulled out a packet of tissues, holding it out to her. "I honestly doubt she was. Did you see how thin she was? If she was already pregnant in December, she'd have been at least five or six months along now. No way she'd still have that tiny waist at that point."

Gwendolyn pulled out a tissue and dabbed at her eyes, giving me a weak smile. "True. I was as big as a barn by six months with Blake. They thought he might be twins."

No, no, no, no. I would not allow myself to like this woman. That was too slippery of a slope. "Why was he in such a rush to marry her? Especially since he didn't seem to love her. If not for a baby, then why?"

"I would have no idea about that." She stiffened, the smile falling from her face. "Blake and I weren't very close, as you know."

I stared at this woman, who had gone from somewhat sentimental at describing the first phase of the path to motherhood to being an ice block about her relationship to the child she had borne. Maybe Blake wasn't the only one hiding something. What did she know about him that she didn't want to let slip, and was it the reason they weren't close any longer?

"Is that why you didn't come to the rehearsal dinner on Friday night? The night Missy disappeared?"

Gwendolyn sat silent for several moments, her gaze locked with mine, her lips pursed. Finally she took a quickly inhaled breath and squared her shoulders. "I was otherwise engaged at a charity function I'd heard about in the local area."

"Charity function?" I racked my brain trying to remember if I'd heard of anything like that. If it had been in Hokes Folly, it would have been at the inn. They facilitated several charity dinners per year.

"Yes, a bingo tournament to benefit a new women's shelter they're building. It was in the basement at a Methodist church a few miles from here." She held her head high as if daring me to comment on the incongruity of this elegant woman playing bingo in a church basement.

"Oh, well. I'm sure Blake understood." I picked up my water glass and took a sip, more for something to do with my hands, to cover the uncomfortable silence, than because I was thirsty.

"I didn't tell Blake." She fidgeted with her flatware again, this time straightening her plate and napkin as well. "I had intended to be at his rehearsal dinner, but I lost track of time." She looked up, her brows drawn together. "If I'd only been there on time, all of this wouldn't have happened."

I sighed. "Look, I really can't help you." I held up a hand before she could interrupt, almost regretting shattering the fragile tendrils of friendship that had momentarily stretched between us. "I won't be at his bond hearing as I truly have nothing I could add."

"But they'll keep him in jail." Her voice came out as an almost wail. "They'll say he has no ties to the community and has money, making him a flight risk."

I flinched, recognizing the same reasons the judge had kept me in jail without bond until my trial. They'd assumed I had stashed a ton of embezzled money away somewhere, and they decided I'd cut and run given the chance to do so. However, the fact remained that there was nothing I could do or say to sway the court. "The best I can do is promise to let you know if I see or hear anything that might clear Blake." I stood again. "I'm sorry you're going through this."

She stood and threw her arms around me, this time kissing my cheek for real. "I wish he'd married you and hadn't gotten tied up with that thing he almost married."

I reached my hands up and awkwardly patted her back. "Um. Okay."

Gwendolyn released me and sat down, smoothing her hands over her slacks. "Thank you. Even if you don't find anything. Thank you for not telling me I'm crazy."

I smiled at her, hoping it looked more genuine than it felt. "It's okay. I understand." What I understood was this woman was losing her marbles over all of this. Maybe she'd lost them before. But her distress was genuine. Whether they were close or not, she seemed to love her son. At least someone still did.

I strode from the room, almost bumping into Rita as she hurried across the lobby. "Wow, you're wearing street clothes. Why aren't you dressed like the belle of the ball today?" I referred to her usual state of dress in early 1900s styles.

"I've been on my hands and knees all day, hemming gowns. The two girls who usually do it both called in sick. Frankly, I think they just skipped out on work today." Rita pointed at the slight discoloration of her white slacks. "I'd rather ruin these than one of the inn's expensive dresses if I'm going to crawl around on the floor like a two-year-old all day."

"I don't see how you do your job at all wearing those period costumes." I imagined trying to run the bookstore wearing huge skirts and buttoned boots.

"It's part of our contracts. And you do get used to it." Rita pointed at her feet. "Honestly, I'd be happy if we could at least wear comfortable shoes. But nope, it all has to be period based." She shrugged. "What brought you by today?"

"Gwendolyn Emerson asked me to lunch." I gestured toward the dining room.

Rita's jaw dropped. "You ate lunch with that woman? Does Keith know?"

"No, I didn't." I shook my head. "We chatted for a few minutes and I left. And no, Keith doesn't know."

Rita pantomimed zipping her lips. "My lips are sealed." She looked over my shoulder and waved at someone. "I really wish I had time to hear about that conversation, but I'm swamped today. I'd better get back at it, or I'll never make it home tonight." She squeezed my hand. "We'll talk soon, and you can fill me in on all the dirt."

After she rushed off, I walked out the hotel's tall doors, stopping on the porch to inhale the spring air. As I took in the beauty of the lawns and the strolling couples, many of them in period dress, I caught sight of Tom Jackson and Connie Plott sitting on a bench at the far end of the porch.

Connie, her ankles crossed, had her legs pressed up against his, one hand on his thigh and one on his chest. Tom, however, sat with his head turned away and his arms crossed. Pressing her breasts against his upper arm, she moved closer and whispered something in his ear. Gads, she was laying it on thick.

Tom jumped to his feet and whirled to face her. "You just don't get it! I don't want you! I still love Missy! That doesn't magically go away just because you want it to!" He rushed the length of the porch, heading to the stairs in front of me.

As he approached the carriages, I shook myself out of my frozen surprise and scurried after him, determined to share the ride back to the parking lot.

Just in time, I swung up and into the carriage, seating myself across from Tom. "Oh, hello. Guess we're both heading out." I smiled.

Tom brushed a lock from his forehead and crossed his arms, pushing back into the carriage seat. "Yeah, okay. Whatever." He stared sullenly out the side of the carriage.

Wow, rude much? I somehow doubted he was trying to enjoy the scenery, so I attempted to engage him again. When would I have another chance? "That hotel is sure something. Wish I could afford to stay there. Are you a guest?"

He swung his gaze around to meet mine, his eyes shimmery with unshed tears. "No. I know someone who is . . . who was . . ." A tear slid down his cheek.

I dug in my purse for that tissue pack, glad I hadn't simply given it to Blake's mother. My fingers brushed it, and I pulled it out, offering it to the young man who shared the carriage with me. "Was the person you knew that bride who was killed?" I mentally swatted away my imaginary Mom-voice, which was all but having a coronary over my bluntness. The ride was just too short to be gentle and take my time.

"Yeah." Tom snatched a tissue and rubbed his eyes with it, honking his nose into it before wadding it in his hand and stuffing it into a pocket. "She was the love of my life."

"I'm so sorry. Were you the groom?" More swatting at my mother's voice. "I heard she was here to get married."

"No." He seemed to sink deeper into the cushions, drawing in on himself. "She was marrying some other dude."

"Oh." I stuck the tissue packet back into my purse. "But I thought . . ." I let the unfinished statement hang in the air.

His lip trembled, and he closed his eyes, breathing slowly and deeply until the trembling quit. "She was marrying someone else. I don't know what he had on her or why she would leave me. We were in love until he showed up."

"I'm sorry." Where could I go from there?

Before I could ask another question, he pounded his fist on his thigh. "If she'd just listened to me. If she'd just let me talk to her. If she'd just come home with me." A sob ripped from his chest. "Now she's dead because she wouldn't listen. I'll never love anyone again. Ever!"

The carriage pulled up in the parking lot, and Tom leapt from its door and ran across the lot to his car, his loud sobs punctuating his flight.

I descended and tipped the driver with an extra-large tip. "Thanks."

He nodded in the direction of Tom's car. "That guy gonna be okay?"

"Eventually." I offered the horses my last two carrots from a baggie in my purse before heading to my car, hoping I hadn't just lied to the carriage driver.

* * *

Less than four hours after I'd seen a distraught Tom rush to his car, sobbing over his dead ex-girlfriend, Connie Plott stood in my store, asking for a copy of the new wedding planner.

My stomach tightened, and I hoped this wasn't what it appeared to be. "Oh, are you getting married?"

Connie glowed and bounced on her toes. "Yes, I am. But not for a while yet. I just want to get the planner so I can get started on my perfect wedding."

Was this girl for real? I took in her appearance, disappointed to see Connie had exchanged her sparkly purple nail polish for nails that looked identical to the ones Missy had sported. The similarities didn't stop there. She'd obviously spent the last few hours going to salons and digging through her sister's clothes.

Her hair had been styled and colored to match Missy's platinum-blonde tresses, and her makeup, which I was pretty sure had been completely absent before, was thickly and expertly applied. An elegant burgundy, mid-thigh-length dress, which I'd seen Missy wear, hugged Connie's lithe form, although the bust seemed a bit loose, and she stumbled a bit in the matching three-inch heels, which didn't seem to fit her.

I leaned on the counter and smiled. "Ooh, let me see your ring. I love engagement stories. How did you meet?"

She narrowed her eyes and pointed at the display window. "Can I just have the book?"

I sighed. It was what I feared. "Connie, are you sure?"

Her brow wrinkled. "How do you know my name?"

"I heard your sister yell at you that you were out of her wedding last week." I came out from behind the counter. "The day Tom begged her to marry him."

The girl flounced her hair back over her shoulder in a Missy-like move that made her look even younger rather than more mature. "I don't care what he did last week. Tom is going to marry me."

Was everyone connected to that wedding insane? Did no one understand the concept of finding someone who actually loved you back? "Let's go sit down and chat for a minute, okay?"

"Fine." She walked toward the seating area, her hips swaying in what I was pretty sure was an attempt to imitate her sister's seductive sashay, marred by her slight wobble in the spiked heels.

I sat across from her, watching her fidget, obviously not yet comfortable in her new look. My heart broke a little for her, this girl fighting to be seen as a woman yet clueless how to go about it. For a moment I was taken aback by the strength of my motherly instincts that came to the fore. First Mason a few months ago, now this girl? Was this how motherhood felt? Not that I was in any hurry to find out. Eddy was quite enough for now, thank you very much.

We continued to sit, and I waited for the haughty look to melt and the wholesome girl to reappear. I didn't have to wait long.

"I just want him to love me like he loved her," she whispered.

"Why?" I let the heavy question hang in the air.

"Because . . ." Her lip trembled and her voice picked up a waver. "Because . . . I just do, that's all."

"Connie, if you wear her clothes and cut your hair and paint your nails like she did, do you really think Tom will see you?" I propped my elbows on my knees. "Or do you think he'll only see a fake Missy?"

She flounced her hair again and glared at me. “I don’t care. I love him, and if this is the only way to get his attention, then that’s how it is.”

“But who is really getting his attention? As long as you look like her, he can’t see you. He can’t love you. He can’t want you.” I reached for the tissue box and held it out to her. How many people were going to cry on me today?

She snatched one out of the box and inexpertly blotted at the tears that had begun to flow down her cheeks, leaving smudged streaks in their wake. “I’ll make him forget her. She didn’t love him. She didn’t deserve a guy like Tom. But he kept chasing and chasing her, even after she was mean to him and told him to go away. And now that she’s gone, he has no choice but to look at me.”

I set the tissues back on the table. “But isn’t that the same thing you’re doing? Chasing him even after he’s told you to go away?”

Even with the remaining makeup, I could tell her cheeks had paled. “You don’t know that.” A sob escaped her chest. “You don’t know anything! He has to love me. After everything I’ve done, he just has to!” She jumped to her feet and staggered from the store on her borrowed shoes, wearing her borrowed dress and borrowed face.

Chapter Seventeen

I'd just unlocked the store's front door on Thursday morning when Rita rushed in.

"Where's Mason?" She craned her neck and walked across the front of the store, peering down aisles. "Mason?"

Mason walked out of the back room, wiping his hands on a paper towel. "Sorry, I was in the kitchen in the back making a sandwich. I overslept and didn't have time for breakfast. What's up?"

"You're handling the store alone for a while." Rita turned to me. "You're coming with me. The shipment of ribbon didn't arrive. Some snafu with the order being accidentally cancelled. Even with expedited shipping, a new order won't be here before the weekend, and we can't decorate for the wedding."

"Um, okay, but I don't have any ribbon." I headed for the stairs to my apartment. "I'm happy to look, though."

Rita prodded me up the stairs from behind. "No, I mean you're coming shopping with me. I have to do a craft store crawl to get enough ribbon for this week. Grab your purse." She turned and yelled back down to Mason. "Is it okay to leave Eddy with you?"

"Sure!" Mason shouted back over a mouthful of his sandwich.

"There, all taken care of. Now let's get going." She hurried me through the apartment and out the front door. "If I have to spend the day in craft stores, you're going with me, so you can tell me what I've missed over the last few days."

I laughed and all but ran to keep up with her rush down the walkway toward the parking lot. "Oh, I get it. This is a grilling session."

"Of course." She unlocked the doors as we approached her car, motioning with her hands for me to hurry up and get inside. "How else am I going to learn anything?"

I buckled my seat belt as she pulled out onto the street. "Slow down a bit, will you? I'd like not to have a heart attack over your driving."

Rita laughed and loosened her death grip on the steering wheel. "Sorry. I've been in such a mad rush the last few days. Honestly, I should have sent someone else to do this, but I needed to get out of there for a while."

"I'm sure." I settled back into my seat. "How's Elliot doing? Did he make the foie gras?"

"Nope, no foie gras." Rita put on her blinker and turned onto the highway toward the next town over. "Not even a decent pâté. He handled it quickly and firmly in his usual unflappable style."

"What happened?" I asked.

"When Missy went missing and the police started showing up, he insisted they be very low-key." Rita changed lanes to go around a large truck struggling up a hill. "Even after she died, they seem to be abiding by that request. After Missy's body was found, the media tried to come to the hotel to get a story. Elliot told his carriage drivers that under no circumstances were they to be allowed a ride to come harass paying guests. He had his PR manager issue a statement saying the only connection the hotel had to the murder was that Missy had been staying there and was scheduled to get married there the day her body was found. Any other connection the media hounds tried to make would be libel, giving the hotel's owners the grounds to sue."

"Go, Elliot." I grinned. "At least he's not stuck staying at the hotel nonstop and stressing himself into an ulcer like he did a few months ago."

"Yes, but that time, someone really did die at the hotel." Rita reached forward and adjusted the air conditioner. "His poor partner didn't see him for almost a week. But they've been together too long for Matthew to let it get to him. I swear, that man's a saint."

"Glad to hear it." Freezing air hit me in the face, and I groped forward, turning the vent away from me. "What's with the snowballs?"

"Sorry." Rita reached out to turn all the vents on her. "My hot flashes have been hitting me night and day with all the current stress at the inn."

While my friend didn't look a day over thirty-five, I knew she was in her mid-forties. "Sucks to be you."

"Really?" She cut me a sidelong glance. "Just wait until it's your turn. I'll be smiling at every little bead of sweat that pops out on your forehead, girlie."

"Truce." I grinned and stuck my hands in the air in a surrendering gesture.

"Uh-huh." Rita pulled to a stop at a light and turned to me. "Okay, spill it. Why were you meeting Blake's mother for lunch?"

"She wanted to ask me again if I would talk to the police for her and convince them he was innocent." I pushed away the tiny tendrils of guilt the sentimental side of Gwendolyn pulled out of me. "I told her I couldn't help her."

"Wait. You said again." Rita eased the car through the intersection and looked over her shoulder to merge right.

"Oh, I forgot." I chuckled. "You never heard about the first time. She's basically trying to guilt me into sticking up for Blake, as if I owe him something. I supposedly know him better than anyone else. She even asked me to go to his bond hearing."

"You know you don't owe him, right?" She pulled into a parking lot and slid the car into an empty spot.

I nodded and unbuckled my seat belt. "Of course I know that. After all that went down, I have no connection to, nor do I want to have a connection to, Blake Emerson."

Rita laid a hand on my arm to stop me from getting out. "Are you really okay with all of this? You were with him for a very long time."

I flopped back in the seat and crossed my arms. "Why does everyone assume I'm pining away for him? *He* wanted *me*, not the other way around."

"You weren't even a tiny bit tempted?" Rita's earnest tone hung in the air.

"Absolutely not." I shook my head, holding steady eye contact with my friend. "Even if there were no Keith, I would have no desire to return to a relationship with a man who dumped me when the going got tough, just when I needed someone to depend on, someone to have my back."

Rita held my gaze a moment longer before nodding and reaching for her own door handle. "Good. I won't ask again. But you have to admit, his coming on to you is weird. Why would he think you'd run back to him, especially when he showed up here with a fiancée?"

"I keep asking myself that question." I stepped out of the car and shut my door, resting my forearms on the roof of the car. "I've had no contact with him since the day he gave me the key to the storage warehouse. I mean, I guess it would be different if we'd communicated in some way, but there hasn't even been a text, much less an email or a call or a visit."

Rita flashed a grin as she came around the car and hooked an arm through mine. "Maybe it's your devastating good looks and massive amount of sex appeal and charisma, and he just couldn't resist you when he saw you after all this time." She tugged me toward the front door of a mega craft store.

"Yeah, okay, we'll go with that." I rolled my eyes, letting her pull me along. "Seriously, though, it's almost like he was marrying her because she had some hold on him that he couldn't escape. Look at it. He comes on to me hard and heavy. He tells her she's bleeding him dry. Why did he let her? He tells me he dumped me and is marrying her because he had no choice. He made an odd comment about how he'd leave her and marry me in spite of the consequences. What consequences? I even asked his mother if Missy was pregnant."

"Oh my God, you didn't!" Rita squealed with laughter. "What did she say?" She grabbed a shopping cart from beside the front door and headed inside.

"She got all huffy and then teary about the possibility of a grandchild. I thought she was going to pass out or something. I had to convince her it was highly unlikely that Missy was pregnant." I followed Rita through an aisle lined on one side with bolts of fleece and imagined cuddling up under something like that with Keith while we watched a movie, and I barely missed running into Rita's back when she stopped at the end of the aisle.

Rita ran her fingers across a pale pink, filmy material. "If she was, she didn't show it. And that would have made it even more awkward if he hooked up with you again. Can you imagine her being his baby mama? Talk about drama." She hefted the bolt and slid it into the cart. "Are you sure this is really Blake and not some doppelganger? This doesn't sound like the tightly wound, controlling, i's dotted and t's crossed guy you told me about before. This guy, who told you he wanted this long engagement after having already lived with you for years, dumps you with no explanation. Then he lets let Missy walk all over him and was getting married to her within a few months. It just seems so out of character."

"You know, as strange as it was that Blake was marrying Missy when it didn't seem like he loved her, wasn't it equally weird that Missy was marrying Blake?" I thought of Tom's description of the Missy he had known. "Tom said she was this sweet person who was the love of his life. He's convinced Blake had something on Missy and was forcing her to marry him, but Blake said he's the one who had no choice."

Rita looked up from another bolt of material, this time in pale leaf-green. "Tom? Isn't that the guy who proposed to her in the street outside your store? When did you talk to him?"

I nodded and ran my hand across a bolt of pale pink satin. "Yep, that's him. I rode back to the parking lot in the same carriage with him yesterday. He was all broken up, crying, saying that if Missy had listened to him, if she'd just come home with him, she'd still be alive. He said he'd never loved anyone else, and he swore he'd never love anyone again. Which sucks for Connie."

"Connie?" Rita dropped the green bolt into the cart and turned to face me. "Missy's sister? What does she have to do with this?"

"That's who Tom was with before we shared a carriage." I raised my hands as in a don't-shoot-the-messenger gesture. "I know. It's a mess. But she came into the store a few hours later to buy a wedding book."

"For what? Or rather for whom?" Rita seemed to have forgotten the materials for the moment as she wrapped her hands around the far end of the cart and propped a foot on its lower rack.

"Tom." I grinned when her jaw dropped. "Told you it was a mess."

"I thought you just said Tom said he'd never love anyone else." She narrowed her eyes and cocked her head.

"Yep." I shrugged. "But she's convinced she can make him fall in love with her. She was wearing Missy's clothes and had spent the time and money getting a manicure, haircut, and dye job to match Missy's. She's trying to *become* Missy in order to snag Tom. She said he had to love her after all she'd done for him."

"Wait. Let me see if I have this straight." She ticked off her list on her fingers as she turned and rounded the corner into another aisle. "Blake says he's still in love with you and will leave Missy for you. Missy wants Blake. Tom wants Missy and thinks his life is over now that she's dead. Connie wants Tom and hopes to take Missy's place. And, of course, you want Keith. That's quite the love triangle going on."

"Wouldn't that be a love hexagon, since there are six of us?" I followed her with the cart. "The only thing stopping it from being a true triangle-style issue is that Keith isn't trying to get with Connie."

"Good grief, I need a whiteboard and a set of sticky notes to keep track of all of this." Rita stopped, sweeping her gaze down a row of ribbon spools. "I think my brain is broken now."

I laughed and pulled a book of crochet patterns from a rack at the end of the row, flipping through it to look at the variety of scarves and blankets. My grandmother had taught me to crochet a couple of basic stitches when I was in second grade, but I hadn't touched it since then. If I was going to spend many more evenings without Keith, I needed to do something with my hands other than munch while I watched TV, or I was going to end up wider than my couch.

Rita dropped a few ribbon spools into the cart and moved down the aisle. "Where does this love hexagon leave us?"

I slid the book back into the rack and pulled out another one with potholders and dishcloths on the cover. This was a bit more my speed, which was barely above zero. "I'm honestly not sure. All I know is that I just can't see Blake killing anyone, even Missy. Don't get me wrong. He's a real jerk. But a killer? No." I shook my head and walked down the aisle to put the book in the cart.

"If not him, then who?" Rita dumped a few more spools in and shifted the cart again. "Do you really think Tom or Connie might have done it?"

"I don't know." I shrugged. "Dana thinks it's Connie."

"Dana Nichols at the bakery?" More spools went into the buggy.

"Yes." I walked to the wall at the end of the aisles, where crochet hooks hung in a variety of colors, materials, and sizes. "She says Connie and Tom were in her store. Connie was badmouthing Missy, saying Tom deserved someone who would love him and not care if he was rich or not. Tom gave her his line about Missy being the love of his life and said he couldn't live without her."

"Pretty much the same things they both said to you." Rita wheeled the cart to where I stood and grabbed a variety pack of aluminum Susan Boyle hooks. "If you're going to take up a hobby, use these." She dropped them into the cart. "And I expect a set of potholders for Christmas."

I grinned. "Thanks. Will do." I snagged a couple of skeins of deep blue yarn on the way toward the checkout lanes. "Connie said something weird, though. She asked Tom if Missy wasn't around, would he stop living. He said as long as they were both breathing, there was hope. He walked out, but Dana heard Connie mumble something like 'what if she's not breathing anymore?'"

Rita stopped the cart abruptly and turned to look at me. "That puts her squarely on the suspect list. Especially when you combine it with her comment about Tom having to love her after all she'd done for him. Maybe she wasn't talking about her makeover."

"Maybe." I dropped the skeins in the cart. "But couldn't we also interpret Tom's comment about how if Missy had just listened to him and come home with him, she'd be alive in the same way? Maybe he went down the alleyway, circling back to talk to her, and she could've pushed away from him and fallen and hit her head on that concrete block."

Rita shook her head and maneuvered the cart, once again heading to check out. "No, if he did it, he shoved her. Remember what Tish said? She said there was bruising that showed someone had slammed their hands into her chest to push her."

"But none of them wore anything with big buttons." I slapped my hand to my mouth. Crap on a cracker. I'd promised not to tell.

Rita took a few minutes to chat with the man behind the register as he rung her up, and I took my crochet supplies to another open lane. Maybe she hadn't heard me. My hopes were dashed, however, as we walked out the door together.

"What's this about a button?" Rita pushed the cart across the parking lot toward her car.

"I wasn't supposed to tell anyone, so don't let Tish know I let it slip, okay?" I opened the passenger door and dropped my purse and shopping bags into the car when Rita triggered the door locks with her key fob and opened her trunk.

Rita looked at me over the trunk lid. "Button? What button? I don't know anything about a button." She grinned.

I rolled my eyes and walked to the rear of the car to help her load her purchases. "Tish says they found a fancy gold button about this size"—I held my fingers up in an imitation of Tish's gesture—"where Missy was. They can't tie it to Blake. Keith thinks it's been there for a while and is just a coincidence. Oh, and Blake didn't have any blood on him anywhere. They checked the clothes he had on that night."

"Which is why his mother wants you to help prove his innocence." Rita slammed the trunk lid and put the buggy in the cart return, which she had parked next to. She opened her car door and got in.

I slid into the passenger seat, rearranging my bags at my feet. "I guess I can see her point, since they don't have anything definitive to hold him on except that he was the last person to see her that night, and they'd just had a public fight."

"Well, if it's not him, that leaves the wanna-be sister and the lovesick ex-boyfriend." Rita stuck the key in the ignition and started the car. "I found all I needed here, so I'll drop you off at your store and head back to the grind."

I nodded absently as I thought of Connie and Tom. I couldn't see either of them killing Missy any more than I could Blake. "Any one of them could have done it. They were all out of sight during the window of time when she was killed. But I don't want any of them to have done it."

Rita slid out of her slot and headed us back toward the historic district. "You always want to believe the best in everyone. Honey, sometimes folks look amazing if you take them at face value. But you have to have learned by now, even if it's just since you've lived here, that some folks hide a soul-deep ugly that will do hideous things and sink back to hide behind that pretty veneer when it's all over."

"I know." I slumped down into my seat, silently mulling over Rita's words for several minutes. She did have a point. "I know I'm too trusting at times."

Rita snorted and turned into the historic district parking lot.

"Okay, a lot of the time." I sat up and unbuckled my seat belt as she slid into a parking spot. "But I don't want to change. I don't want to become suspicious and paranoid."

"Honey, there's a happy medium. You don't have to look for monsters around every corner. But you have to start accepting that monsters do exist, and not just in those books in your store."

I opened my door, got out, and bent down to look at my friend. "I don't like condemning anyone unless I have proof, not conjecture."

"Then what we need to do is get you some proof." She reached to turn the AC back up to full blast. "We have to find the garment that's missing Tish's button."

Chapter Eighteen

Friday afternoon, I stood in the lobby of Hokes Bluff Inn, waiting for Rita. As the wedding for that Saturday had now been postponed until June, the hotel was a lot calmer. No bridal parties rushed around, wedding planners weren't measuring rooms, and decorations weren't going up. Instead, the feel was one of hushed anticipation, a quiet, uneasy peace, as if the other shoe was yet to drop.

"Jenna!" Rita seemed to float across the lobby in her turn-of-the-nineteenth-century day dress.

I gave my friend a quick hug and stepped back. "That's gorgeous on you. What material is that? It's not satin."

"Faille." She grinned. "Like it?" She twirled slowly. "It's from the late 1890s and was the first thing that resembled a business suit for women."

A jacket in a rich, chocolate shade ended at her waist, tailored to fit. Long sleeves were snug to the armpits, where they poufed out almost as big as Rita's head. Chocolate velvet covered the wide lapels and cuffs, with a bit of cream lace extending from the bottom of the cuff. A silk shirt decorated with small flowers peeked out from between the front lapels of the jacket, with a high collar that ran up under Rita's chin. The skirt was the same chocolate brown faille with a hem of velvet, neither slim nor belled, but somewhere in between.

"It's gorgeous on you, but it's hard to believe that's business wear," I said.

"Oh, but it was, and women were thrilled." She grinned. "At the time, women were finally allowed to participate in business, and some were even going to college."

I shook my head. "Hard to believe that it wasn't really that long ago when women had absolutely no rights." I looped my arm through hers and turned toward the elevators. "At least that one looks like you'll be able to help search rooms without tripping over a big skirt."

"Why do you think I wore this one today?" She winked at me as the elevator doors slid open and the attendant offered his arm to help us into the car.

His assistance wasn't really necessary, but it was how things were done in 1900, and the corporate owners insisted on period accuracy, even in this. "Where to, ladies?"

Rita told him our floor, and we silently rose to the designated stop, where the attendant assisted us from the car into the hallway.

When the doors closed, Rita leaned in, lowering her voice to just above a whisper. "We have to be fast. Elliot's called a meeting for the wedding party members who are still here. I think Tish is here to give them an update on when they can go home, or something like that. It won't last long, and we have three rooms to search."

"Three?" I followed her sweeping skirts down the hallway. "I thought there'd be more than that."

Rita shook her head, stopping at a door and using an electronic keycard, one of the few concessions to modern security the hotel had allowed. A soft snick signaled the door had unlocked, and Rita pushed it open. "There were, originally. But when Missy died and Blake was arrested, Blake's mother moved into their room to protect Blake's things. I think it was really because it has a way better view than her original room. Anyway, Connie came and took all Missy's stuff to her room. The groomsmen, who had only arrived in town Friday night, just in time for the dinner, and were all accounted for the entire evening, went back to Charlotte. And to keep costs down, they stuck the three bridesmaids into one room, although they're not happy about it."

"Whose room is this?" I peered around the feminine room, with the bed's high canopy edged in delicate lace, the triple-mirrored vanity table with a dainty stool padded in pale cream silk, and the filmy curtains framing the windows overlooking a rose garden.

"Gwendolyn Emerson's room, the one that was Blake and Missy's." Rita strode to a tall wardrobe in the corner and swung the door open. "Don't just stand there, woman. Help me search."

I walked to the writing desk tucked in a corner near the windows and pulled open a drawer. Elegant stationary filled the space, and I fingered the thick paper before shaking myself. This was not a sightseeing tour. I slid the drawer closed and opened the other. Empty. The nooks and crannies in the desk yielded zip. "Any luck in the wardrobe?"

"Not a whit." Rita shut the door and reached for a drawer beneath. "Just the typical stuff you'd see someone like her bring. Dresses and pantsuits, none with buttons like you described."

"I wish I'd seen a picture." I knelt on the floor and flipped up the dust ruffle, peering into the dimness under the bed.

Behind me, Rita slid a drawer closed. "Nothing here. Anything good under there?"

"I'm not sure." I reached into my back pocket and pulled out my phone, tapping the screen to turn on the flashlight. A small leatherbound book lay just under the edge of the bed near a night table, as if it had fallen down between the table and bed and had been accidentally kicked underneath. I crawled on my knees to get closer and fumbled under the bed until my fingers closed on its cover. I pulled it out and tapped my light off.

"Looks like a day planner." Rita took the burgundy binder from me and flipped it open. "Oh my god. It's Missy's."

I scrambled to my feet and took the book to the little desk, laying it open and flipping a few pages until I found the days she'd been in Hokes Folly. "There's nothing here but appointments with you for dress fittings, notes about flowers, and a list of gift ideas for her bridesmaids." Disappointed, I closed the book.

"I think we should put it back where we found it, but we should tell Tish and Keith where it is." Rita pointed back to the corner of the bed. "It's probably just here because Connie missed it when she cleaned out her sister's stuff."

I picked up the book, walked to the bed, knelt, and with a quick flick of my wrist, slid the book back into its corner beside the night table.

Rita sat at the vanity table, the lid of an old-fashioned train case flipped open revealing the toiletry items of an older woman. Facial creams were tucked in among curlers and bobby pins. Makeup designed to diminish wrinkles lay on the table next to the case, along with a loose powder and a set of brushes.

"Doesn't look like there's anything there." I peered down into the case, reaching in to tug the pockets open, just in case a button was hiding somewhere, although I wasn't sure why one would be, or if there was, how a similar one would have gotten into an alleyway.

"That's it for this room." Rita stood and looked at her watch. "We'd better get moving. Two more rooms to go."

When we got to Connie's room, Rita again let us in with her master keycard—I didn't ask her how she got it—and moved to the wardrobe to swing open the doors.

My heart sank. "I think those are all Missy's clothes."

Rita slid the outfits aside one at a time. "Where are Connie's?"

I spied two suitcases in the corner, walked over, laid one on its side, and unzipped it. "They're here." All of Connie's things, her identity, her sense of self and style, had been hidden away in her attempt to turn into her sister.

"Didn't she keep any of her things out?" Rita peered over my shoulder as I opened the second bag and rummaged through it.

I shook my head. "Doesn't look like it. And no, before you ask, nothing in these bags would have had that kind of button. How about on Missy's stuff?"

"Nope." Rita walked to the writing desk and checked the drawers and nooks. "Nothing here either."

After zipping the suitcases, I crawled to the bed and flipped up the dust ruffle, finding nothing but darkness underneath.

On the makeup table, we found a small, zippered makeup bag with discount brands of makeup in bright colors, a few bottles of cheap nail polish, and a set of fingernail clippers. Next to it lay an elegant bag in gold satin. Inside were expensive boutique makeups, brushes, tweezers, and masques.

"I guess we can tell which one was Missy's." I zipped the gold bag closed.

Rita nodded. "But still no button."

I followed her to the room where Mandy, Molly, and Mickey were staying. When she swung the door open, my jaw dropped. Clothing was scattered in piles on the floor, draped over the writing desk and chair, and flung across the bed. The wardrobe doors stood open, and the vanity table was a jumble of bottles, jars, compacts, brushes, hair products, and styling tools.

"How do they live like this?" Rita strode to the wardrobe and peered in.

"At least we won't have to worry that they might notice if we move things around a bit." I walked to the vanity table and looked at the jumble. "I don't even know what half this stuff is for."

Crossing the room, Rita laughed. "Maybe you'd better let the makeup expert handle this one, and you take some of the piles."

I backed away, hands up. "It's all yours." On the bed, I tried to keep the same sense of messiness while I pawed through the heaps of tossed-aside clothing, looking for anything that might have large gold buttons. No luck.

Rita moved to the writing desk. "Nothing here."

"Nothing under the bed either." I crawled on my knees to the closest pile on the floor.

"I guess I'll hit the wardrobe after all." Rita gently began sliding the clothes aside, looking at each outfit.

We had just finished when we heard loud voices in the hallway.

"What a crock. Now we're stuck in this backwater, nowhere town until they close the case," said a voice I was pretty sure was Mandy's.

Another voice, softer and more tentative answered. "She said we're witnesses and may have to testify."

"Damn it." Mandy's voice was now right outside the doorway. "I can't find my keycard. One of you get yours out."

It hit me that they were entering their room, and Rita and I were still here. I frantically scanned the room for a hiding place, catching sight of Rita waving an arm at me from an open doorway. But how long could we hide in the bathroom? Maybe they were just coming in for a minute and we could sneak out after they left. I moved as quickly as I could without making noise and stepped through the door behind Rita.

Rita flipped a switch, and light flooded a hallway, and I realized we were in the secret passageways the hotel had kept from the original plans. She held her finger to her lips and stayed at the door, her ear pressed to its surface.

Following her example, I heard the bed creak as if someone had flung themselves, rather than more clothes, on it.

"I'm so over all this mess. Leave it to Missy to screw it up for everyone," Mandy said.

One dissenting voice piped in. "Mama says you shouldn't speak ill of the dead."

A snort. Then Mandy said, "Missy was a dumbass. She had the brass ring but she just had to be stupid about it all. She needed to shut the hell up and get Blake Emerson to the altar. Then, if they'd disrespected her, she could have tortured his mother and his ex all she wanted."

"I thought her ring was a diamond."

I barely kept in my guffaw. Guess we could tell which one of the remaining three wouldn't win an intelligence award.

Mandy's voice soured. "You're dumber than a box of last year's eyelash extensions. I said brass ring. You know, as in the big prize? She hit it big when she hooked up with Blake Emerson, and now look where she is."

Rita elbowed me and pointed down the hallway, turning and softly moving away from me. I followed through twists and turns until Rita opened a door into a wide, two-story library. We stood on a railed walkway on what would have been the second story of the room if there'd been a full floor. Instead, the walkway ran the full circumference of the room, with sliding ladders that could be moved to retrieve books. Spiral staircases curled down from each corner to the main floor, where a large fireplace sat facing a long bank of tall French doors looking out on a wide lawn.

"This is where I want to be buried." I sighed.

"At the hotel?" Rita turned and narrowed her eyes at me.

"Nope." I shook my head. "I mean right here. In this room."

Rita laughed and turned toward a staircase. "I don't think they'd appreciate that."

I followed her down to the main level and through another set of French doors that led to the main lobby. Elliot met us as we exited the library and bent at the waist to kiss the backs of Rita's and my hands.

Rita grinned and handed him the keycard. "Thanks."

He slipped it into his waistcoat pocket. "Any luck? I tried to keep them busy as long as I could."

Now I knew where the keycard had come from. I shook my head. "None. Although whoever is cleaning the bridesmaids' room needs a raise."

"I've heard." Elliot rolled his eyes.

"They almost caught us," Rita said. "We had to leave through the passages."

"I figured as much when I saw you leaving the library." Elliot looked back over his shoulder. "I think they're all gone now, though, so you"—he looked at me—"can leave without any of them knowing you were here." He nodded at a front desk clerk who was waving at him. "I have to go."

As he strode across the expansive room to the front desk, Rita and I followed at a slower pace.

"If anyone had any garment with a button like that, it's long gone now." Rita's voice mirrored my own disappointment.

"The only person we couldn't check was Tom." I stopped at the front doors. "Maybe I need to find out where he's staying and check his room."

"I don't think Keith would like you breaking into someone's room." She hooked her thumb toward Elliot. "He can't give you a keycard to get in, and you won't have secret passages to get away." She gave me a quick hug. "Just be careful, okay?"

Rita swept away in a rustle of skirts, and I stepped out onto the porch, half expecting to see Connie and Tom again, as I had on my last visit. The porch benches, however, sat empty today.

I stepped from the stairs onto the drive and walked toward the carriage station. As I reached to pet a horse's nose, movement caught my eye at the tree line near one of the walking paths. Tom stood staring at me for a moment before turning and running down the path out of sight.

Chapter Nineteen

I skirted the carriages, race-walked across the lawn to the path's opening, and plunged into the woods. Tom had disappeared. Running footfalls echoed through the trees, and I gave chase. I jogged down the dirt path, not even processing the incredible beauty around me. I crested a rise in the path and caught a flash of a yellow jacket where a figure left the path and crashed through the undergrowth.

I jumped off the path, pawing my way through brambles and brush, angling in the direction I'd seen Tom take. After a couple of minutes, I stopped, rapidly sucking in deep breaths. Hot peppers on a pancake, I was out of shape. After wheezing for a good minute or two, I straightened and listened.

The forest had gone dead silent. No birds sang. No squirrels chattered. Nothing moved. The hair on the back of my neck stood up. My father had grown up near the woods, and he said when the trees went silent, there was a predator nearby. He, of course, meant a black bear or a coyote, but I was more afraid of a two-legged predator.

I'd gone running into the trees after a possible killer. No one knew where I was. I looked around. Hell, I didn't even know where I was at this point. I'd zigged and zagged, trying to skirt briars and fallen trees, until I wasn't sure which way to go to get back to the safety of the inn.

A twig snapped behind me, and I jumped and whirled, uttering a soft scream. Silence met me again, and the forest took on a sinister feel. My gaze scanned for a hiding spot, somewhere safe. The trees were too tall, their lowest branches too high for me to reach to climb. Nothing was bunched in a way where I could hide. There were no overhangs or huge rocks I could duck under or behind. Just silent trees watching me, waiting for something to move.

Could I have been any dumber? Was I out for the idiot-of-the-year award? Keith would kill me when he found out. If Tom didn't do it first. At least I thought I'd been chasing Tom. What if I had been wrong? Who knew who or what was in these woods?

Panic clawed at my chest, and a full-blown scream erupted when another twig snapped. I whirled again.

Tom stood within three feet of me, his eyes narrowed and his balled fists hanging at his sides. "Why are you chasing me?"

I staggered back, and my knees buckled. I gasped for breath as my heart tried to force its way out of my chest.

"Hey, are you okay?" Tom reached down and grabbed my arm, shaking gently.

I shook my head, tears threatening to fall. This. This moment. This was why Keith got so angry at me. I acted before I thought. I sucked in staccato breaths and blinked rapidly to clear the tears.

Tom held on to my arm and pulled me to my feet. "Do I need to get a doctor or something."

"No," I managed to gasp out. "You just scared me half to death."

He laughed, but there was no humor in the sound. "I scared you? I've just been chased through the woods, and I don't even know why." He led me to a log and lowered me to sit on it.

I bent forward, my head down, concentrating on my breathing and trying to stop myself from hyperventilating. *In. Out. In. Out.*

I sat up, forming words around my gasps. "Just wanted. To talk. To you."

His brows drew together. "Why?"

"About Missy." The words came easier that time as I continued to force my breathing to slow.

"Missy?" Tom squinted at me. "Hey, I know you. You rode in my carriage to the cars the other day."

I nodded and held out my hand. No reason I couldn't be polite to a possible killer, just in case it swayed him toward letting me live. "I'm Jenna. I own a bookstore in town."

His eyes widened. "You're the woman who was dating Missy's boyfriend."

"Emphasis on was." I took another breath and let it out slowly. "We broke up before he got together with Missy."

He took a small step back. "I heard you stole a bunch of money and killed a guy."

Wait a minute. I was supposed to be afraid of him, not the other way around. "I don't know where you're getting your information, but yes, while I was suspected of those things, I was acquitted of all charges, or I wouldn't be sitting here. I'd be in jail."

He curled his lips into a thoughtful frown and nodded. "I get that. So why are you chasing me?"

"Why are you hiding in the woods?" My breathing had finally slowed to a normal rate, and my heart was no longer beating loudly enough to be heard by the whole state. I heaved myself up from my log seat in case I needed to run or defend myself.

"I have nowhere else go to." Tom raked a hand through his hair. "I used all my savings on the ring I bought for Missy. The police told me I can't leave until this is all over, and I can't afford to stay at the Days Inn out by the interstate anymore. So I pulled out my tent and sleeping bag and found a nice spot here in the woods."

"You brought a tent with you?" Who the hell was this guy? As I looked at him, I realized he was older than I'd first thought, at least my age.

"I hunt." He shrugged. "I always keep my gear in the truck, including a small tent."

"I hope you're warm enough. It gets cold here at night this time of year." I refrained from telling him that the whole "don't leave town" schtick the police ran was not a law. If he wasn't under arrest, he could leave when he wanted to. For now, though, I wanted to keep him here. I had to find out who killed Missy.

He nodded and looked back over his shoulder. "I have plenty of blankets and a thermal sleeping bag. I'm fine."

"Do the police know where you are?" I tried to see past him, looking for his tent and landmarks in case I needed to tell Tish and Keith.

"No." He rammed his hands into his pockets. "They have my cell number, though."

"Okay." I wondered if the police really could track him through his phone. If that was the case, I wouldn't have to remember how to get back to this spot in the woods. "But what about your job?"

Tom looked at his feet and scuffed a toe in the leaf cover. "I quit my job to come here. I was planning on finding a job in Charlotte. Everything I own that matters to me is locked in my truck at the hotel."

Stunned, I sank back onto the huge log, patting the gnarled wood beside me. "Why would you do that?"

He took a step and eased himself down beside me, propping his elbows on his knees. "I wanted Missy to be happy. I knew she didn't want to be in Hickory anymore. She wanted the big city life and the glamor of her fancy job. I wanted to fit into her new world."

As gently as I could, I said, "But she didn't want you there."

Tom shook his head. "No. She didn't. But I had to try. She was my whole world. I met her when she was just nineteen. She started working at the plant on the line. I was the foreman by that time. I'd been there four years. That first time I asked her out and she said yes? It was the most perfect thing that had ever happened to me."

Was he talking about the same bitchy woman, labeled a bridezilla by store owners and hotel staff alike, who had screeched hateful things at Tom, Blake, and Connie, even striking her sister in public?

Tom must have caught on to my confusion. "She wasn't always what you saw here. She was sweet and kind and loving and giving. We dated for five years, and then something snapped. I don't even know what. One day, Hickory wasn't good enough for her, and I wasn't either."

"And she moved to Charlotte and met Blake." But why him? Blake wasn't as rich as others in the company. He might be at some point as he moved up the ladder, though, and maybe she had been planning ahead.

Tom looked away, a light breeze ruffling his collar-length hair. "He was everything I wasn't. He was cultured and educated." He shifted his gaze to his hands. "I'll bet he's never even had dirt under his fingernails from hard work."

I laughed. "You have no idea. Blake got a manicure every week without fail. I think he would have passed out if he had to do something dirty with his hands."

Tom let his hands drop to his lap. "See what I mean?"

"Why, when she let you know she didn't want you any more, did you keep chasing her?" I hurt for this man, and the longer we talked, the more convinced I became that he couldn't be the killer. Damn it, here I was being a sap again. Someone had killed Missy, and I had no proof it hadn't been the man sitting next to me.

"I kept hoping it was an act, something to make me jealous." He reached into his pocket and pulled out a small box, flipping the lid open to look at the tiny diamond atop a gold band nestled in its folds. "I knew she wanted to get married, and I thought she was just trying to show me what it was like without her. Like she expected some huge gesture on my part to win her back." He flipped the lid closed and stuffed the ring back into his pocket. "But all I have now is a useless ring."

"What about Connie?" I shoved aside Mom's voice telling me not to butt in any further.

"Connie?" Tom shook his head. "She's just a kid. She's only seventeen, and I'm ten years older than she is."

"That kid thinks she's in love with you," I said softly.

"I know." His shoulders slumped. "And I don't know how to get her to stop. She's convinced if she hammers at me long enough, I'll fall in love with her like I did her sister. But she's not Missy."

I thought of the young girl, older than I'd thought, older than she seemed, who wanted so badly to be someone she wasn't. "No, she's not." I hesitated. If I kept doling out advice, I'd need to get a job at the local paper writing an advice column. I sighed. "Can I make a suggestion?"

"Sure." Tom shrugged.

"Be gentle with Connie. She's trying to find out who she is. Living in Missy's shadow couldn't have been easy for her. She needs to be reminded that who she is, apart from Missy, is something good. Remember, just like you lost your ex-girlfriend, she just lost her sister and will be fighting her own sense of guilt over the fight she had with Missy where she said . . ." The full impact of what Connie had said hit me.

"What did she say?" Tom's brow furrowed.

"She said . . . some hateful things to Missy that she can't take back." I stood and brushed off the back of my jeans. "Now she'll never be able to make peace with her."

"Yeah, I guess." Tom heaved himself up and took a few steps. "Come on, I'll show you the way back to the hotel."

Grateful to have a guide, I followed him as he pushed aside branches and brambles, and stepped on briars to let me cross. We finally emerged out into the parking lot, and I turned to thank him, but he was already disappearing into the woods, leaving me alone with the words Connie had yelled at Missy ringing in my head: "I hate you. I wish you were dead."

Chapter Twenty

Breaking glass shattered my restless sleep, and Eddy leapt to his feet in the bed, barking furiously. I jumped out of bed, scrambling for my jeans and a shirt and shoving my feet into my shoes. I grabbed my phone. Two AM. I dialed Keith's number as I walked out of the bedroom.

"Jenna?" Keith's sleep-muddled voice came over the line.

"I'm sorry, I should have called Tish." I hung up and scrolled through my contact list, interrupted when the phone rang in my hand. I tapped the screen to answer Keith's call.

"Jenna, what the hell is going on? You wake me up and now you're going to call Tish?" His voice was wide awake and tinged with worry and irritation.

"I think someone is breaking into my store." I strode over to Eddy, who stood rigidly by the door to the spiral stairs, his hackles raised. "Eddy does too."

"Jenna, listen to me. Do *not* go downstairs."

My hand froze where it rested on the bolt to unlock the door. "I can get my bat."

"No! Stop! I want you to do exactly what I say. I need to call this in. When we hang up, I want you to call Rita. Tell her you're coming immediately. Then I want you to get Eddy and run from your door to hers. Don't look back. If you're not at her door within thirty seconds after you call, she's to call me."

Fear lanced through me. "You think they'll come up here?" I backed away from the door, tugging Eddy with me, turning to scan the room for where I'd tossed my jacket.

"It's possible. Now promise me you're going to Rita's."

"But I—"

"Jenna, promise me!" Keith barked the order as if talking to a perp in cuffs.

"Fine, I promise!" If only to get him to stop yelling at me.

The line went dead, and I instantly dialed Rita's number.

"What's wrong?" Rita's voice held no hint that she'd been asleep.

"Someone may be breaking in downstairs. Keith said to call you and have you call him if I'm not there in thirty seconds." I grabbed Eddy's leash and clicked it on, scanning the kitchen for my purse and keys, finally snagging them off one of the barstools.

"Wait, don't hang up. Just keep the line open and get over here. Now."

I listened at my door, cracking it open when I heard no sound. The walkway outside was empty, and I scampered through, banging it shut and locking it. Eddy ran ahead of me into Rita's open doorway, and she slammed it closed, turning the bolt and the doorknob lock before turning to lean on it.

"Are you okay?"

I took in the chenille bathrobe and matching slippers, the foam curlers wrapped tightly in her hair, and the eye mask pushed up on her forehead. "I'm sorry I had to wake you, but Keith made me promise."

Rita slid the mask off her head and walked through her apartment, a mirrored duplicate of mine, and dropped it on the kitchen bar. "Don't be ridiculous. I'd have been pissed if you hadn't done what he asked."

A siren wailed in the distance, and I hoped it was on Keith's car. "I'll be out of your way in a few minutes."

"Oh no, you don't." Rita strode toward her bedroom. "You're going to sit right there until I'm dressed and Keith comes to this door. Understood?"

"Yes, ma'am." I walked to her living room and sank onto a wingback chair facing her fireplace.

A knock sounded at her front door as Rita exited her room, curlers gone and fully dressed, and she strode through her apartment to look through the peephole. "It's Keith." She unlocked and opened the door.

Keith nodded at Rita as he brushed past her, making a beeline to where I sat. "Jenna."

I stood as he approached. "What happened downstairs? Was anyone there?"

"No. But you need to come with me."

Minutes later, I stood across the street from my store, my mouth gaping open and a knot forming in the pit of my stomach. "Who would do this?"

Rita slung an arm around my shoulders. "We'll fix it, honey."

The words *bitch*, *whore*, and *murderer* had been spray-painted across my front door, which remained intact. My front window had been shattered, and two bricks lay inside the display. The same red paint had been used to spray random patterns back and forth across the items in the display. "But it's all ruined. The new wedding planners. The antique books. Even the veil and material you loaned me."

"You can stop worrying about those things." Rita squeezed me again. "They don't matter at all right now."

I drew closer, careful as I felt glass crunch on the sidewalk under my feet. "Why? I don't understand."

Keith, who had been talking with two uniformed officers, approached. "They need to check the store to make sure no one is inside. Can you unlock it for us?"

I fumbled in my jacket pocket for my keys, slid the correct one into the front door, turning the lock, and stepped back to let the officers pass.

Rita appeared at my side, peering in through the door. "Doesn't look like anyone did any damage there."

"The door was still locked, so unless they climbed in over broken glass after making a huge racket, they didn't come inside," Keith said from behind me. "There's also no sign of torn clothing or blood on the jagged edges of the glass remaining in the window frame."

I watched numbly as an officer disappeared into the back room and reappeared a moment later, shaking his head.

Keith placed a hand on my shoulder. "Doesn't look like the back door was jimmied either."

I longed to lean into Keith, but he still seemed so standoffish. Instead, I turned back out onto the sidewalk, surveying the damage to my window and the slurs sprayed across my storefront. My chest squeezed, and a lump rose in my throat. I swallowed several times, determined not to break down. A glint of gold caught my eye in the window, and before anyone could stop me, I reached past the broken glass, easing the shards away from the gold, and picked up my aunt's and uncle's wedding rings.

My fingers closed around them, and the floodgates opened. Sobs ripped from my soul, and I would have fallen to my knees if Keith hadn't caught me.

He swept me into his arms, carrying me to one of the benches. Gently, he eased me onto the wooden slats and sat beside me, not releasing his hold on me. "Jenna, it can be fixed." He slid a hand up and down my spine. "It'll all be okay."

I shook my head, sobbing out the words. "No. It. Won't." I pushed deeper into his embrace and stopped fighting the emotional onslaught, safe in his arms, at least for the moment.

When I finally came up for air, reluctantly pulling out of Keith's arms, I came face to face with not only Rita, who had plopped into a tailor position on the sidewalk, but also Shelby, who knelt in front of me, dressed in pink silk pajamas, a matching kimono, and a pair of flip-flops.

"Honey, I'm so sorry," Shelby said. "Are you okay? Is there anything I can do?"

"No." I took a deep shuddering breath. "Not unless you can wave a magic wand and make it all go back to normal."

Keith's arm, still tight around my shoulders, pulled me back against him. "We *will* fix this. I promise."

"How?" My heart clenched again as I surveyed the damage. "Even if they fix the window and clean the door and bricks around it, I can't unsee this. I can't undo the fact that someone intentionally vandalized my store. And it wasn't random. This was deliberate and aimed at me."

Shelby stood and grabbed my hand, pulling me to my feet. "Stop that." She turned so she stood beside me, facing the store. "Now take a good look and tell me what you see."

"Ugly words, broken glass, and ruined books and items I borrowed from Rita." My fists clenched at my sides. "I see days of being closed. I see days of losing money because I can't make sales."

"Uh-huh." Shelby signaled to Rita and Keith to be silent. "Do you want to know what I see?"

I sniffed and nodded.

"I see a brand-new window with elegant framing. I see a better platform for your displays. I see a new store sign decaled across the glass. I see newer shelves behind the counter, maybe in oak, with carvings on their backs, so they'll be part of the display." She turned to face me. "I see a chance to rebuild, to make it better than it was before, to show whoever did this that they did you a favor, demolishing the old so you could build the new."

As she spoke, images of the changes I'd long wanted to make flitted through my head. "Maybe." I sniffed again.

"She's right." Rita stood on the other side of me and took my hand in hers. "It'll be like *The Six Million Dollar Man*. We'll build it bigger, better, faster."

Keith softly sang, "Do . . . do do do doo," from the theme song of the 1980s show.

A half giggle, half-hiccupped sob bubbled up, and I leaned back into Keith where he stood behind me. "You guys are great. What would I do without you all?"

Keith wrapped his arms around my waist from behind. "You'll never have to find out."

"Well, now that that's settled"—Shelby turned toward Keith—"introduce me to your friends. Can I assume, based on the fact that he can't keep his hands off of you and that you're not going all ninja on him, that this is your hottie detective you were telling me about?"

Bless that woman—she knew how to break some tension. My laugh this time was genuine. "Yes, this is Keith Logan." I nodded toward Shelby. "And Keith, this is Shelby Foster. She owns the new candle store in one of the Hokes sisters' slots and lives on the other side of Rita." I gestured toward the redhead, who was staring at my vandalized door.

"We've met," Rita mumbled. "I always meet my neighbors when they move in." She cocked her head to one side. "Why use those words? I mean, this is someone accusing you of murdering someone. Is someone dragging up your past in Charlotte? And if so, why call you a bitch or a whore?"

"If it was just the stuff from Charlotte," Shelby said, "I wouldn't have put it past those kooky ladies from the Women's League on Public Safety."

I shook my head. "The other two words don't fit, though. Even if they wanted to force me out because I'm bringing crime into the area by causing another crime at my store, I don't see either one of them calling me a whore."

"No," Rita said softly. "But someone would if they thought you were trying to get Blake back. Think about it. Those three bridesmaids tried to set fire to your store. What's to say they didn't do this, too, because they're trying to point a finger at you?"

Keith dropped his arms and snorted. "Can anything happen in this town these days that's not connected to your ex?"

I turned, catching his icy expression and the uncomfortable glance Rita and Shelby gave each other. I gave Keith a glare of my own. "Can we not do this now?"

Rita stepped between us. "I think now is the perfect time." She turned to face Keith. "You, sir, are being a dumbass."

My jaw dropped. Rita didn't generally use profanity, and for her to actually call someone a name like that was huge.

I laid a hand on her shoulder. "Rita, wait—"

"You hush up." She whirled on me, her Georgia accent, usually hidden unless she was in extreme distress, in full bloom. "I've had just about enough of you two. You"—she jabbed Keith in the shoulder with her finger—"need to stop punishing Jenna because some jerk from her past decided to start making trouble for her. If she wanted to be with him, she would've tried long ago, or at the very least, she would've fallen into his arms when he played all gropey-feely the other night at her store. She wouldn't have given him a knee to the groin, run from a grocery store to get away from him, and raced straight to the police station so you could help her. Are you that dense that you can't see it's you she's turning to?"

Keith's mouth worked open and closed, as if he wasn't sure how to respond.

"And you." Rita whirled to face me. "You've moped around, cried, lost sleep, and worried you were losing Keith because you were convinced he didn't want you anymore because you had a boyfriend in the past. Big deal! We all had boyfriends and girlfriends in the past."

"But you said to give it time for him to come around." I looked back and forth between Rita and Keith. "So I waited a day or so and took cake pops to the station, and Keith still didn't want to make up." Gads, I sounded like a whiny child.

"That's not true." Keith put his hands on his hips. "I was worried about you and didn't want you involved in any kind of investigation, but here you are, right in the middle of it all. Again!"

"Stop!" Rita held up a hand in front of both our faces. "Enough from both of you. This has been going on for a week, and it's time for it to be done. Just deal with it. Now." She looped her arm through Shelby's and led her toward another bench.

I caught motion out of the corner of my eye and realized lights were on behind several apartment windows on either side of the street. Great, now we were creating a Missy-style scene in the street in front of my store at almost three in the morning.

Keith shoved his hands in his pockets. "I just don't want you sucked into the middle of this mess. You went through enough at Blake Emerson's hands in Charlotte, and here he is, dragging your emotions through the dirt again."

"Blake's not the one dragging my emotions through the dirt." I crossed my arms. "You are."

"I am?" His brow furrowed, and he shook his head. "How am I doing that?"

"You keep implying I want to be with Blake, and you refuse to listen when all I'm trying to do is give you some insights into the man, a man that I knew for a very long time, whether you like it or not. And when I try to even mention anything to do with this whole situation, you clam up, get angry, and leave, and last weekend, you threw me out of your house." By this time my hands were balled at my sides. "How can that *not* screw with my emotions?"

Keith sighed and pinched the bridge of his nose with his fingers, his eyes closed and head bowed. "Jenna, how can you not know how deeply I love you?" He brought his gaze up to meet mine. "Do you not have any idea how devastated I would be if anything happened to you? If I lost you? After everything that's happened in the last few months, do you really doubt that?"

Tears sprang to my eyes again. "Keith, I . . ."

He opened his arms, and I stepped into his embrace. His lips lowered to meet mine, pouring all his passion, his fear, and his love into that one kiss.

"It's about time." Rita clapped as if watching the ending of a theatrical production as she and Shelby approached. "Can we get back to figuring out who did this to Jenna, without a bunch of unnecessary drama getting in the way?"

"Yes, ma'am." Keith grinned at Rita but didn't release his hold on me.

"While y'all were busy, I had a look around." Shelby pointed her finger up and down the road. "How many of these businesses do you think might have security cameras?"

"I've already instructed one of the officers to come back in a few hours and canvass the stores," Keith said. "However, having a camera doesn't mean it would get a shot of Jenna's window."

"No," said Rita. "But it might catch someone running by at the right time, which means whoever that was either did it or they saw who did."

"I agree." Keith nodded. "If we can get a clear picture, we might have something we can go on."

"My money's on Missy's friends." Shelby pulled her thin robe closer around herself. "They did try to burn the store down, and that was before Missy was dead. I could see them blaming her death on Jenna."

"I don't know." Rita sat on the bench and crossed her legs. "The way those three have been acting since Missy was killed, I wouldn't put it past one of them to have killed her. I think her name is Mandy. She's become queen bee now, and she is as bad as, if not worse than, Missy ever was."

"You think she might have killed Missy to take over the group?" Keith shook his head. "That's a weak motivation at best. Plus, she had an alibi. She was in full view of the entire dinner party when Missy was killed."

"There goes that idea." Rita rolled her eyes and tossed her hands in the air. "Maybe Blake really did do it."

I shook my head. "Without a lot more proof, I just don't see it."

Keith tensed against me, and I mentally kicked myself. Was this little bit of peace we'd made so easily undone?

"It's just that I know this man," I rushed to add. "If he's a murderer, it means I'm the biggest idiot on the planet. I never once saw him even kill a spider. He'd catch them in a glass and put them outside."

Keith sighed and kissed my cheek. "Sweet, trusting Jenna. You have to understand that most of the people I've arrested for murder over the years have been nice, gentle people who wouldn't kill a spider, until someone pushed just the wrong button at just the wrong moment."

"Maybe." I pulled out of his arms and turned toward my store, sweeping an arm across the view. "But at the end of the day, we know for a fact that Blake didn't have anything to do with this . . . this disaster someone made of my store."

An officer signaled, and Keith strode over to talk to him.

"We're not going to solve this thing by standing in the cold street in the middle of the night." Shelby wrapped her arms around her middle. "I need to get warm."

"I, for one, am wide awake now," Rita said. "I'm going to put on a pot of coffee and watch an old movie if either of you would care to join me."

"I'm in." Shelby raised her hand. "Lead the way."

"I'll be along after I say goodnight to Keith." I waved them on and turned to where Keith stood on the sidewalk across the street.

He crossed the cobblestones to where I stood. "I've stationed an officer inside the store for the remainder of the night. We can't secure that window until tomorrow when we can get some plywood."

"Plywood." I sighed. "Can we put a few panels over the painted words?"

Keith chuckled. "I can, but no one could come inside if I did that."

"Right now, I'm not sure if I want them to." I laid a hand on his chest.

"The store be damned." He slipped his fingers through my beltloops at my hips and pulled me forward, lowing his head to kiss me. "Everything over there is replaceable. You're not."

I snaked my arms around his waist and laid my head on his shoulder. "If I'd known all it took to remind you of that fact was a break-in at my store, I'd have thrown bricks through the front window days ago."

A harsh chuckle barked past his lips. "You say that, but Jenna, someone was trying to hurt you. They've tried to burn you out. Now they've demolished your window and painted graffiti on your storefront. Even if they didn't mean to physically injure you, they meant to harm your business and your home. You shouldn't be so flippant about it."

"I know, I know." I raised my head to look at him. "Can you stay?"

He shook his head. "I need to go write reports on this and prep everything for tomorrow's canvassing."

"Okay." I brushed a kiss across his lips. "Be safe."

"Really?" He squeezed me and released me, a grin on his face. "After all that's happened to your store in the last few days, you're telling *me* to be safe?"

"Fine, I'll be safe too." I chuckled and waved as he headed toward the parking lot.

A yawn popped up. I needed to sleep, but I was too wired. The warm glow in Rita's windows pulled at me. I had to go over there anyway because Eddy was still there.

When I knocked on her door, a muffled "Come on in" was the response. I pulled it open, stepping into the warmth of the apartment. Striding across the room, I slipped off my jacket to drop it on a dining chair.

Eddy didn't bother to get up and greet me. Instead, I got a tail thump from his position on the couch between Rita, who was scratching his back ridge, and Shelby, who was feeding him bites of popcorn while he lay with his head in her lap.

"Man, my dog sure has it rough." I laughed and plopped down into an easy chair at an angle to the couch and TV.

Shelby bent down to Eddy's face and kissed it. "Don't you listen to her, baby dog."

He licked her nose and rolled to his side, paw in the air in a request for a belly rub. She obliged, dropping another piece of popcorn in his mouth.

I shook my head and turned toward the screen. "What are we watching?"

"*Breakfast at Tiffany's.*" Rita handed me a popcorn bowl. "I made a bowl for you."

I took the bowl, munching as we watched the iconic Audrey Hepburn film about a socialite whose past kept getting in the way every time she tried to move forward with her life, wishing my own past would just leave me alone.

Chapter Twenty-One

"Wake up, sleepyhead." Rita gently shook my shoulder. "You dozed off and missed the ending."

I yawned and stretched, massaging my cramping neck. "It's official. This chair should not be used as a bed."

Shelby laughed. "Girls, this has been fun, but I have to get home and grab a couple more hours of sleep." She fumbled in her robe pocket for her keys.

I stood and hugged Shelby. "Thanks for being there for me tonight."

"Any time." Shelby chuckled and shook her head. "Wait, let me clarify that. I'd rather tonight's events be a one-time shot, but I'm here if you need me."

"Here's what else is official. We all need sleep if those are the things going through our brains." Rita walked into her kitchen. "Need a cup of coffee for the road before I empty the pot?"

"Nah." Shelby headed toward the door. "I'll make a pot in a few hours when I wake up. But thanks!" She let herself out.

"I guess I'd better head home too." I walked to the dining area and grabbed my jacket off the floor. Guess I'd missed that dining chair with it when I took it off.

"Wait." Rita turned. "Stay. I don't like the thought of you being over there alone after what happened tonight."

"Are you sure?" I knew Rita had a spare room, and the thought of staying was far more appealing than jumping at every sound while I slept in my own bed. "I don't want to be in your way in a few hours when you're trying to get ready for work."

"Yep, I'm sure. And I'm off today, so you won't be in my way at all." Rita skirted her island and walked into her guest room to flip on the light. "The bed's made, and it's okay if Eddy sleeps with you. The bedspread isn't anything special."

"Thanks." I walked past her into the room, smiling at the homey feel. Soft light spilled from the Tiffany lamp on the nightstand, sending small blotches of color to rest on the walls and ceiling. A lavender bedspread hung to the floor on either side of the queen-sized bed and covered plump pillows. A tall chest of drawers stood in one corner, and a bentwood rocking chair sat in the other.

"If you need more blankets, they're on the top shelf." Rita gestured toward the closet door. "Help yourself."

"I will, thanks." I wiggled my fingers at her in a goodnight gesture as she strode out the door.

Eddy padded into the room and took a sniffing stroll through the space, ending at my feet. He whuffed, as if to ask what we were doing up, and hopped onto the bed, turning three circles before settling into a ball.

I sat on the bed and scratched his head. "I couldn't agree more." I kicked off my shoes and stood to shimmy out of my jeans, pulling my bra off without taking off my shirt. As the covers fell over me, my eyes drooped, and I barely got the lamp turned off before sleep took me.

When my eyes opened again, the room was still dark, but the smell of fresh coffee wafted in through the open door. I stretched, stood, grabbed my clothes, and headed to the bathroom. After dressing, I splashed water on my face and used another bit to tame my hair, which stuck out at odd angles from my restless sleep.

Finally feeling human, I strode into the main living area. "What time is it?"

Rita turned, a mug of coffee in her hand. "Seven thirty, and good morning to you too."

"Sorry." I laughed. "I'm not a morning person." I grabbed my jacket from the barstool where I'd dropped it when she'd asked me to stay.

"You headed home to grab a shower?" Rita turned, a mug of coffee in her hand.

I nodded. "Yeah, after Eddy gets his turn to go potty."

"I already took him out." The microwave beeped, and Rita turned to open its door. "He woke up when I did, and I didn't have the heart to make him wait."

Eddy's tail moved in a slow wag. He stared intently at Rita as she pulled her breakfast from the microwave.

"No, baby. This isn't for you." She shuffled past him to the dining room.

Eddy followed her, and she gave him a scratch on the head as she sat.

I searched for the leash, snapping it onto his collar when I found it. "Come on, let's go get our own breakfast." I looked up at Rita. "Thanks for letting me stay."

"Don't mention it." She smiled and waved as I left.

The crisp, late-March breeze cut through me as I walked across to my front door in the last minutes before the sun rose. I shook my head. Daylight savings had started the weekend before, and I still wasn't used to the time shift.

I unlocked my door and stepped inside, grateful for the warmth that enveloped me. Moving through my morning routine, I showered, dressed, fed Eddy, and had settled at the bar with a bowl of cereal when my phone rang.

"Hello," I mumbled over a bite of Raisin Bran.

"Lily just called me." Mason's stressed tones echoed over the line. "She had to go in early today to help with a catering event. She said the store is all messed up and there's a cop outside. Are you okay?"

I swallowed my cereal. "I'm fine. Eddy's fine. The store's not. Someone tossed a couple of bricks through the window and spray-painted everything in red paint."

"Wow," Mason said. "I'll be there to help you clean up as soon as I can get dressed. She said there's glass everywhere."

"There is, and thanks." I started to say more, but Mason had already hung up.

After wolfing down the last of my cereal and putting on my shoes, I grabbed a jacket and Eddy's leash, and we headed downstairs. I stood in the store, surveying the damage from the inside. From this vantage point, the only truly visible damage was the shattered window glass and the red paint splashed all over the shelves and the display.

I sighed and moved to the coffeepot to brew us some liquid strength for the upcoming tasks. I jumped when I heard a noise from the back room. "Who's there?" I shouted.

"It's Officer Todd," came the muffled reply, punctuated by a flushing toilet. He appeared in the doorway to the back room. "I had to . . . you know." He hooked a thumb back over his shoulder.

Relieved to find yet another person wasn't trying to mess with my store, I poured a cup of coffee and extended it to the approaching officer. "Anything happen last night?"

He shook his head. "Nope. It was dead quiet. We really didn't expect anything, though. I was mostly here to keep anyone from deciding to jump in and grab a five-finger discount."

"Sounds like a wonderfully boring evening." I poured myself a cup of coffee and took a sip.

"Nah. I love to read, and you had an old Richard Bachman book I hadn't read yet." He picked up a worn paperback from the counter. "I didn't quite finish it, though. How much to buy it?"

"Consider your time here as payment enough." I recognized Stephen King's alter ego and couldn't imagine sitting here in the middle of the night, window open to a deserted street, reading a horror novel. "How long will you stay today?"

"Now that you're here, there's really no need." Officer Todd yawned and shook his head. "Sorry. I normally work the night shift, but I'd usually have been home getting ready for bed by now." He took a long draught from his mug.

"Then by all means, head on home. Someone will be here all day today, and I hope to have something up over the window before tonight." I poured myself a cup of coffee and took a sip.

"Thanks." Officer Todd gulped down the remaining coffee in his mug, grinning as he set the mug on the counter. "Gotta have some go-juice to get me home." He wiggled the paperback at me as he walked out the door. "And thanks for this. Now I just have to resist reading the rest of it before I go to sleep."

Alone in my store, I took a deep breath and surveyed the damage in the light of day. As with a King novel, things had seemed scarier in the dark. I stepped to the end of the counter. Shattered glass covered the carpet, and a few shards gleamed on top of and in the recesses underneath the counter. The top of the bookshelf had a layer of glass chips, interspersed with large chunks, which had cut nicks into the wood. Red paint created what would be odd patterns on the surface once the glass was removed.

A low whistle outside drew my attention, and I looked out to see Mason surveying the damage from the cobbled street.

"Man, this is worse than I thought it would be." Mason shaded his eyes in the morning sun. "This is going to be a bear to clean up."

"There's coffee to get you going." I gestured over my shoulder.

Mason walked a wide circle around the glass on the sidewalk and entered the store. "When Lily said the window had been broken, I didn't realize she meant it was completely gone."

I poured a cup of coffee and handed it to him, knowing he liked it black. "Yeah, and get a load of the glass back there." I pointed behind the counter.

"We'll be vacuuming up glass for the next month." Mason stepped closer and leaned in. "At least the books on hold and the reference books weren't damaged, just the top and back of the shelf."

"I guess we'll have to replace that." I mentally tallied up damages for my call to my insurance agent.

Mason shook his head. "Nah. That shelf is solid wood. They don't make them like that anymore. All it'll need is a good sanding and a nice coat of paint, which, to be honest, it's needed for a long time."

"True." I sipped the last of my coffee and picked up Officer Todd's leftover mug to take to the sink in back. "We'd better get started."

Mason swigged back his coffee and strode to the back ahead of me, passing me on his way out with the broom. "I'll get the sidewalk cleaned up so no one gets glass stuck in their shoes or nobody's pet steps on it and gets hurt."

I walked to the sink and put the mugs down, then returned to the desk in one corner of the back room. A file in the cabinet held the insurance information, and I called my agent, explaining the extent of the damage.

"Be sure to take a lot of photographs of the damage before doing anything," she said. "Then do whatever you need, such as putting wood over the window, to make sure no further damage occurs. It'll be Monday before we can get an adjuster out to look at it."

"Can I at least clean the painted words off my front door and surrounding bricks?" I pictured gasps and hands held over children's eyes as people shopped the district. "This is a busy shopping district."

"Of course," she agreed. "Just be sure to have pictures. And make sure anything you do, any expense you incur, is well documented. We will reimburse you for anything that's needed to ensure the security of the store, stop damage from continuing to happen, and make certain people entering and exiting are safe, as long as those charges are deemed reasonable."

We ended the call, and I returned to the front room and headed to the front door. As I was about to pull it open, Shelby swept in, wearing jeans and a sweatshirt that said, "It's always a bright idea to burn a candle."

"The troops have arrived." She set down two buckets containing cleaning supplies. "I wasn't sure what we'd need."

"Wouldn't that be 'troop,' since there's only one of you?" I grabbed a pad of paper, ready to write down anything we used to clean up. If the insurance company didn't cover it, I would.

"The rest are outside." Shelby thumbed over her shoulder toward the door.

I stepped out to see Rita and Phillie Hokes standing across the street, and I crossed the cobblestones to join them. "Pretty bad, huh?"

Phillie's hand was at her throat. "Oh my."

Rita chuckled. "She's said that four times now."

"That about sums it up, though." I pointed at my employee. "At least Mason has most of the glass swept up, so passersby won't get hurt." I pulled out my phone and took several pictures of the damage, zooming in on the graffiti for a couple of extra shots. "The insurance lady said we can clean up for safety, and we can board up the window to keep further damage from happening. I got her to agree we can clean the graffiti off too. But I have to keep a careful tally of everything we spend. She said they'd reimburse me for anything reasonable."

Phillie pointed to a cardboard box near the door. "I brought over some leftover containers of wipes used to clean paint off of brick. I'll have to see if I still have the receipt."

"You guys are the best." I grinned. "But with this many people helping out, I'd better put on another pot of coffee."

Two identical little girls, their dark hair pulled back into ponytails, ran out the bakery door, carrying paper bags as they scampered toward us.

"Hi, I'm Anna." She shoved a bag at me, elbowing the other girl to get her to do the same. "Mama said to bring you these and to tell you she's sorry she can't come help since it's Saturday, and Saturdays are always busy, but she'd help if she could."

"Is Dana your mama, honey?" Rita took one of the bags and peeked inside.

Anna nodded. "Yes, and this is Izzy, my sister."

Izzy smiled and cut her gaze at Eddy. "Can I pet your dog?"

I knelt by Eddy, who seemed as enthralled by Izzy as she was by him. "Sure. His name is Eddy." I kept my hands on him, just in case there was a problem. I shouldn't have worried, however.

The moment Izzy touched Eddy, he became a ball of wiggles and wags and a flashing tongue as he bounced around the child, showering her with kisses. Her squeals of laughter seemed to encourage him, and he continued his excited play.

"Izzy wants to be a dog trainer when she grows up," Anna said solemnly. "She watches this show called *Canine Intervention*, and for our eighth birthday last October, Daddy bought her the *Dog Whisperer* series on Amazon Prime."

"And what about you? What do you want to be?" I was genuinely interested.

"I'm going to do what Daddy does. He's a contractor. He builds things and fixes things. Sometimes he lets me help him, and I'm really good at it, he says." Anna grinned. "And I want to have boots like Daddy's. Izzy and I can stomp on his feet and he can't feel it because there's metal in them. But nobody makes them for kids, so I have to wait until I grow up to have some."

Rita laughed around a mouthful of muffin. "Now there's as good a reason to choose a career as any I've heard."

"And don't you let anyone tell you that you can't do it either." Phillie snatched one of the bags from Rita and pulled out a bear claw.

Izzy looked up, a huge grin splitting her face. "Can we stay and play with him?" She threw her arms around Eddy's neck.

"Mama said we had to come right back." Anna crossed her arms.

Shelby walked up, taking in the scene. "Why don't you let me handle that?" She strode down the sidewalk toward the bakery, where Dana could be seen hovering just inside her door, watching her girls. A moment later, Shelby returned. "Your mama says you can stay, since we really need someone to take Eddy upstairs and keep him company while we work. Do you think you girls are up to that?"

Izzy jumped up and squealed again. "I am, I am, I am!"

Anna rolled her eyes. "Geez, we get it." She turned to Shelby. "Sure. We can help. If we go back to Mama's store, she'll make us sweep and wipe tables. This is funner."

I took Dana's daughters and my dog upstairs and gave them the remote for the TV, showed them where the bathroom and refrigerator were, and made sure the front door was locked. Leaving the door to the stairwell open, so I could hear if there was a problem, I went back downstairs.

Shelby handed me a paper bag. "Hope you like muffins. The blueberry one is all that's left."

I pulled it out and took a huge bite, moaning as I chewed the moist breading and juicy blueberries. "It's perfect."

"I got the glass off the sidewalk." The black trash bag in Mason's hand tinkled as he walked. "Want me to vacuum the floor next?"

I brushed off my fingers and popped the rest of the muffin back into the bag. It would have to wait beside the coffeemaker until I found time to spare, which likely wouldn't be soon. "Please do." I pointed toward the trash bag. "Leave that with me. Shelby and I will pick up the bigger pieces so they won't tear up the vacuum cleaner."

Carefully stepping behind the counter, I began gently dropping jagged chunks of glass into the bag Shelby held open. "Who knew a window could break into this many pieces?"

Shelby laughed. "Did your grandma not have Corelle dishes when you were little? They're not supposed to break, but try dropping one of those cereal bowls. Those things literally explode into a thousand tiny shards."

"Note to self. Don't get Corelle dishes. I'm too clumsy." I motioned Shelby over and brushed glass from the top of the bookshelf into the open bag she held.

Done behind the counter, we moved for Mason to vacuum, and I caught sight of a sparkling clean front door, and through it, Phillie Hokes, long rubber gloves covering her hands and forearms, scrubbing the bricks with what looked like a heavy-duty wipe. Beside her, Rita used a gloved hand to pull another wipe free from its container.

"I finished the door." She stepped up beside Phillie. "Show me how to do the bricks." Her voice wafted in through the gaping hole that used to be my window.

"If you use smaller motions, it seems to get into the crevices better." Phillie scrubbed the wipe across the bricks in tiny circles. "Then we'll power wash the residue away."

I stepped outside. "Phillie, you shouldn't be scrubbing bricks."

"I'll do what I want." Phillie stuck her tongue out at me.

My jaw dropped. Had I really just seen that?

Rita elbowed Phillie. "You really shouldn't let the kids in your youth gardening classes at the nursery teach you bad habits."

"But it worked. See? She stopped telling me what to do." Phillie pointed a gloved finger at me. "I'll have you know, Livie and I cleaned paint off the entire back of the house one year. Daddy had painted it years before, and we wanted to go back to the natural brick. Now that was a job. This? This is nothing. I'm just glad we still had these leftover wipes made to clean paint off of brick. Otherwise, I'd have been driving to Asheville to pick up new ones."

"Is it like this?" Rita caught Phillie's attention, scrubbing in circles across the brick.

"Put a little more oomph into it, dear. We're not drying dishes." Phillie scrubbed her own wipe across the bricks, dissolving the red paint.

Clinking glass caught my attention, and I turned to see Shelby dropping chunks from the display area into the trash bag.

"Here, let me help." I took a step and grabbed the bag, holding it open.

"No," Shelby said. "Swap me. You know what you want done with this stuff." She pointed at the ruined books.

Gently, I picked up one of the wedding planners, red paint sprayed across its front and nicks dug into its cover from exploding glass. "This one's trash." Careful not to drop any glass on Mason's neatly swept sidewalk, I placed the book in the bag Shelby now held.

One by one, I removed the displayed books. In spite of the red paint, I hoped some of the antique books of poetry could be salvaged. After sweeping the glass shards into the trash, I laid them in a small pile on the walk. "Rita, what do you want me to do about this material and the veil you loaned me?"

Rita, gloved hands held out to her sides, as if trying to avoid touching anything with chemicals on her hands, stepped to my side. "Looks pretty bad. But see if you can shake the glass out. Then bag it all up, and I'll take it back to our cleaners. Maybe they can get the stains out."

"If they can, I need a bill for the insurance company. If they can't, I need the value of the items." I carefully pulled the veil from the bottom of the display, shaking the shards from its folds into the trash bag.

"Are you going to stand there all day, or are you going to help me with this wall?" Phillie asked. "We're almost done."

Rita grinned. "Duty calls." She returned to making small circles on the bricks with a wipe.

By the time Shelby and I had completed the window, Phillie had dragged a garden hose from the cardboard box she'd brought and had fed it through my store to the spigot on the outside wall in the alleyway.

I watched as she expertly attached a power washer and signaled to Rita to turn on the water. "You've done this before."

"I've always washed the windows and doors at the house once a year." She swept the sprayer at a sharp angle, ensuring no spray entered through the window opening. "Now, with the greenhouse? I use hoses for all kinds of things every day. I'd say I'm an expert at this point."

She paused long enough for Shelby and me to slip inside. Shelby headed for the back door to take the glass trash out. Unable to make myself go to the dumpster without seeing Missy's body in my mind, I excused myself and headed upstairs for a kid and dog check-in.

The TV was the only sound as I stepped into my apartment. *The Princess Bride* played on the large screen over the fireplace. I grinned when "As you wish," came from Westley's lips as, dressed in all black, he tumbled down a hill, a frantic Princess Buttercup running down after him.

Turning, my grin widened. Eddy lay sprawled between the girls, with both of them folded in snuggling him. The three of them were fast asleep. Eddy elicited a soft snore, then faintly yipped, wiggling his feet, probably dreaming of his playtime with his new friends.

Quietly I tiptoed to the bedroom and pulled two lap blankets from the shelf, returning to lay one over each girl. Stepping softly, I slipped down the stairs, holding a finger to my lips and motioning Shelby away from the base of the stairs. "They're all asleep," I whispered when we were several feet away.

Shelby laughed. "Girl, you haven't been around kids much, have you?"

"No, not really." My mother's sister, Aunt Irene, hadn't had any children, so I'd never had cousins to play with. My father had been an only child, as I was. "Extended family wasn't very extended for us."

"My family is huge. We have to rent a church hall for family reunions just to fit us all in." She pointed upstairs. "Let me tell you, when most kids that age fall asleep, you could take a marching band through that apartment, and they wouldn't wake up."

Rita walked through, slowly rolling the hose while Phillie made sure any excess water emptied on the street. "We've cleaned up as much as we can. Honestly, you can't see it if you didn't know it was already there."

Shelby and I followed her outside. As we stepped from the store, Lily walked out of The Weeping Willow, a tray balanced in one hand, and a pitcher in the other.

"Lunch." Lily held up her offerings.

Mason rushed past me to her side, taking the tray from her hands and planting a chaste kiss on her cheek. "Hi."

Color flooded her cheeks, and a playful smile tugged at the corners of her mouth. "Hi, thanks." She slid her free hand under the pitcher of what looked like lemonade. "I figured you guys would be hungry, and I guilted Willow into letting me bring over some simple sandwiches."

Once inside, Mason placed the tray on the counter, and I grabbed disposable coffee cups from under the coffee table.

"Should I wake the kids?" I asked Shelby.

"Nah." Shelby shook her head. "We'll save sandwiches for them." She grabbed a plastic-wrapped sandwich from the tray and unwrapped it.

As I watched my friends munching on a quick lunch, I realized this was what life was about. It wasn't jobs and bills and events and groceries and housework. Life was about the moments when the people you loved came together in support, whether for good times or bad. I just wished the bad would stop coming for a while.

* * *

Hours later, I stood looking at my "repaired" window. Dana's husband had brought plywood, a roll of weather stripping, and the tools to attach it all to the wall. Who knew you could screw wood to brick?

Rob Nichols tore a page from a notebook and handed it to me along with the receipt for the materials he'd used. "Here's a list of what I see. Make sure you point it all out to the adjuster. Don't let them skip over any of it."

"I won't. Thanks." I pointed up at my apartment windows. "Ready to gather up your girls?"

He nodded. "I hope they weren't too much of a bother."

"They were actually a big help." I led Rob into the store and toward the stairs. "To be honest, they did me a favor by keeping Eddy company. He had some trauma before I got him a few months ago, and he gets a bit antsy when he's alone for too long."

"Dana said it helped her out too." Rob followed me up the stairs. "The kids were scheduled to go to a friend's house to spend the weekend. But the friend got sick, and I had to work, so Dana had to bring them with her. No way to make last-minute plans."

When we stepped into the apartment, we found all of the dining room chairs had been turned to face outward. The blankets I'd tossed over the girls earlier had been hung on the chair backs, making a fort under the table. I knelt and peeked inside to see Eddy sprawled on the rug. Both girls sat beside him, each brushing Eddy's coat with one of my hairbrushes. The dog rolled to bicycle a leg when one of them hit a spot that felt really good.

"Time to go, ladies." Rob knelt down and stuck his head inside the fort.

"But we're playing doggy beauty parlor," said one of the twins.

"Eddy's our best client," said the other, stroking his chest with my brush.

"I'm sure he is." Rob chuckled. "But Mama's cooking dinner, and we don't want it to get cold, do we?"

Amid groans of protest, the girls hugged and kissed Eddy goodbye and headed back down the stairs, leaving me alone with my dog, who hung his head in a pout.

"Don't get used to that kind of treatment." I chuckled and pulled the blankets from the dining chairs, giving Eddy a quick kiss on the nose. After folding them and putting them away, gathering up my brushes—I'd never get all that dog hair out of them—and turning all my chairs around, I clipped on Eddy's leash for a walk. "Handsome guy like you with a fresh do needs to strut his stuff."

After a spin around the grassy area near one of the parking lots, I dropped some kibble in his bowl and left him eating while I returned to the store to find only Rita remaining.

"Mason and Lily had a date tonight, so I sent them home." She gestured to the bookshelf sitting on a tarp in the middle of the floor. "This has to dry overnight anyway, so there wasn't much else he could do."

I looked at the soft sage-green paint, which blended so well with the warm woods in the room. "You guys did a great job. It's needed a makeover for a long time, but I never had time to do it."

"See?" She grinned. "That's looking at the positive in all of this."

I looked at the wood covering my window. "I'm positive I wish none of this had happened."

"Stop it." Rita swept her arm around the store. "You have all of this. Your store. Your books. Okay, so someone damaged the window and a very few items. But it's fixable. Stop looking at the worst of it."

"You're right." I sighed. "I'll just be glad when all of this is over."

"I know, honey. And it will be soon." She stepped on the first treads of my stairs. "Now come let me out your front door, so I don't have to walk all the way around the building. I'm pooped."

After I closed my door, I turned. Eddy sat near the kitchen, wagging his tail.

"Nope, you already had your dinner." I walked to the fridge and pulled it open, Eddy at my heels. I laughed. "And you know you'll get part of mine."

I fixed a quick sandwich, too tired to do much else, and plopped in front of my TV to binge watch a few episodes of *Perry Mason*, reveling in how he always brought the killers to justice.

Chapter Twenty-Two

"I'm not letting you sit at home all day, moping about your store." Keith tugged me up from the couch.

I held up my crochet hook attached to half a slightly lopsided potholder, blue thread dangling to the ball on the couch. "I'm not moping. I'm making Rita's Christmas present."

"It's March, Jenna." Keith took the craft items and laid them on the coffee table. "I think you'll have plenty of time to finish . . . whatever that is."

"But—"

"No buts." Keith shooed me toward the bedroom door. "We haven't been out in several weeks, thanks to my job and yours. We need this."

I refrained from adding it was also thanks to the fact that we'd been having problems. "Fine." I walked into the bedroom and opened my closet door. "Where are we going?"

Keith sat on the bed, patting the spot beside him until Eddy joined him. "There's a new club out by the interstate. I thought we could go dancing, and I hear their food is great too."

“But it’s Sunday.” I pawed through my closet, looking for something cute to wear. “Are you sure they’re open?”

“They’re open until ten. I called.” Keith reached past me and pulled out a smokey-blue dress. “Wear this. It’ll match your eyes.”

“Out. I need to get ready.” I gently pushed him out of the room and closed the door.

“No fair that Eddy gets to stay,” he called through the door.

“Eddy won’t try to distract me.” I laughed, digging through the floor of the closet for my charcoal-gray, peep-toe pumps with a low heel. No way was I dancing on stilettos.

“Whatever.”

I quickly dressed and stepped to the bathroom to dab on a bit of makeup and fix my hair. Satisfied, I walked to the living room, twirling in a circle to flare the filmy skirt that stopped mid-thigh. “How do I look?”

Keith wolf-whistled. “You look amazing.” He stood up from the couch and reached for my hand, pulling me to him in a spin and brushing my lips with a kiss.

“I thought we were going out to dance, not staying in.” I grinned.

“Don’t tempt me, woman.” He stepped back, my hand still in his, raking his eyes across me. “The way you look in that dress . . .”

I laughed. “Let’s go, handsome. I want to show you off.”

“Are you sure you won’t get cold in that?” He fingered the material of the cap-sleeved bolero jacket.

“I’ll be dancing with the sexiest man in the room.” I strolled toward the door, swaying my hips. As I reached for the doorknob, I threw a glance over my shoulder. "I'm sure he'll keep me very warm."

"Wait, who is this guy?" Keith grabbed his jacket off one of the stools. "Is he buying my dinner too?"

"I'll ask him when we get there." I headed out the door.

When we arrived at the club, Keith left his jacket in the car, so he wouldn't have to keep track of it, and stuck my ID and lipstick into his pocket. I tucked my purse under the back seat and stepped out into the parking lot to the beat of music as it thumped out through the walls of the building.

Keith grinned and extended his arm. "Shall we?"

I tucked my hand through his elbow, glad to have his support, since my low heels didn't like the gravel parking lot.

Keith pulled open the door and guided me through. The music rose and fell in an almost hypnotic beat, and Keith pulled me onto the dance floor. The song ended and the music slipped into a slow beat.

I slid into Keith's arms, his hand on my low back as he guided me through the slow dance. We swayed together, lost in the embrace until the tempo changed. After several fast dances and a couple more slow ones, we finally stepped from the floor, needing a break.

"Go grab us a booth, and I'll see if I can scare up a couple of menus." Keith gestured toward the bar. "What do you want to drink?"

Shelby's analogy popped into my head. "A dirty vodka martini with garlic olives." I grinned.

"Coming right up." Keith weaved his way through the crowd toward the bar.

Spotting an open booth, I headed for it and slid onto one of the bench seats, grateful to be off my feet for a bit. I craned my neck, looking for Keith, ducking back when I spotted Elizabeth North and Helen Grigby from the Women's League on Public Safety headed my way with drinks in their hands.

I slid deeper into the booth, scanning the crowd for Keith and looking for another table. Spotting one, I eased forward, about to rise when I heard one of the women.

"I've been just dying to tell you. I saw the dead girl's sister yesterday, and you wouldn't recognize her."

I slid back into the booth, turning sideways in the seat as if watching the dance floor. I bobbed my head and swayed my shoulders a bit, my ears trained on their conversation while I watched them from the corner of my eye.

Helen took a sip of her drink. "She was gussied up like a hooker with all that makeup and those tight clothes."

"Oh my lord, that poor child." Elizabeth shook her head.

"She was prancing around on high heels with those other three women. You know, the ones who were supposed to be in the wedding? I thought her name was Connie—that's what the newspaper said—but they were calling her Kiki and acting like she was one of them. But when her back was turned, they were rolling their eyes and making fun of her."

Elizabeth tapped a finger on the table. "You know what I heard? The woman at the bakery said she thinks that girl might have killed her sister to steal the sister's ex-boyfriend."

"Why would she need to kill over an ex?" Helen tilted her head and furrowed her brow. "Which means he's technically a free man." She waved a hand. "No, if she killed him, I can tell you why. Money. That's why."

"Money?" Elizabeth sipped her drink. "What money?"

"I was at the hairdresser yesterday." Helen touched her curled hair. "And Mary Louise Bellhaven was there. She and her husband were having dinner at the steakhouse over on Mulberry Street. You know, the one with the big sign with horns out by the road?"

"They have the best salads," Elizabeth said.

"Yes, they do." Helen nodded. "Anyway she said those girls had come in and were eating dinner. And when Kiki got up to go to the bathroom, the others were talking about how she was going to get a bunch of insurance money and how maybe she'd killed her sister for it. Seems the dead girl was trying to force her to stay in Charlotte and get a job when Kiki wanted to go back to wherever they came from. Said she'd throw Kiki out on the street without a dime if she didn't do what she was told."

"Now there's a reason for murder." Elizabeth tsked. "From what I've heard about how her sister treated her, I wouldn't blame Kiki one bit for wanting to go back home and have her own life."

"That man they arrested? Blake Emerson? His mama was there too. Wearing clothes that looked ready for the rag bag. With all his money, he needed to at least make sure his mama wasn't wearing worn-out clothes." Helen sniffed. "She was hanging on every last word like her life depended on it."

"Can you blame her?" Elizabeth sipped her drink. "Even murderers can have mamas who love them."

"True." Helen turned her head and scanned the room. "Oh, there's Lavinia. We've got to tell her about this and see what she thinks."

"Thank goodness." Elizabeth slipped from the booth, with Helen right behind her. "She promised to be the designated driver tonight."

Keith appeared out of the crowd and passed the women, a drink in each hand and two menus tucked under his arm. He slid into the booth across from me. "Sorry it took so long. The bar's slammed tonight."

I bit my lip, knowing what I was going to say would not go over well. "I think you need to go talk to those three women." I pointed toward a bar top table across the room.

Keith's smile slipped. "Why? What's wrong?"

"You know I don't go looking for this stuff." I pushed out the words, hoping he wouldn't assume I'd intentionally stuck my nose into the investigation again. "But they have information you should probably hear."

"About?" Keith sighed and crossed his arms, leaving his drink untouched.

"A big reason why Connie Plott might have killed her sister." I took a swig of my drink, needing something to look at other than the cloud that passed over Keith's face.

He snorted. "And here we go again."

"It's not my fault. They came and sat in the booth next to me." I pointed back over my shoulder. "What was I supposed to do? Tell them to shut up?"

"No." Keith shook his head and picked up a menu. "I suppose not. I'll try to set up appointments with them this week."

"You should do it now while they're all chatty from drinking." I pointed them out again. "They're with the Women's League on Public Safety, and I guarantee if you tell them you're with the police and make them feel important, they'll spill their guts to you about it all."

He stared at me over the top of the menu for several moments. "You're serious. Our first date in over two weeks, and you want me to go interrogate three women in order to help get your ex out of jail."

"That's not fair." I pulled the menu out of his hands and threaded my fingers through his. "I love you, and I know you would never forgive yourself if you didn't dot every i and cross every t to make sure you have the right person, whether that's Blake or not."

Keith's gaze softened and he raised one of my hands to his lips. "I love you too, and I know you're not going to let this go." He stood and crossed the room, taking his drink with him.

I watched as he propped an elbow on their table, and wished I could hear the conversation. Instead, I sipped my drink and perused the menu.

Within ten minutes, Keith slid back into the booth. "I think one of them pinched me on the butt."

I barely managed to swallow the garlic olive I was chewing without choking on it. "That's hysterical. Did you at least get any good information?"

He picked up a menu. "I did."

When he didn't say anything else, I prodded him again. "And did they tell you about the insurance policy?"

"Yep." He flipped the menu over.

"And about how Connie wanted to go home, and Missy was going to cut her off if she did?" I put my hand on the menu and flattened it against the table.

He nodded and picked up his drink to take a sip.

"Are you going to tell me what you think about it all?" If he thought I was going to sit here and pretend he hadn't just gathered new information, he had another think coming to him.

"Is this you staying out of the investigation?" He pulled the menu out from under my hand.

"Keith, come on." I grinned at him. "I'll let you take me out on the dance floor again, and I promise I'll be the one pinching your butt this time." When all else failed, it was time to flirt my way into his good graces.

He sighed. "Fine. Yes, you were right. It's a valid motive that needs to be explored."

"I knew it." I propped my elbows on the table. "See, I can be useful at times."

He wiggled the menu at me. "Can we get back to the date portion of the night?"

We ordered food and ate, returning to a light but slightly strained banter. Determined to get our earlier mood back, I pulled him from the booth when the Cupid Shuffle was played, leaving our empty plates behind.

"Are you sure about this? We just ate." Keith followed me to the dance floor.

I slipped into line with the others on the floor, stepping to the side in rhythm. "I love this song. It's fun."

By the time the song ended, we were laughing, and Keith pulled me into his arms for the slow song that played next. We spent the next hour dancing until our feet wouldn't take any more.

In the car, I slipped off my shoes and bent forward to rub one foot. "If we're going to do that again, I need more comfortable shoes."

"I don't see how anything that looks like that can be comfortable." Keith pulled out of the lot and turned toward the historic district.

I pointed at his dress shoes. "Can you imagine those things going with a dress like this?"

"To be honest, when you're in a dress like that, I'm not looking at your feet at all." He grinned and winked at me.

My stomach flipped and a slow smile spread across my face. "And just what are you looking at instead?"

Keith rubbed his chin with one hand, the other still on the steering wheel. "Your elbows. You have really cute elbows, and those short sleeves show them off."

I crossed my arms. "Really? Elbows? That's where you want the evening to go?"

"To be fair, elbows are a lot closer to certain other parts than feet are, and elbows definitely smell better." He turned into the historic district parking lot and slid into a spot.

I forced my aching feet into my shoes and reached behind my seat for my purse before stepping from the car. "Now we're talking about foot odor? Are you trying to spoil the mood?" I laughed.

Keith draped his jacket over my shoulders against the chill that had descended with the night. "Sweetheart, I am a professional at mood spoiling. Want me to share more secrets on how?"

I giggled. "Stop it." We walked across the upper walkway to my door and were greeted by Eddy when we stepped inside.

"Can you stay?" I pulled Eddy's leash from behind the door and snapped it on.

"For a while." Keith took the leash. "But only if I get to take you out of that dress." He winked at me as he headed out the door to give Eddy his nighttime walk. "I like unwrapping presents."

I laughed as I padded barefoot through the apartment, pulling a bottle of wine from the small wine chiller under the bar and pouring two glasses before adding a scoop of kibble to Eddy's bowl. I lit a fire and pulled up Pandora on my phone, connecting to the speakers in the living room. If Keith was in a romantic mood, I could at least set the stage.

When he returned, the wine remained untouched. Instead, he strode across the room, scooped me into his arms, and carried me into the bedroom.

Chapter Twenty-Three

Monday morning, I woke to an empty apartment. I rose and dressed, still floating on a cloud after my time with Keith, and stepped into the kitchen. A tented note sat on the counter, a heart drawn on the front. I opened it and read.

Jenna, I hated to leave, but I had to be at work early. I tried not to wake you. I miss you already. You should wear that dress more often. I love you. Keith

A grin popped across my face, and I ate my breakfast with gusto, one of my crooked potholders cushioning my cereal bowl. Maybe I'd make placemats next. The emotional high I felt did wonders for offsetting my previous doom-and-gloom attitude, and I leashed Eddy for our prework walk with a light heart. Today would be a fantastic day, and I'd open the store, window or no window.

We took our time on our walk, Eddy sniffing his trees, posts, benches, and grass, and me enjoying the feel of the morning sun on my face and the crisp, invigorating breeze. As we passed by the alleyway behind the stores across the street from us, Eddy pulled hard, dragging me forward a few steps.

In the alleyway stood the bedraggled orange cat he'd chased before, it's back arched. Eddy play-bowed and yipped, wagging his tail furiously.

I knelt beside him and put an arm over his shoulder. "Baby, that kitty doesn't want to play with you." I dropped a kiss on his nose.

My heart broke for the cat, and I imagined how terrible it must be to be a stray, alone and always on guard. I made a mental note to call the local no-kill animal shelter and see if they could trap the cat and find it a home. As I stood, I noticed a white plate tucked into a corner next to a cat carrier. If someone was feeding the cat, maybe it had a chance after all.

Keeping a firm grasp on Eddy's leash, as I had no desire to repeat the recent alleyway chase, I tugged my dog past the corner of the building and started down the walkway. As I passed the Cookie Cutter, Dana waved at me from behind her counter, gesturing for me to wait where I was.

"Sorry, I can't let you bring Eddy in." She wiped her hands on her apron as she stepped outside. "With my luck, that would be the day I had a surprise health inspection."

"No problem." I gave her a quick one-armed hug. "What's up?"

"I wanted to thank you for letting the girls play with your dog yesterday." She reached down to scratch his ear. "It was the highlight of their weekend. They were still talking about it this morning before school."

"It was fun for Eddy, too." I chuckled. "He was apparently their best client at their doggy day spa."

"Yep, those are my twins." Dana shook her head and grinned. "Want to hear the highlight of my weekend? When we arrived and saw the damage, I had to explain to my eight-year-old daughters what 'whore' meant and that you really weren't a murderer. *That* was a fun Saturday activity." She rolled her eyes.

"Oh no. I'm sorry." I winced. "I didn't even think about them seeing the graffiti."

"Don't be." Dana laid a hand on my arm and gave it a gentle squeeze. "That part of our day was done and over long before anyone else got here. Remember, a baker is at work while everyone else is still asleep."

"At least it's all cleaned off now." I turned my gaze toward my store and the ugly plywood covering what had been my window.

A customer walked in through the bakery door, and Dana glanced inside to make sure her employee had greeted them at the counter. "A baker's work is never done."

"Dana, before you leave, can I ask you something?" I thought of the little plate and the cat carrier. "Do you know who's feeding that big, orange cat?"

"You mean Mr. Fluffy?" She grinned. "That's what the girls have already named him. If it is a him. We're not sure."

"The plate and the carrier are yours?" I asked.

She nodded. "Annabelle saw him last week and told me about him. I was just going to feed him until we could get someone from the shelter out to trap him, but Isabelle has begged to keep him. Rob is going to buy a cat trap this week."

I imagined the cat sprawled under a table fort, Dana's twins brushing him. "That cat has no idea what he's in for." I grinned.

"Rob grew up around cats, so he's pretty excited too." She stepped aside as a couple walked into her store. "We're getting the second wave for the morning. I'd better go. I just wanted to say thanks for Saturday." After giving me a quick hug, she dipped back into her store and disappeared behind her counter.

By the time I got to the store, Mason had arrived, and the painted shelves had been settled back in place behind the counter.

"Morning, boss." Mason raised his coffee mug to me from behind the counter. "I made a pot, if you want some."

I unhooked Eddy's leash and headed for the coffeemaker. "Thanks. You look chipper. What's up?"

He grinned. "I aced both of my midterms."

"Oh wow. With all that's happened, I completely forgot. Congratulations." I poured a cup of coffee and blew on the hot brew.

"Thanks." He plopped back onto one of the stools. "Today is the first day of spring break, and I plan on enjoying it. No studying, no books, no classes."

"Good for you. Anything planned with your free time?" I tentatively took a sip of my coffee, scorching my tongue.

"Yeah, I was going to ask you about that." He set his mug on the counter. "I'd really like to take Lily to Asheville to tour Biltmore one day. She's never been. Wednesday is her day off, and if it's okay with you, I'd like that day off too."

"Sure." I grinned at him. "Anything for love."

Mason rolled his eyes, a slow blush creeping up his cheeks to contradict the gesture. "I'll let her know. Thanks."

The door bells jangled, and the day advanced with a steady flow of customers. Mason and I split our time between selling books and answering questions about the plywood gracing the front of our store.

Around four PM, Rita popped in. "Hey, boys and girls. How's it going?"

Mason set a stack of the bridal planners on the counter. "Just selling books and taking names." He grinned and moved off to help another customer.

"I swear, if I have to say 'the window was damaged and we're replacing it soon' one more time, I'll go crazy." I picked up the stack of planners and slid them into the shelves behind the counter. "How was work?"

"Not too bad. This week's bride is really sweet. And Elliot finally hired two new full-time employees to help with the weddings, which means no more late nights for me." Rita propped her elbows on the counter. "Want to go grab an early dinner with me? Today was slammed, and I forgot to eat lunch. I'm starving."

Before I could answer, my back pocket buzzed, and I reached to pull out my phone. "Hang on. It's Tish." I tapped to accept the call. "Hey, Tish. What's up?"

"Jenna, we have a problem." The strain in Tish's voice was as clear as her words. "I need you to come to the station as soon as you can."

Chapter Twenty-Four

My heart thumped the backs of my ribs and my breath caught in my throat. My first thought was that Tish somehow knew I'd spilled the beans about the button. But that was days ago, and how could she?

My second thought was more dire. "Is Keith okay?"

"Yes, he's fine." She heaved a sigh. "On the testy side, but fine nonetheless."

"What's the problem, then?" I met Rita's questioning gaze and held a finger up in a silent request for her to be patient.

"I really don't think I should get into it over the phone. Can you please come?" Tish's frustration and weariness echoed over the line.

"I'll be there as soon as I can." I ended the call and grabbed my purse from under the counter. "Tish says she needs me to come to the station immediately."

Mason approached the counter to ring up a customer, and I quietly filled him in.

"Go." He waved me out the door. "I've got the store covered."

I stepped outside and headed to the parking lot, Rita at my side. "Where are you going?"

"To the police station with you." Rita shot a look in my direction. "Duh."

"I thought you were starving." I aimed a thumb back over my shoulder toward The Weeping Willow. "Weren't you headed out to eat?"

"I'll be fine." Rita waved a dismissive hand. "And this sounds like you may need a friendly face."

"What if they realized Blake didn't kill Missy, and now they think it might have been me?" I put voice to the fear that had crept into the back of my mind as I unlocked my car and slid behind the wheel. "I mean, Tish did say Sutter was harping on how I could have killed her, I guess because that way I could have Blake."

Rita snorted and dropped into my passenger seat, sliding the seat belt across to buckle it. "The way that man was coming on to you, you could have had him whether or not Missy was still in the picture."

I started the car and pulled out of the lot. "Then what, if not that? What if the Women's League on Public Safety actually got me banned?" What would happen to my store? For that matter, where would I live? I'd have to sell everything and move.

"The Women's League? Those crazies? What are they up to now?" Rita signaled and changed lanes.

"Shelby said they came into her store with a petition to get me kicked out of the neighborhood." I fought the knot in my stomach. Tish had sounded serious. "She says they're trying to get me banned from the district because of all of the crimes centered around me and my store."

"Oh, that's what Shelby meant when she said she wouldn't put it past them to have damaged your store." Rita laughed. "Don't worry about them. No one listens to those ladies anyway. Tish probably called you because they found out who threw a brick through your windows, so stop worrying. We'll be at the station in another minute or two, and we'll find out."

Those last ninety seconds seemed like half an hour as my mind created scenario after scenario for why Tish wouldn't tell me the reason I needed to come to the station. By the time we pulled up, I was on the verge of tears, even though I knew I was being ridiculous.

I strode up the stairs with an exterior confidence I didn't really feel, entering the building to find Sutter behind the glass again. He buzzed us through without even making eye contact. What the hell?

A uniformed officer met us as we walked into the bullpen and asked us to follow him. We moved down a hallway and stepped through the indicated doorway.

"Someone will be with you soon." The officer shut the door, leaving us in an interrogation room, the sound of the lock clicking into place pounding in my ears.

Rita rushed to the door and yanked on the handle. It didn't budge. "Are you kidding me?"

"Maybe they did listen to Sutter." My stomach tightened, and my mind spun as my past experiences in interrogation rooms flooded in. I fought the panic I knew I shouldn't be feeling, unsure of how to get it to stop.

Rita knelt in front of me and took my hands in hers. "Honey, your hands are ice cold." She rose and stomped to the huge glass mirror that took up most of one wall. Raising her fist, she let it fly against the glass. "I watch TV. I know what this is. I know you're in there and can see us. I want to see Keith Logan or LaTisha Riddick *now*!" She pounded the window again.

Within seconds, the door swung open, and Tish strode in. "I'm sorry, guys. The officer was supposed to put someone else in here. You were supposed to be escorted to the conference room." She held the door open and stood to the side. "If you ladies will come with me, please?"

I shot out of the chair and all but leapt toward the door, mumbling a thank-you at Tish as I passed.

Rita looped her arm in mine and slowed me down. She leaned in to whisper in my ear. "Calm down. You don't want someone to think you're trying to escape from custody and tackle you."

I slowed my pace and clamped a trembling hand over hers where it gripped my arm. "Thanks. I just don't do well with interrogation rooms."

Tish strode out in front of us and led us down another hallway to a small conference room. The wall held a city map rather than a mirrored window to another room, and the seats looked a lot more comfortable.

I slid into a chair and crossed my legs, clenching my hands together in my lap. "Tish, what is going on, and where's Keith?"

"Keith is . . . elsewhere." Tish picked up a folder from the table and opened it, pulling a piece of paper from inside. "To be honest, there was doubt about whether he would be able to keep his cool about all of this, so he's been given another assignment for the moment."

Rita sat beside me and slipped her hand over mine. "Why did you ask Jenna to come?"

Tish leaned back and steepled her fingers, elbows propped on the chair's arms. "We received an anonymous tip about a day planner belonging to Missy Plott, which we then retrieved from Gwendolyn Emerson's room."

Crap on a cracker. After the vandalism at my store, I'd forgotten to tell Keith we'd found it. Based on Rita's tensed grip on my hand, I figured I knew who had called it in.

"Due to sensitive material inside, we checked fingerprints on the cover." Tish leveled a glare at me. "Guess whose we found?"

I winced and took a deep breath. "Mine. But there's a reason."

"I'm all ears." Tish tilted her head, a guarded expression on her face.

"Rita and I went to see if we could find any clothes that fit the button you told me about." Oops, maybe not the best way to open.

Tish's jaw clenched and unclenched. "The one I asked you to keep confidential?"

I nodded. "But I didn't mean to tell her. It sort of slipped out. And she had a way to get a keycard, so we didn't break in or anything."

Tish tipped her steepled fingers back to pinch the bridge of her nose and closed her eyes. "And did you find anything during your search?"

"No." I shook my head, even though I knew she couldn't see me. "Just the day planner."

Rita cleared her throat. "I called in the tip. I thought Jenna was going to talk to Keith about it."

"But then my store was vandalized, and I sort of forgot." I slumped back, feeling like a kid in the principal's office. I guess

I knew now why Keith was upset. He was probably angry at me again for getting involved.

Tish was silent a moment before heaving a deep sigh. "It has certainly muddied the waters." She reached forward and tapped the paper she'd pulled from the folder. "Did you read the letter?"

"What letter?" Rita asked.

I shook my head again. "We saw it was Missy's and put it back where we found it. We figured it had been knocked off the table when the room change happened. I really did mean to tell Keith about it."

Tish slid the paper across the table until it rested in front of me. "This is a photocopy of a letter found tucked into the front cover of the planner. This won't be easy to read, but as it involves you, I think you have every right to see it."

I looked down and focused on the page. White-hot rage and a hurt so deep I couldn't find the bottom washed over me. "Is this real?"

Rita pulled the paper from in front of me and read it aloud. "To whom it may concern, If I am dead, Blake Emmerson killed me." She looked up at me. "Oh my god."

I opened my mouth, managing to push out a few words. "Read the rest."

Rita stared at me for a long moment before turning her gaze back to the page she still held in her hand. "I took a job with Brinks and Judson, a marketing firm, in the administrative pool. One day, while I was working late on an assigned project with a deadline, I discovered Blake messing around on one of the computers. At first, I didn't think anything about it. But then I saw the screen. He was transferring funds out of the company accounts. I asked him about it, and he was furious with me. He threatened to blame me if I told anyone he had taken money. When the company started snooping around, Blake went to meet with Joe Saunders, one of the senior executives. Now Mr. Saunders is dead, and Blake planted evidence that got Jenna Quinn arrested for both the embezzlement and the murder. I told Blake I was going to the police, and he told me he'd found a way to frame me for all of it if I tried. Then he told me I had to marry him, because then I couldn't be made to testify against him if he got caught. I said I would, and I wish I hadn't. And if you're reading this, Blake killed me to keep me from telling anyone. Sincerely, Missy Plott." Rita dropped the paper to the table and threw her arms around me. "Honey, I don't know whether to do a happy dance or cry with you."

My own emotions warred. Relief at black and white evidence that I had done nothing wrong in Charlotte warred with rage at all Blake Emerson had put me though for his own selfish gains. Guilt whirled through it all. The unkind thoughts I'd had about Missy ran through like a scrolling marquee. She'd been just as stuck with all of this as I had. My heart broke for this girl who had just wanted a good job to take care of her sister and had been swept up in Blake's crimes, just like I had been.

Tish cleared her throat. "Jenna, there's more."

Rita pulled back from me, and we both turned to face the detective.

"Blake says it's all lies. He states he will give us a full statement, but he'll only do it if you're in the room." Tish reached for the paper and slid it back into her folder.

I jumped from the chair, knocking it backward. "Are you kidding me?" I shoved away from the table and paced the room, needing to release the roiling ball of angry energy in my soul.

"He actually wants me to be in the same room with him right now? Is he insane?" I whirled to stare at Tish, planting my feet, my arms and hands gesturing wildly. "If you put me in there, I'll kill him. Then I really *will* be a murderer!"

Tish rose, holding up a hand and shaking her head at the officer who had thrown open the door when my shouts had apparently powered through the thin walls. "Jenna, I understand. Please, can we discuss this?"

Rita reached a hand out toward me in a silent entreaty for me to take it. "Jenna, please."

Her soft tones broke through my blinding fury, and I grasped her hand, clutching at her fingers as she gently drew me back to my seat.

As my backside hit the chair, the anger plunged to the bottom of my heart, forcing my soul to weep. The floodgates opened, and sobs ripped from my chest. I dropped my head to my forearms on the table and let the tears flow unchecked.

Rita rubbed my back, mumbling soft words I couldn't understand. I barely registered the soft whoosh of the conference room door as it settled into place as the officer left.

Within moments, the door swung open again, and I looked up to see Keith framed in the opening. Three strides brought him to my side, where he dropped to his knees, spun my chair to face him, and gathered me into his arms, planting kisses on my hair.

"Logan, I thought we discussed this." Tish's frustrated tones cut through my emotional onslaught, and I turned my head to look at her.

Keith's arms tightened around me protectively. "I don't care what we discussed. I'm not leaving. If you don't like it, then you can leave," he growled out at her.

Tish threw her hands in the air in surrender. "Fine. But if you're going to be involved in this, you have to control yourself." She narrowed her eyes at me. "And that goes for you too, Jenna."

My first instinct was to tell her what she could do with herself. But I reality-checked myself, seeing it from her perspective. Here I sat like a crazy woman, screaming out my anger, waving my arms, threatening to actually kill someone, and throwing myself into a sobbing pile. Surprisingly, my inner Mom-voice hadn't begun to berate me for creating a scene in public. I guess even my sense of decorum knew when to shut up and let me have a good old-fashioned Southern come-apart.

I wiped the sides of my fingers across my eyes, glad I rarely wore makeup. At least I wouldn't have the indignity of huge mascara streaks on my face and blotchy foundation. I pulled out of Keith's arms, instantly missing the warmth of his chest. Closing my eyes, I mentally counted to ten while I took slow, deep breaths.

"I'm good." I opened my eyes and placed my hands flat on the table. "Sorry about the drama."

Tish chuckled. "Honestly, I think you took it better than I would have. I'd have gone hunting through the building for him by now."

The laughter that burbled up eased a bit more of the tension, and I forced my anger and hurt deeper into my memory, where I could deal with them later. "Why does Blake want to talk to me?"

Keith stood and paced. "We honestly don't know. He won't tell us anything. He said he will explain everything but only if you're present."

“Jenna, didn’t you say he kept saying he needed to tell you something important?” Rita pointed at the folder in front of Tish. “Maybe this is what he was talking about. Maybe he just wanted to come clean and ease his conscience.”

Keith snorted and crossed his arms. “Right now, I really don’t care about his conscience. But being able to record his confession will make it easier to put him away for a long time.”

I looked up at Keith. “Will you be there?”

“No,” Tish answered. “He’ll be behind the glass so he can’t beat the snot out of Blake.”

A laugh barked out of my chest. “I kind of like that image.”

“Don’t tempt me,” Keith growled.

“The question is, are you up for this?” Tish picked up the folder. “If you’re not, we need to find another way to go at him.”

I looked down at my hands, one of which used to wear Blake’s ring. “I think I need to do this. I need to ask him why.”

“Good.” Tish strode across the room and opened the door. “I hope you get the answer you need.”

Chapter Twenty-Five

We followed Tish down the hallway, back to the interrogation room where we'd first been brought.

As we approached the door, Keith stopped me, turning me to face him. "Are you sure you can do this? If you can't, we understand."

I nodded. "I'm okay." A cold calm had settled in my stomach, smothering all emotion.

Keith kissed my forehead, and he and Rita walked to the next door down the hall and entered what I assumed was a viewing room.

Tish held the interrogation room open for us, and I steeled myself to come face to face with Blake.

As we entered the room, Blake stood. "Jenna. Baby, I—"

"Don't." I held up a hand. "Don't ever, ever call me that again. You lost that right when you—" My throat closed over the rest of my words, and I swallowed back my emotion, searching for the cold calm again.

A guard stepped forward, laying a hand on Blake's shoulder. "Please sit, Mr. Emerson."

Blake turned his head to look at the man and nodded, settling back into his chair before looking at me. “You read Missy’s letter.”

“I did.” I took one of the seats across the table from him, my back to the huge mirror, even though the thought of being this close to him made my skin crawl. “And I just want to know why, Blake. Why would you use me like that? Why would you set me up to go down for murder? What did I ever do to deserve that?”

Blake leaned forward, propping his arms on the table. “It’s all lies. I swear.”

I eased back, putting more air space between us. “Like the way you lied every time you told me you loved me?”

Blake reached across the table as if to take my hand in his.

Tish stepped forward and grabbed his wrist. “No contact.” When he withdrew his hand, she sat next to me. “You stated you would give us a full statement if Ms. Quinn was present.”

“I just need Jenna to understand.” Blake looked at me, deep sorrow etched across his face.

“I don’t.” I wrapped my arms around myself as if I could physically hold in my emotions. “I don’t understand any of this.”

A heavy sigh pushed from Blake’s chest, and he hung his head for a moment. “It started about three years ago.” He raised his eyes to look at me. “I . . . A situation arose, and I needed money fast. I didn’t know where else to turn, so I creatively borrowed it from the company.”

“Creatively borrowed?” I snorted. “You mean you stole it.”

“I didn’t steal it.” He shook his head. “I put every dime back. But then a few months later, another situation arose.”

“And what were these situations?” I clenched my fists in my armpits. “Just what was so important?”

"It doesn't matter now." Blake sagged back in his chair, his hands in his lap. "I borrowed money again."

"Using my credentials?" How could I have been blind to all of this?

"Not at first." He clenched his fists together and hung his head. "But eventually, yes."

"Why?" I shook my head as if I could shake away the confusion. "Were you intending to hang me with all of this?"

His head popped up, his intense gaze boring into me. "Never. I swear." Another sigh whooshed out, and his shoulders slumped. "Missy caught me one day as I was in the account putting the money back and making entries to cover the changes in balance. She'd been assigned to our group. When she figured out what I was doing, she told me I had to keep doing it and give her half. If I didn't, she said she'd tell everyone. I'd have lost my job and would have gone to jail."

"Instead, you let me lose mine and go to jail for you." I turned my head away and gritted my teeth. "Thanks for that."

"I knew I couldn't keep using my own credentials or I'd get caught. I was desperate. I'd seen you type in your login information enough times to know it by heart."

"Did you really hate me that much that you'd steal my information and blame me for everything?" I stood and began to pace. "What did I ever do to deserve that?"

Blake reached a hand toward me. "Jenna, I didn't hate you. I loved you. Deeply and desperately, and I still do. We were getting married. We had it all planned out, and me losing my job and going to jail would have destroyed it all. I couldn't let that happen. Don't you understand that?"

I whirled to face him. "Did you think if I went to jail it would be better for us as a couple? If that was the case, if you loved me so much, why toss me out?"

"I didn't have a choice." His voice came out barely above a whisper.

"Didn't have a choice." I snorted and crossed my arms. "Yeah, you said that a few days ago about marrying Missy. You were the one with all the choices, and you took all of mine away. Is that why you killed her? Because she was calling the shots?"

"I swear I didn't kill her, Jenna. I don't know who did." He started to stand but glanced over his shoulder at the guard and lowered himself back into this seat.

"How am I supposed to believe that, when you killed one of the company executives? Is that what would have happened to me if I'd found out? Would I have ended up dead too?" The reality of my words hit me, and my knees weakened. I staggered to my chair and sat.

"I didn't kill him." Blake shook his head. "Missy did. She'd been keeping her ear to the admin grapevine, and there was scuttlebutt that he'd found out who was responsible for the doctored books. She dug deeper and found out who he was and went to his home that night. She told me the next morning she'd fixed our problem. I didn't know what she meant until she told me she'd killed him."

"And you thought, 'Hey, that's a turn-on, I think I'll propose to her'?" I shivered, horror at his motivations running through my soul.

"I never wanted to propose to her. As a matter of fact, I didn't." He raked a hand through his hair. "I told her I was going to the police to come clean. That's when she told me she took one of my sweaters with her when she killed him. She wore it when she stabbed him, getting his blood on it, but she wouldn't tell me where she hid it. If I tried to go to the police about the murder, she'd use it to prove I'd killed him. But I swear, I didn't know she was going to intentionally point the finger at you."

"And when they did, you did nothing." Ice formed around my heart with a cold so deep I didn't think I'd ever be warm again.

"That's not true." His voice trembled. "I was the one who pointed out that every time the embezzlements happened, you were not in the building, based on your keycard swipes. I tried to protect you."

Rage pushed through me, and I jumped from my chair. "Protect me? You call letting me rot in jail for three months for crimes you knew I had nothing to do with protecting me? What is wrong with you?"

"I knew they would never be able to convict you." Tears formed in Blake's eyes, and he turned his head away, blinking rapidly. "But I couldn't go to jail for murder either. I was afraid, and I let my fear hurt you. Missy said I had to marry her so I couldn't testify against her. She gave me no choice."

I looked at this man I'd almost married, and my stomach rolled. "Let me see if I have this straight. You stole money. Missy caught you and insisted you steal more, which you went along with. You then used my login information to steal even more. Missy murders the man who was about to blow the whistle on you, and she threatens to frame you. Instead, she frames me for all of it, and I go to jail and have had this hanging over my head for all this time." I cocked my head at him and crossed my arms. "And you did all of this because you loved me."

"I'm sorry, Jenna. You don't understand how sorry. For all of it." He looked down at his hands. "I wish there was a way to take it all back, to erase it all, and we could go back to where we were."

"I'm not even sure where that was." I thought back through the relationship. "The fact that you could even consider doing any of this means I never knew you at all. And the fact that you thought that I would be understanding about what you've done means you didn't know me either." I gripped the back of the chair, propping myself up with it. "You know the stupid part about marrying Missy?"

Blake's brow furrowed. "I know I shouldn't have let her bully me into it. I should've stood by you. Then maybe we could've fixed it."

"That's not what I mean." I shook my head. "What I mean is the part about not testifying. You do realize that only covers a spouse being forced to testify, right? I mean, you do know you can testify against your wife if you want to, just that they can't make you do it if you don't."

His eyes widened and tears filled them. "Jenna, I . . ."

I stood and nodded at Tish. "I'm done here." I strode to the door, waiting for the soft snick of the lock releasing before I pulled it open and walked out.

Chapter Twenty-Six

"Do you think he's telling the truth?" Rita turned into one of the historic district parking lots and turned off my car.

When she'd held out her hand for my keys, I'd dropped them into her palm without question, knowing I was too distracted to drive. The trip home had been silent until now.

"I honestly don't know." I reached to unbuckle my seat belt. "If you had asked me that question yesterday, I'd have said he never lied. But now?" I shook my head and got out of the car.

We climbed the stairs to our apartment walkway, and Rita matched her stride to mine.

"Want to come over?" she asked. "I can order takeout from The Weeping Willow, and we can watch an old movie."

I stopped at my door and slid my key into the lock. "I'd rather just be alone for a while."

Rita rubbed my shoulder. "Honey, if you need anything, no matter what time it is, even if it's just a need to vent and cry, call me or come over. Okay?"

I nodded and mumbled a quick thanks before slipping through my door and closing it.

Eddy greeted me with his usual excited wiggles and wags, and I knelt to wrap my arms around his neck. I'd left my apartment door unlocked, and Mason must have put him up here after the store closed. I wasn't even sure what time it was.

I stood and looked at the microwave over the stove. Six thirty. No wonder it was dim in here. But the waning light suited me. I dropped a cup of kibble into Eddy's bowl and walked into the bedroom, flopping onto the bed and rolling myself into the comforter like it was a cocoon.

Eddy jumped on the bed and curled up at the small of my back, his warmth lulling me to sleep.

Darkness filled the room when I woke. Soft sounds came from the kitchen, and the smell of cooking food wafted in. I sat up, keeping the comforter wrapped around myself, and hobbled to my bedroom door.

Keith turned, a cooking spoon in his hand. "I made spaghetti."

I nodded and padded to the couch, curling up in one corner.

I listened to the clicks and sounds as Keith set his spoon on the counter, turned off the burners, and moved pots away from the heat. Footsteps approached, and he lowered himself to the couch beside me, gathering me into his arms. "Are you okay?"

"I will be." I closed my eyes and listened to his heart beating beneath my ear. Solid. Steady. Calming.

"I'm sorry you had to go through all of that today." He kissed the top of my head and laid his cheek on my hair. "Do you want to talk about it?"

I shook my head and snuggled deeper into his embrace. We sat in the silence, the sound of his heartbeat my only focus.

After a while, I asked, “What time is it?”

Keith shifted, turning his wrist. “Nine. Are you hungry?”

“Not really.” I pulled back and sat up. “But I should eat anyway.”

Keith settled me at the table and moved into the kitchen. “It’s a little cold now, but I’ll pop it in the microwave.”

I looked up at him. “Why?”

“Because I’d prefer to eat hot food.” He grinned. “Wouldn’t you?”

I shook my head. “No. I mean why would someone who said they loved you do something that horrible to you?”

Keith pressed buttons on the microwave’s touchpad, and the appliance hummed. “I honestly have no answer to that. In all the years I’ve been doing this job, understanding how some people can get to the point where they hurt others and justify it has never been my strong suit.”

I propped my elbows on the table and rested my forehead on my palms. My relationship with Blake played like a movie reel in my head. “I know you’ve asked me several times if I still love him.”

“And do you?” Keith pulled a plate from the microwave and set it on the counter.

I sighed and leaned back. “My answer is still no. But at this point, I’m not sure I ever did. How could I, when I obviously didn’t even know him? But whether I loved him or not, betrayal is a bitter pill to swallow, especially when it’s this deep.”

Keith walked to the table and set down two plates. He slid into the seat beside me and took my hands in his. “You know I would never betray you.”

A lump formed in my throat, and I swallowed it back, refusing to let Blake Emerson ever make me cry again. I looked into Keith's chocolate eyes and let myself be pulled into their depths, into the warmth and love that waited there. "I know."

"I love you." Keith raised my hand and kissed it.

"I love you too." I touched my forehead to his. "More than you know."

Keith rubbed my hands and blew warm breath on them. "Your hands are like ice."

I quirked the corner of my mouth up. "I can always warm them on your stomach."

Keith jumped up. "No way, woman. Love only goes so far." He laughed as he walked to the kitchen, returning with forks and napkins.

"I see how you are." I tried to laugh, even though it didn't reach my heart.

"Let's just see if we can get some food into you." Keith inched my plate closer to me. "I know you love Italian food."

I ate about half of what Keith had put in front of me, tasting nothing. "I think I need to lie down again."

Keith settled me in bed and returned to the kitchen. I listened to him clink around in the kitchen, putting food away, rinsing dishes and loading them into the dishwasher, and wiping down counters. He called Eddy, and I heard the click of the leash clasp before Keith called out that he was giving Eddy his bedtime walk.

I dozed in and out, trying to feel numb, trying to push away any memories of Blake and any emotion they brought, until I felt the thump of Eddy jumping onto the bed beside me.

Keith stooped over to kiss me, stroking my hair back from my face.

"Stay." I grasped his hand, tugging him closer.

He rolled onto his side behind me and wrapped his arms around me. "I'm here, baby. I'm not going anywhere."

Sunlight streamed in through the windows when I next opened my eyes. Eddy barked from the kitchen, and Keith shushed him, softly laughing.

"I can't give you any more if you're going to get noisy and wake your mom."

I eased out of bed and headed for the shower. Once clean and dressed, I padded on bare feet into the kitchen. "Morning."

Keith turned and smiled. "Morning. You feel better?"

"A bit." I slid onto a bar stool and propped my arms on the bar top. "I'm still processing."

"Well, wait until you see what I have for you." He wiggled his eyebrows up and down.

I chuckled, grateful for his attempts at levity.

Keith set a plate in front of me. "Spinach and feta omelet covered in hollandaise sauce." He reached back and grabbed a second plate, placing it next to the first one. "And for dessert, we have fresh crepes with a light dusting of powdered sugar and a glaze of raspberry reduction."

I stared at the feast. "Okay, Julia Child, when did you get here, and where is my boyfriend?" I slid a bite of the omelet into my mouth and moaned. "This is delicious."

Keith grinned and shrugged. "I was up early, so I watched some YouTube videos on how to make this stuff. I also called Mason and told him you'd be late today." Keith wiped his hands on a towel and leaned against the sink facing me. "I figured you might need a bit more time."

"Thanks." I ate a bite of the crepes, which were even more delicious than the omelet, hoping it would stimulate some semblance of an appetite. "I guess it's just hard to realize someone you lived with, stood up for, at one point loved, could have murdered two people."

"Yeah." Keith sighed. "We're still working on that."

"There's no real way to prove whether he did or didn't, is there?" I ate another bite of the omelet. I didn't need a blood sugar drop on top of everything else.

Keith shook his head. "We're looking at all angles. At the very least, we can hold him on charges of embezzlement, which he does not deny. But the murders have boiled down to a he-said, she-said thing. We have her letter saying one thing and his statement, which directly contradicts it. How do we know who to believe, especially with Missy dead and unable to give more details?"

I pushed the food around on my plate with my fork. "I know this will sound bad. But even if there were serious doubt that he'd done any of it, there's a part of me that wishes he'd spend time in jail like I did, sitting there with no one to believe him, no one to help him, and no way to convince anyone he's been unjustly accused."

"Fortunately, at least part of it isn't unjust, legally speaking." Keith rounded the bar to sit next to me. "Right now, the DA is prepping two cases. The first is in the event we find evidence that he undoubtedly killed Missy and the man in Charlotte. The second is if we find evidence that proves he's telling the truth and he killed neither of them. This second case means he's still guilty of the embezzlement and is also an accessory after the fact in the murder of your company's executive. Either way, he's going to jail for a lot longer than three months."

I laid my fork on the bar top and crossed my arms in front of my plate. "I guess you're right. It's just hard to accept that I could have been that blind to who he really was and what was really going on."

Keith ran a hand up and down my back. "I know, honey. I wish I could make it easier for you."

"Time will do that, I guess." I straightened my spine and plastered on a smile I didn't feel yet. "Are you off today?"

He shook his head. "Sadly no. I've got to head out in a minute. The Charlotte DA is pushing for us to turn Emerson over to them for prosecution. Depending on where he committed what crimes, we may need to let them take him."

"It's okay. I understand." I picked up the fork and ate another bite. "I'll finish breakfast and head down to the store. Mason will be there. I won't be alone with my morbid thoughts."

"Good to know." Keith stood and reached for his jacket, which was lying across another stool, and slid his arms into the sleeves. "I'll call you later and check on you. I promise."

I turned my lips up to meet his goodbye kiss. "I'll be fine. Go, so you're not late."

As the door snicked shut, the smile slid from my face, and I turned back to look at my plates. I'd promised Keith I would eat. I sighed and picked up both plates, carrying them to the living room coffee table. At least I could watch Perry Mason put bad guys away while I ate.

Chapter Twenty-Seven

Two episodes later, I headed down to the store, Eddy running down ahead of me.

Mason met me at the bottom of the stairs. "Hey, Keith told me what happened. You okay?"

I smiled, feeling that one a bit. "I am. Just still going through a lot in my head."

"Yeah." Mason nodded, his brows drawn together. "I get that."

"How are sales this morning?" I stepped behind the counter and reached for the receipt bag. "Anything good?"

"Meh. It's a Tuesday." He pointed at his phone on the counter. "Plus, I looked at the weather, and it's supposed to rain today. And you know people don't like coming out here in the rain."

"True." I looked at the wood panels secured over my window and hoped the weather stripping would hold and I wouldn't end up with water damage on top of everything else. "Oh no. I forgot about the insurance guy."

"Don't worry. I handled it." Mason grinned. "One less thing for you to have to do." He reached under the counter and pulled out a business card. "He said he didn't need you here anyway."

"But I wanted to make sure he saw everything." How could I have completely blanked on it yesterday?

Mason held up a sheet of paper. "I made sure he saw everything Rob wrote down."

I sighed in relief. "Thank you. What would I do without you?"

"Let's see." Mason scratched his head in fake concentration. "You'd have to be here on time every day. No sleeping in like you did today. You'd have to walk your own dog. You'd likely still be cleaning up glass everywhere. You probably wouldn't have finished inventory yet."

"Stop." I held up a hand. "I'm assuming you no longer want to go to Asheville tomorrow?"

"Hey, now." Mason laughed. "I already bought tickets, so you can't change your mind."

"Uh-huh." I gave him a mock stern look, spoiled when I couldn't keep the grin at bay. "Keep talking, buddy. I can change whatever I want to."

"Fine. I give." Mason turned when the door opened.

Tish strode in, heading straight to the counter. "I have news."

"Did they find more evidence about Missy?" My heart squeezed, afraid of the answer either way it turned out. I didn't know how much more I could process in one day.

Tish shook her head. "No, and it may be a while before we work all of that out. In the meantime, we've discovered who vandalized your store."

"Who?" Mason leaned on the counter next to Tish.

"We pulled video footage from several of your neighbors, and we have clear shots of four perpetrators, one of whom was nonparticipatory and ran away before the damage was done." Tish pulled out her phone and tapped the screen. She turned it to face me. "Look familiar?"

Three slender frames draped in dark hoodies and sweatpants stood outside my store. One held a spray can, the photo freezing her in the act of spraying my walls with red paint. The other two each held a can and a brick. One had turned back to look toward the parking lot, her face clear in the streetlamps. "Mandy."

Mason craned his neck to see until Tish turned the phone. "Aren't those the chicks who tried to burn down your store?"

"We questioned them about that when we brought them in. They're claiming there was no fire when they left the store, and they have no idea what happened." Tish tapped her screen off and slid her phone into her jacket pocket.

"But they've admitted to throwing bricks through my window?" I thumbed back over my shoulder at the plywood.

"No." Tish sighed. "We only have Mandy's face, which means we can't one hundred percent prove the others were involved. And all Mandy will say is her father is on the way. Apparently, he's some high-powered attorney."

"You mean they might get away with it?" Mason thumped a fist on the counter. "Man, that's just wrong, I don't care how you look at it."

"That's the way it works sometimes." Tish pointed at the coffeepot. "Mind if I get a to-go cup? The coffeemaker at the station is broken."

"Help yourself." I gestured toward the pot. "The cups are underneath on the left-hand side."

Tish walked over and opened the cabinet under the coffeepot, pulling out a Styrofoam cup and plastic lid. "Molly and Mickey will likely skate. But we do have proof Mandy threw one of the bricks and sprayed paint across the window's contents. It's a class one misdemeanor, but if her dad's a good attorney, he'll get her off with community service and a fine."

"She should have to pay for the damage." Mason crossed his arms. "It's not fair that she did this and gets a slap on the wrist."

"She may." Tish stirred sugar into her coffee and took a sip before putting on the lid. "In cases like this, we provide the guilty party's information to the injured party's insurance company. Their legal teams will go after her for reimbursement of their costs to fix your damage." She cocked her head. "Jenna, you might be able to sue them as well, getting something for pain and suffering as well as lost potential income while the store is damaged."

I shook my head. "No. I just want it all to be over. The insurance company is going to pay for the repairs. I don't need to capitalize on their crime."

"Your choice." Tish shrugged. "I'd better get moving. It's my lunch break, and the guys expect me to come back with some of those cake pop things. I figured I'd stop in and tell you in person while I was down here."

I chuckled as Tish left. "I've created a monster."

"Speaking of lunch . . ." Mason looked toward The Weeping Willow.

"Go." I shooed him toward the door. "Tell Lily I said hi."

Mason scurried out the door and across the street, not waiting for me to finish my sentence.

I stepped out from behind the counter and turned to look at the sage-green shelf, amazed at how different it looked just by changing the color. I ignored the fact that part of that difference was likely the dimmer light due to my window being blocked by plywood.

The door bells jangled, and I turned, doing a double take when I saw who stood there.

"I . . . Can I talk to you?" Connie Plott stood just inside the door, her hands clasped together as if she wasn't sure what to do with them.

"Sure." I rounded the counter and sat on one of the stools. I had a feeling I knew what this was about, and I wanted her facing the damaged window while we talked.

Connie stepped toward the counter, her brows drawn together and her lips pursed. "I want to say I'm sorry."

"For?" I crossed my arms and tilted my head.

"For being rude the other day." She hung her head. "Mama used to say to always be polite to people because you never knew what kinds of things they were dealing with."

That wasn't what I expected her to say, but I'd roll with it. "Sounds like something my mom would say too."

Connie relaxed her hands and offered a tentative smile. "You were right about Tom."

My heart squeezed. To be that young and having to deal with so much loss. "I'm sorry. But you're a great girl. I'm sure you'll find someone who will love you for you." I inwardly cringed, realizing how tacky I sounded.

"Maybe." Connie shrugged.

"I'm glad you're not wearing all that makeup today," I tried again, hoping to open a true dialogue with the girl. I couldn't imagine being that young and completely alone.

"Yeah, it was breaking my skin out." She slid a hand across her cheek. "I didn't like the way it felt anyway."

I nodded. "I don't wear it very often either."

"I'm keeping her clothes, though." She ran her hand across the tan slacks she wore. "Some of them are nice."

"Blue's a good color on you." I gestured toward her shirt, wondering how long we'd have awkward small talk before she'd get to her point.

"I don't really want to be Missy." Tears filled Connie's eyes.

I reached under the counter and pulled out a box of tissues, extending it across to her. "I'm honestly glad to hear you say that."

"I just don't know who I am without her." She pulled out a tissue and dabbed at her eyes. "I thought if I dressed in her clothes and hung around with her friends and tried to be like them, I'd get the things she had, and someone would finally think I'm special."

"And did you get those things?" I edged her closer to what I suspected was her real reason for wanting to talk to me.

Connie shook her head. "No. I realized Missy worked hard for what she got, and she wasn't always a nice person. And her friends are mean. They . . ."

I sighed, realizing I was going to have to push her into her confession. "They threw bricks through my window and spray-painted my wall."

Her eyes widened and the color drained from her cheeks. "You knew?"

"That you were the fourth person in the video?" I nodded. "It was an easy guess."

"I didn't know what they were going to do. They just said they were going to make you pay for trying to break up Missy's engagement and for killing her. I believed them. That you had killed Missy, I mean." She looked past me at the plywood. "I didn't know they were going to throw bricks and paint those words. I was just so angry, and I didn't think before I said I'd go with them."

"I had no reason to kill your sister." I rested my arms on the counter. "I didn't want to get back together with Blake. I already have a great guy in my life."

Connie's brows drew together. "I know. The part about not killing my sister, I mean."

"It's okay. I get it. I know what it's like to feel your world fall out from under your feet." It hadn't been that long ago when I'd lost everything, but at least I'd been an adult with an education and a place to go. "What will you do now?"

Connie straightened her shoulders. "Tom is being really nice. He said he'd help me get a part-time job at the furniture plant in Hickory and will help me pay my bills until I graduate in two months and can work full time. He wants to honor Missy's memory."

Chalk one up for Tom.

Before I could answer her, Mason strode in, a drink cup in his hands. "I brought you a sandwich." He held out a paper bag as he stepped behind the counter.

Connie backed toward the door. "I guess I'd better go." The door chimes jingled as she pulled it open. "I really am sorry. For everything."

"What was that about?" Mason asked as she disappeared from view.

"Just a girl trying to find out where she belongs." And I truly hoped she found more peace than Missy had.

Chapter Twenty-Eight

Keith had to work late, so I spent the evening working on a new crochet stitch. By the time I went to bed, I had several more potholders under my belt. Maybe I'd try those placemats soon.

When Wednesday dawned, I was determined to face the day with a positive attitude. My name had been cleared, and I'd been forced to work through the remaining emotions I'd had tied to Blake. I'd even received an email from the insurance company, stating they were covering the losses and had scheduled for a glass repairman to be there before the end of the week.

Eddy and I settled in to work the store without Mason, and the day passed as customers flowed in and out. As the light dimmed toward sunset, I prepared to close the store for the day, happier than I'd been in days.

I took the day's receipts to the back room, startled when I heard the door bells. Striding back out into the front, I called out, "I'm sorry, we're closed."

Gwendolyn Emerson poked her head around an aisle. "There you are."

Hot pickles on a Pop-Tart, why hadn't I remembered to lock the front door? I pasted on a smile. "What can I do for you today, Mrs. Emerson?" I still refused to call her Gwendolyn.

Gwendolyn wrung her hands. "I was hoping you might have changed your mind about helping Blake." Her hair, usually perfectly in place, hung limply to her shoulders, and the burgundy blazer she wore highlighted the dark circles under her eyes.

I gritted my teeth and counted to ten. "I've told you there's nothing I can do."

"I just don't understand." She threw her hands in the air. "After all you and Blake meant to each other, you'd just let him rot in jail for something he didn't do?"

I crossed my arms. "Why is it you think I owe Blake anything after what he did to me? He stole money using my logins, and either he or Missy framed me for it. And if it was Missy, he let her do it. One of them killed a company executive, and they framed me for that, too. He didn't even have the decency to stand beside me as I fought for my freedom. And you think I owe him?"

"But . . . I thought . . ." Gwendolyn's eyes brimmed with tears. "He's all I have. Please, please help me get him out of jail."

I walked around the counter for my tissue box and slid it to her across the counter. "There really is no way for me to help. It's up to the police to find out if he's only guilty of embezzlement and accessory after the fact to murder or if he actually killed anyone. But your son is going to jail."

"This is all that woman's fault." Gwendolyn broke down in sobs, a tissue held to her mouth to stifle her cries. I handed her another tissue, and she snatched it to blow her nose. "She was forcing him to marry her. She was the one who killed that man, not Blake. He told me. He still loves you, not that piece of trash."

I watched Gwendolyn with true sadness in my heart. While I had no desire to be with Blake, she was his mother and seemed to truly love him, flaws and all. "I'm not sure Blake ever loved me. Love is supporting and kind. Love encourages you to be all you can be and shouts its pride from the rooftops when you succeed. Blake smothered any initiative I had and hid me like a nasty secret to keep himself from looking bad."

"But you were perfect for him." Gwendolyn dabbed at her eyes, her sobs subsiding into soft hiccups.

"Perfect?" I snorted. "How so?"

"You're cultured and come from a good family." She swept her arms around the store. "You love good books and have good taste. Missy was . . . tacky. She even had a rhinestone wedding topper with their initials made for their cake. Who puts the initials *B* and *M* on a cake? Bowel movement? For crying out loud."

I burst out laughing, unable to hold it back. "*B* and *M*?"

"See what I mean?" Gwendolyn stepped to my counter and reached for the tissue box, her arm stretching past me.

My gaze slid to her sleeve, where a loose thread hung. "I think you've lost a button."

"I have?" She flipped over both sleeves, and only one held a large gold button. Thread hung from a tear in the sleeve of the other. "What in the world? Now I'm going to have to find one to match it. And on my lucky jacket too."

My eyes widened and I stepped back instinctively before forcing myself to relax. *Act normal, Jenna.* "Lucky jacket?" I kept my voice open and friendly. This must be what she'd worn to the beauty parlor, although I'd hardly call the jacket ready for the rag bag.

She slid her hands down the blazer's front. "I always wear it when I'm going to . . . an event."

"An event?" My mind raced, mentally walking through her hotel room. There was no way we'd missed this jacket in her closet.

"Well, to be honest, bingo. And sometimes I like to take a trip to the casinos in Cherokee." Gwendolyn sniffed and straightened her shoulders. "I know my son is in jail, but sitting at home crying all day won't fix that."

"I'm sure he'd understand." I nodded, a cold fist of fear settling into my stomach. This time I really was alone with a killer. "And you should wear that color more often. It suits you." *Shut up, Jenna.* I had to stop blabbering like an idiot.

Gwendolyn preened a bit. "I'll take it to a tailor when I get home." She held up the torn sleeve with the missing button. "I keep the jacket in my car in case I need it. Maybe it popped off in there somewhere. I'll have to look for it tomorrow when there's enough light to see."

"I'm sure it'll turn up somewhere." I stepped back, putting distance between us. My hand dropped to my back pocket. No phone. Damn it. "Don't let me keep you. I'd hate for you to be late and miss part of the fun." I smiled brightly.

Her gaze slid across my counter. "I know what I can do." She smiled and reached toward the pencil cup sitting beside the register, pulling out the scissors I used to open envelopes. "I can just snip the one off the other sleeve. That way they'll both match again. At least I won't look lopsided until I can get it repaired."

Great. Now she was armed. I took another step back. "I really need to close up now." I smiled at her again and skirted her, aiming toward the door.

"The police have my button, don't they, dear?" Gwendolyn stepped between me and my escape path.

"What do you mean?" I cocked my head, trying to look innocent. "Why would the police have your button?"

"Oh, don't act stupid now," she snarled, taking a step closer. "You may have been fooled by my idiot son for too long, but you can't be that dumb." Gwendolyn lunged, swinging the scissors toward me.

I jumped back, the blades barely missing me. "Gwendolyn, wait. Stop!" I hoped the use of her first name might pause her. I hoped wrong.

"I've killed to protect my son before. Don't think I won't do it again." With a speed that surprised me, Gwendolyn lunged again, toppling me to the ground.

I gripped her wrists, pushing back with all of my strength as she tried to shove the scissors down into my body. As the scissors dipped closer, I tried to remember what Keith taught me to do to get out from under someone. Panic set in.

A blur of red and white flew from the stairs and Gwendolyn screamed as Eddy sank his teeth into her leg. Her body shifted, trying to shake my dog loose, and Gwendolyn let go of the scissors with one hand, swinging wildly at Eddy. Taking the opening, I twisted my hips and shoved, rolling her to her back and straddling her. I slammed the hand that held the scissors into the floor several times until she let the blades go.

She bucked underneath me, writhing and twisting, finally flipping on her stomach to crawl away.

"Enough!" I grabbed her hair and pulled hard, my knee in the center of her back. "I know you killed Missy, but why kill me?"

Gwendolyn sagged to the floor sobbing. "I have to save my son."

"Killing me won't save him." I gritted my teeth, keeping my knee planted. For all I knew, she was waiting for an opening to try again. "If you don't tell the police what you did, your son will go to jail for a murder he didn't commit. And while I might think that's a weird form of poetic justice after all he did to me, can you really live with that?"

Gwendolyn bucked under me. "No one knows. Only you."

"Killing me won't change Missy's letter." I pulled back hard on her hair again. "The only thing that can change it is if the real killer confesses."

"I can't." She stilled beneath me.

"Hey, Jenna. I brought pizza." Footsteps sounded on the spiral stairs. "What the hell?" Keith raced down the stairs.

I climbed off of Blake's mother, and she flipped to her back, sitting up to cradle her bleeding leg.

"Tell him." I pointed to Keith. "Now."

"I . . . I killed Missy." Sobs ripped from her chest.

Keith pulled his phone from his pocket and tapped the screen. "I need an ambulance for a dog bite, and I need a police detail to meet me at the emergency room."

I turned to search the room for my dog, spying him behind the counter. I moved to his side, kneeling to run my hands through his fur until I was sure he was uninjured. "It's okay, sweet. It's all over." I cradled my shaking dog, crooning to him.

I listened as Keith read Gwendolyn her rights and hoped she wouldn't get out of her confession by claiming she wasn't

Mirandized before she spoke. Sirens approached, and Eddy pressed himself into me. I kissed his head and rocked him, relieved when two police officers arrived and I heard the snap of the handcuffs closing on Gwendolyn's wrists.

Keith stuck his head around the counter. "Is he okay?"

I nodded. "He's fine. Just scared out of his mind."

"They're loading her onto a gurney." He looked back over his shoulder. "I have to go with them. I'm sorry." He leaned in to kiss me. "Save me a few pieces of pizza, okay?" He ducked out the door without waiting for my answer.

I stood and gathered my dog into my arms, carrying him up the stairs. It had only been four months since he'd witnessed the murder of his former owner, and seeing me attacked had sent him into a tailspin of fear.

Once in the bathroom, I wet a washcloth and wiped the blood from his face, the only outward sign that he'd jumped into the fray. "There's a good boy. I'm okay. You saved me. I'm not leaving you." I kissed him on the head, receiving a tiny tail thump in response.

Too hungry to go to bed yet, I stood and patted my leg. "Come on, sweet puppy." I stepped forward, coaxing him out of the bathroom toward the couch, where I tapped its surface. "You sit here and let me get some pizza for us."

I retuned with several slices and sat facing him, feeding small bites of cheese and pepperoni to Eddy in between my own bites. Exhausted and full, I changed into my pajamas and crawled into bed with Eddy curled up against me.

A sound from the kitchen startled me awake. I slipped out of bed and padded to the bedroom door. "You're back. What time is it?"

Keith glanced toward the microwave. "Two thirteen." He picked up his plate of pizza and walked to the dining table. "I just needed to see you tonight, but I was hungry. Sorry I woke you."

I joined him at the table, Eddy at my feet. "It's okay. What happened after you left?"

"They gave her stitches. Eddy laid into her pretty good." Keith took a bite of pizza.

Eddy perked up at his name, and he laid his head on Keith's knee, begging for a treat.

Keith tore off a tiny piece and gave it to Eddy. "You earned this, buddy. If I didn't know it would be terrible for you, I'd give you the whole pizza."

"Did she make a full confession?" I shooed Eddy away from Keith's plate.

Keith nodded. "She said she'd arrived late for the dinner and saw Missy in the parking lot. She walked over to talk to her, and Missy tried to walk away from her. Gwendolyn chased her, and Missy pitched a temper tantrum, calling her names and threatening her. Gwendolyn snapped and shoved her hard, and her head hit an old concrete block. Gwendolyn panicked and hid the body, but her clothes had blood on them, which everyone would have seen if she'd gone into the restaurant."

"But why kill Missy?" I pinched a piece of crust off of Keith's pizza slice and popped it into my mouth. "She and Blake weren't that close, so why was she stressed out that Blake was marrying a woman she didn't like?"

"It seems Gwendolyn also killed the guy in Charlotte." Keith bit into another slice.

"What?" I sat up and turned to stare at Keith. "Why would she do that?"

"Remember when Blake told you a situation had come up where he'd needed money fast?" Keith asked.

I nodded. "Yeah, and he wouldn't tell me what the situation was."

"It was his mother's gambling debts." He wiped his fingers on a napkin. "She'd gotten in deep with her gambling. She'd been losing a lot at a couple of casinos, and she came begging to Blake. He thought he could just pull the money out and put it back before anyone was the wiser. But then she came a second time, knowing he'd bail her out again."

"Missy must have made the whole situation worse, demanding her share of anything he took and prodding him to steal more and more." I settled back and tucked my feet under me.

"When the executive found out, Gwendolyn killed him to keep the money train flowing. She didn't realize Missy had also come to try to convince the man to keep silent." Keith stood and took his empty plate to the kitchen.

I followed him to the kitchen and slid onto a stool. "But Missy told Blake she killed the guy and was going to frame him."

Keith grabbed the pizza box with the remaining slices, closed it, and slid it into the refrigerator. "She apparently thought she could control him more with the threat of a murder frame-up than with a desire to protect his mother. She knew Blake was paying off Gwendolyn's gambling debts, and she was pushing Blake to cut his mother off once they were married. It's why Gwendolyn stole her bracelet and engagement ring. She hocked them two towns over. We found the pawn ticket in her purse."

"What happens to Blake now? Does it still count as accessory after the fact if Missy didn't really kill the guy?" I stood and followed Keith back to the couch.

He patted the seat beside him and wrapped an arm around me when I sat. "That's a sticky one. Blake will still serve a sentence for the embezzlement, and he'll be transported to Charlotte for processing tomorrow. As for the accessory charge, I'm honestly not sure. That'll be up to the Charlotte DA. Gwendolyn will likely serve consecutive life sentences without the possibility of parole." Keith shook his head. "I just don't get why Blake would keep paying off his mother's debts. You said they weren't close. Why would it matter enough to him to risk going to jail?"

"Image." I thought of how Blake had hidden our relationship and was such a stickler for every little detail in his life. "He would have worried it would make him look bad or that it might have harmed his chances for a partnership offer in the company. It's the same reason he kept her picture on the mantle. He wanted to appear to have a normal, calm life with normal relationships and normal responsibilities."

"Normal can be overrated." Keith dropped a kiss on my hair and squeezed my shoulder.

"Hey!" I pushed away from him, laughing. "I can do normal."

He snorted. "When?" Keith winked and turned up one corner of his mouth. "Besides, if you became normal, life would get pretty boring around here." He sat forward. "I almost forgot. Did you find what I left for you?"

"Left for me?" I searched my memory. "Other than the pizza?"

"Hang on." Keith stood and walked into the bedroom, returning with two wrapped packages. "Here." He held out the larger package as he sat.

I took the package and unwrapped it. "Where did you find this?" A grin split my face as my fingers slid over the cover of *The Five Little Peppers and How They Grew.*

"I spent an afternoon surfing and found a few copies for sale online." He pointed at the golden cover. A black section crossed the front diagonally, and inside were golden silhouettes of children surrounded by golden vines and leaves. "I know it's not quite like the one that burned, but it's a first edition and is in great condition."

I leaned in and kissed him. "It's perfect."

"Now this." He held out a tiny, flat box.

The top lifted off to reveal a lavender key covered in purple hearts and paw prints. I flipped the box over and dropped the key into my palm.

"It's to my house." Keith closed my hand over the key. "I promise you now that I'll never ask you to leave again." He lowered his head to kiss me.

Eddy head butted between us, demanding to be a part of the embrace, and we pulled away laughing. These were the moments that made life amazing.

Keith eased back on the couch and pulled me to his side, pointing the remote at the TV. "I'm exhausted but there's no way I could sleep right now. Anything you want to watch? It's about all I have the energy to do right now."

"What, no offer to take me dancing?" I stuck my feet out and wiggled them. "They're all ready to go."

"In the middle of the night?" He humphed. "Are you going to put on that dress again?"

"Maybe soon." I grinned and took the remote from him and found *The Princess Bride*. It had all the elements of my own story. Love, betrayal, murder, and romance, and the good guys won in the end. "This okay with you?" I looked up at him.

He winked at me. "As you wish."

Acknowledgments

As always, thank you to my husband, George, whose support and encouragement, as well as brainstorming ideas, keep me grounded and moving forward. Thank you to Tris Rohner, my amazing beta reader, brainstorming partner, biggest cheerleader, and best friend. You came through for me again at the last minute. Thank you to Leslie LeMense, former owner of The Cookie Box and baker of the most amazing cake pops anywhere. Thanks for all the answers to my baking and bakery questions. Thank you to Lee Hicks, Allstate insurance agent, for taking the time to answer my insurance questions regarding businesses that had been vandalized. Thank you to the wonderful members of my community in Manning and on Lake Marion, who have encouraged me, supported me, and celebrated with me along my writing journey. Thank you to my incredible agent, Dawn Dowdle, who continues to answer all my questions, soothe my frantic feathers, and offer solid advice. I couldn't imagine doing this with anyone else on my team. Thank you to Crooked Lane Books for the continued opportunities to share my stories with the world.